Reviews for Sizzling

"[A] tasty dish…Mallery's prose is luscious and provocative, and her characters worth following from book to book."
—*Publishers Weekly*

"*Sizzling* is simply dazzling! You'll laugh, you'll hoot, you'll raise your eyebrows, and yes, you'll cry buckets, so have those tissues handy. Susan Mallery is an author not to be missed! Highly recommended!"
—Debora Hosey, *The Romance Readers Connection*

Reviews for *Irresistible*

"Mallery is at her addictive best in the charming second installment of her Buchanan family saga….The bestselling author crafts vivid characters and a winning story about the risk and joy of second love."
—*Publishers Weekly*

"'Dysfunctional' is a good way to describe both the Buchanan and Towers families. Mallery does her usual excellent job of taking characters with issues and making them riveting. This second Buchanan book will make readers hungry for the next chapter of this twisty family drama."
—*Romantic Times BOOKreviews*

Reviews for *Delicious*

"Food and love are a great mix, so it is appropriate that bestselling author Mallery launches a tasty new series based on the lives and loves of a family of restaurateurs. Using her patented blend of wit and humor, Mallery explores deeply complicated family relationships that are laced with love and loss. Outstanding!"
—*Romantic Times BOOKreviews*

"Seasoned with humor, the start to Mallery's new Buchanan series has a wonderful cast of characters….Readers who can't get enough of Nora Roberts' family series will latch on to Mallery's, which is sure to be a hit."
—*Booklist,* starred review

SUSAN MALLERY

Accidentally Yours

HQN™

ISBN-13: 978-0-373-77205-6
ISBN-10:   0-373-77205-X

ACCIDENTALLY YOURS

Copyright © 2008 by Susan Macias Redmond

www.HQNBooks.com

Printed in U.S.A.

Dear Reader,

I have a secret to share. Writing is magic.

I know, I know. If you've ever tried to write a term paper at four in the morning with it due for an eight-o'clock class, it feels like torture. But writing a novel can be magic.

Some book ideas are born out of circumstances and some grow character by character, but some are gifts. They show up in a writer's brain (a fairly scary place for anything to be, let alone an amazing idea) with all the possibilities in place.

So it was with *Accidentally Yours*. I was minding my own business, munching on takeout because my husband was out of town on business, contemplating which chick flick I would watch, when I had a thought. What if a mom was so determined to save her child that she pretended to be a superhero, so her son would believe he had superhero genes floating around in his body? Genes that would save him.

I put down my plate and fork and grabbed a pad of paper. The idea didn't particularly make sense to me at the time. Fake superheroes? Kids? What? But the ideas tumbled one after the other. A mom like that would do anything, risk anything. She was smart and determined and scared and funny and hanging on by a thread. She needed a great guy, but the man who popped into my brain was anything but great. He was difficult and stubborn and pretended he didn't care, because once he'd cared so much it had nearly destroyed him.

I wrote and wrote on that pad. Somewhere around midnight I had the outline of the book you're holding in your hands. It made me laugh, it made me cry, it made me believe. I hope you'll believe, too.

Susan Mallery

To Jake…with love.

Accidentally
Yours

CHAPTER ONE

"GIRLFRIEND, this is not your thing," Lance said as he passed over three napkins, then clucked his tongue.

"Tell me about it," Kerri Sullivan muttered. There was liquid everywhere and a lot of it had come from a very expensive bottle of eighteen-year-old Scotch.

Balancing three drinks on a small tray should be easy, she told herself as she took a deep breath and carefully lifted the tray. The trick was to not think about what she was doing. Or somehow do it better, she added as the tray dipped a little.

This was her third lunch shift at The Grill—an upscale lunch and dinner place in the financial district of Seattle. The decor was simple but elegant, the food totally recognizable. The Grill was the kind of restaurant that catered to the successful executive dining with his associates or an important client.

She was already on probation from an unfortunate incident the previous day. It had involved crab cakes, a large leather handbag jutting out into the walkway and an oil-based sauce landing smack on a shantung-silk jacket.

"At least I can do hair," Kerri reminded herself as she delivered the drinks and took the men's orders. Give her some foil and bleach and she could make anyone look like a movie star. But serving food seemed to be a challenge she couldn't meet.

She'd gotten the job at The Grill by lying about her experience. Her glowing letters of recommendation had been printed out on her home computer.

Lance, a waiter here and in on her plot from the beginning, had saved her butt three times already. If she could just hang on until Nathan King showed up to claim his usual table, she could quit before she got fired. That was why she was here—to confront Mr. King and convince him to help her.

She had her speech prepared. Even more important, she had a DVD with a copy of a program from the Discovery Health channel she planned to flash at him. The small, portable DVD player was stuck down the front of her pants, the oddly shaped bulge hidden by her white apron.

For about the four hundredth time, she glanced toward the table in the corner. It had remained annoyingly empty. But this time when she looked, she saw activity. There were fresh flowers, a wine list and a bread basket.

She raced off to find Lance.

"His table's ready," she murmured as she pulled her tall, model-esque friend into a corner. "That means he's here, right?"

Lance sighed heavily. He was pretty enough to be on a billboard and funny enough to make her want to have dinner with him. Just for the company, of course—Lance wasn't into women and she wasn't into relationships.

"He's here," Lance confirmed. "You're going to get fired, you know that, right?"

"That's okay. So we have a plan. I'll take their drink orders, then show Nathan King the DVD. We'll talk, he'll be charming and agree and all will be well. If it goes badly—" She glanced upward and offered a brief prayer that it *not* go badly…it couldn't. There were no other plans after this one.

She sucked in a breath. "If it goes badly, you come running over and yell at me to get away from your table. Then you complain loudly to the manager that I presumed to take over your station. I'll slip out during the confusion."

"With the DVD player."

"Right." Because she had to return that puppy later. It was expensive and she was, as always, short on money.

"This isn't going to work," Lance told her.

"It *has* to work. I'll make it work." She would, too. By sheer force of will, she could move mountains.

She glanced back at the table and saw four men being seated. Based on her Internet research, she could easily pick out Nathan King. Tall, dark and rich, she thought grimly. A nice combination that made him extremely popular with women of all ages. If only her motives were that simple.

She waited until the men had settled down and were chatting before approaching. Random facts flashed through her mind. Nathan King, age thirty-eight. He'd come from a working-class family and had earned his money the hard way. He was divorced. He had a reputation for being so cold, he froze out the competition.

He'd also lost his son to Gilliar's Disease six years ago. Of all the billionaires in all the world, she'd chosen him specifically for that reason.

"Gentlemen," she said when she reached the table, giving her best smile and flipping her long, layered blond hair. Normally, she wore it pulled back. But for these purposes, she'd curled, teased and sprayed it until she looked just trashy enough to be sexy. With more makeup than usual and a push-up bra doing its best with what she had, she hoped to get Nathan's attention long enough to make him listen. "What can I get for you?"

Two of the men exchanged glances, then looked back at her.

She knew exactly what they were thinking and silently told them, no, she wasn't on the menu. She wasn't here for them.

She looked directly at Nathan King and was instantly chilled by the lack of emotion in his dark eyes. Somewhere she'd read that he'd been described as the kind of man who made sharks nervous. She got the analogy as a shiver tiptoed down her spine.

He was as good-looking as his pictures had promised. Maybe more so, but none of that mattered when the man in question appeared to be lacking a soul.

She had the sudden realization that she could totally blow this, and that if she failed, she had nowhere else to go. Then she remembered why she was here, what she needed, and squared her shoulders.

"Scotch for me," Nathan said, his voice low and clipped.

She thought of the small amount in the bottom of the bottle she'd knocked over earlier and hoped there was more inventory. She carefully wrote down the order, along with those from the other three men.

"We have several specials," she said as she tucked her pad into her apron, reached behind it and pulled out the small DVD player. She opened it, turned it on and set it in front of Nathan.

"If I may?" she asked as she pushed Play.

"This is new," he said, looking at his associates. "The things restaurants will do to keep business."

The other men tried to look at the screen, but Kerri ignored them. The only one who mattered was the one frowning as on the DVD the interviewer questioned Dr. Abram Wallace.

"So you were close to a breakthrough?" the woman asked.

Dr. Wallace nodded slowly. "One can't be sure. In matters of research there are always questions. But with a little more time…"

Nathan glared at her. His eyes were ice, his expression hard. She had the distinct feeling that if he'd had a gun on him, he would have shot her and never blinked.

"What the hell are you up to?" he asked.

"Saving a boy's life," she said, speaking quickly. Time was not her friend at the moment. "My name is Kerri Sullivan and my son has Gilliar's Disease. Your son had it, as well, so you know what he's going through. Cody will die soon if something isn't done. I've been talking to scientists and doctors for years. But there aren't enough sick kids to warrant funding from the government or other private agencies. Then I saw this interview. Dr. Wallace was working on a cure for Gilliar's Disease. He was close, really close. There was an explosion in his lab a few years ago. The lab shut down. He's still working, but it's just him and his assistant. If he had more money, he could find the cure. That's why I'm here, Mr. King. He needs fifteen million dollars."

Nathan King motioned for the manager. Kerri kept talking.

"It's a fortune I'll never have," she said, speaking even faster now. "But you give that amount to charity every year. If you could just give him the money, he could keep on working. He could make a difference.

He could save my son. Please, Mr. King. I'm running out of options and Cody is running out of time. I know you understand. You lost your son. Please help me save mine."

"What are you doing?" the manager asked as he approached. He reached for Kerri's arm. "This isn't your station. Lance takes care of Mr. King and his guests."

Kerri pulled free and ignored her soon-to-be-ex boss. "You have to help. I'm desperate. There isn't anyone else. I've been everywhere, talked to everyone. Your little boy would have wanted you to help me."

Nathan King had remained impassive through her speech, but now he carefully put his napkin on the table and stood.

He was a whole lot taller, so he bent over until they were eye-to-eye and his face was only inches from hers. "Get the hell out of here," he growled. "Get out now, or I'll have you arrested."

"No!" Her voice rose as she was grabbed from behind. "I won't give up. You have to do this. That kind of money is nothing to you. Why won't you save a child? He's just a little boy. He doesn't deserve to die."

Kerri fought against the men dragging her out, but they were bigger and stronger. She found herself propelled through the front door and actually thrown onto the sidewalk. She went down on one knee and stayed there, trying to catch her breath.

"You're fired," her boss screeched. "Fired. You're a lousy waitress. I'll bet your recommendations are all fake. You're lucky I don't have you arrested."

She slowly stood and stared at the short, fat man frothing at her.

"I've already been threatened with that today," she said, suddenly exhausted. "You'll have to try something else."

"I'm not paying you for the last three days. I'm ripping up your time card and your application. You never existed."

Kerri waited until he'd stomped back inside before leaning against the brick building. It was spring in Seattle, which meant cool air and a constant threat of rain. She needed to drag her butt back inside to get her purse, her coat and the DVD player. Although how she was going to accomplish that without being seen seemed hard to imagine.

But it was easier to deal with logistics than face the reality of failure.

Nathan King hadn't just said no—he'd refused to listen. How was that possible? He knew exactly what she was going through. He'd suffered, he'd felt the aching sense of helplessness. How could he not be compassionate?

Tim, Nathan King's chauffeur, approached. "He didn't listen?" he asked.

Kerri shook her head. "You said he wouldn't."

Tim had actually said more than that. He'd

warned her against her plan and told her his boss liked to support his charities from a distance. He sent a check—he never got involved.

"You had to try," Tim reminded her.

"I'll try again."

"How?"

Good question. She'd been so sure Nathan would help her. She'd put all of her energy into getting to him. She'd tried infiltrating his secretarial staff, but her office skills were more pathetic than her server skills. Next she'd attempted to become one of his maids. But while the company that took care of his many buildings had been willing to offer her a job, she'd found out that she'd need seniority to work anywhere close to the boss. She didn't have years to work her way up the food chain.

As a last resort, she'd attempted to seduce Tim and when that hadn't worked, she'd tried to bribe him. The five hundred dollars she'd put on the table—all the money she had in the world—hadn't impressed him. Still, he'd listened as she talked about Gilliar's Disease and Cody and how Nathan King could be the one miracle they were waiting for.

Tim had offered to introduce her to his significant other—and Lance and the lunchtime ambush had been hatched.

"I'll come up with something," she said. "I'm a great ideas person. Maybe I could kidnap him and hold him for fifteen million in ransom."

"You wouldn't like prison," Tim said. "Plus, I'd be forced to shoot you and that would be a drag for both of us."

Despite everything, Kerri had to smile. Tim was about six four, two hundred and fifty pounds of muscle. He wouldn't have to shoot her—he could simply crush her like a soda can.

"I'm open to any suggestions you have," she said.

"Mr. King doesn't like publicity he doesn't control. It makes him very angry."

"Okay." Interesting, but not helpful. "And?"

Tim hesitated. She suspected he was weighing his loyalty to his boss and thinking about the afternoon he'd spent with her son, remembering Cody didn't have as many afternoons left as other children.

"Sometimes it's more helpful to ask for forgiveness than permission."

Did he have to be so cryptic? "For those of us not flirting with a one-sixty IQ, that means?"

"Say you already got what you want. Then maybe you'll get it."

Before she could absorb that, Lance burst out the front door of the restaurant.

"I'm not supposed to be doing this," he said as he thrust her belongings at her. "I have to get back to work. Nathan King is fuming. The staff is in an uproar and some of the customers want to know why they didn't get to see their specials on a DVD player. Speaking of which…" He handed the player to her. "Don't forget your receipt when you return it."

Kerri hugged him briefly. "I owe you. Seriously. Anything. It's yours. A kidney? I'm so there."

"I know you are." Lance smiled at Tim. "See you later, big guy."

Tim grinned. "I'm counting on it."

Lance ran back inside. Kerri shrugged into her coat. She had turned to Tim to clarify his slightly confusing suggestion when the door opened again, but this time Nathan King was the one stepping outside.

He looked from her to Tim.

"What's going on?" he demanded.

"I tried to bribe your chauffeur into letting me slip into the back of your car," Kerri said quickly, not wanting the man who had helped her to get into trouble. "He said no. You have very loyal employees, Mr. King."

"I pay for loyalty."

She briefly thought about debating the merits of paying versus earning, but let it go. There was only one greater good here.

"Please help me," she said. "I will do anything to keep my son alive." She hesitated. "I'll find a way to convince you."

He folded his arms over his chest. "How?" He nodded at the DVD player. "If that's the best you've got, you've already lost."

She stiffened. "I've only begun this battle."

His face was unreadable, and his body language screamed that he was unapproachable.

"I don't get it," she said. "It can't be about the money. You give away millions. Why not to this cause? Why don't you care? Why don't you want to fix this?"

His dark gaze bored into her, digging down to her soul. "My son is dead. Why the hell should I care about yours?"

KERRI DROVE east on I90, turning off twenty miles below the summit at the exit for Songwood, the small town she and Cody had moved to three months ago.

The once-thriving mountain community had taken an economic and emotional nosedive three years ago when the large biomedical research facility run by Abram Wallace had exploded on a dark, snowy night.

A case of bad electrical wiring had caused the disaster, killing the four-member janitorial staff, two security guards and three scientists. They had all been local—leaving the two hundred other employees and the town keenly feeling their loss.

Dr. Wallace had shut down the lab and become a recluse. Songwood had tried to limp along, gathering up a few tourist dollars during the winter ski season and attempting to lure the outdoor types to hike and stay in the area during the summer.

As soon as Kerri had discovered that Dr. Wallace had been working on a cure for Gilliar's Disease,

SUSAN MALLERY   21

she'd packed up Cody and moved to the town. So far she'd been unable to meet the researcher himself, but she'd become friends with Linda, his assistant. Linda had been the one to tell her about the lack of funding.

Which was still Kerri's problem. She rented a chair at the local beauty salon. Even on the best of weeks, her tips would never get her to the needed fifteen-million-dollar mark.

She drove into town, honked and waved at Frank, the guy who owned the gas station, and turned left at the library.

Songwood might be close to going under, but like an elegant Southern woman, she would go down looking good. The storefronts were all freshly painted, the flowers and bushes trimmed and tidy. It was the kind of town that had pumpkin festivals and hay rides. Kerri had lived in a lot of places in her life, and this was one of her favorites.

She parked behind the dry cleaners, then hurried around to the front.

"I'm late," she announced as she entered, then handed Millie a five-dollar bill.

Millie, a gray-haired former teacher, passed over the costume. "Everything's in place. You can change in back."

"Thanks."

Kerri ducked under the counter and headed for the tiny restroom at the rear of the building.

In a matter of minutes she'd replaced her black

pants and shirt with a white skating skirt, white boots, blue tights, a long-sleeved dark blue T-shirt with a sequined *W* on top of an *M* in the middle of her chest and a bright red cape. It was amazing what one could find at a decent thrift store.

She brushed the hairspray out of her hair, pulled it back into a ponytail, then grabbed her street clothes and raced to her car, her transformation from regular person to almost-mythical Wonder Mom complete.

"Thanks, Millie," she yelled as she went.

"You give that boy a hug for me," Millie called after her.

Kerri waved, then jumped in her car and drove the three blocks to Michelle's house. Cody was playing with Michelle's son, Brandon, and Kerri planned to use that as an opportunity to flaunt her extra-special powers. Well, technically she was a single mom in a cheesy outfit, but in the right light it was almost like having superpowers.

Right on time the back door opened and Michelle appeared with the family cat in her arms.

"Good luck," Michelle whispered as she passed over the plump tabby.

"Thanks."

Kerri stared at the sturdy tree beside the house and at the ladder Michelle had put in place. Climbing the ladder was scary enough. Climbing it with a less-than-cooperative cat in her arms could be challenging. But she needed to make an appearance as

Wonder Mom and this was the best idea she'd been able to come up with on short notice.

She stroked Tiger until the cat was purring, then started up the ladder. The purring stopped. A couple more steps and the cat began to struggle.

"Cut me a break," Kerri whispered quietly. "If we fall you'll land on your feet and mock me. I'll be lying flat on my back with everyone looking up my skirt. Worse, I'll probably break something."

The cat seemed unimpressed by the argument and continued to try to twist away.

Kerri kept hold of her, careful to grab on to the back claws to avoid having them slice through her stomach, which only left her one hand for ladder clutching. Not a good thing.

She finally reached the thick branch more than halfway up the tree. After getting into position on the branch and doing her darnedest not to fall off, she kicked the ladder free.

"We're committed now," she told the unamused cat. Kerri battled very legitimate fear. What had she been thinking? A cat? A tree? Was she insane?

From inside the house came a cry of distress.

"Tiger's gone," Michelle said loudly, sounding desperate and worried. "Did she get out? What if she climbed the tree? She always does that, then she can't get down. Oh, no!"

The blinds at the rear of the house opened and two boys stared out into the backyard.

Kerri took that as her cue. She pushed Tiger onto a higher branch. The cat clung on, swaying and meowing in protest.

"I've got you," Kerri told the unhappy cat. "Hang on, Tiger. I'll save you. I'm Wonder Mom and that's what I do."

She retrieved the cat, who glared at her and tried to swipe Kerri with her claws. But Kerri kept clear of the weapons. She lowered Tiger to the branch at her feet and watched as the disgruntled feline made her way to the ground. Then Kerri turned her attention to the trampoline carefully positioned just below the tree.

She slowly eased along the branch, grateful she'd taken her thrift-store boots into a shoe-repair shop for a gripping sole. When the limb narrowed and began to dip, she paused, sighted the trampoline, ignored the knot of fear in her stomach and jumped.

She hit the trampoline, rose in the air, managed an ungraceful flip before hitting again where she landed on her back. After catching her breath, she crawled to the side and climbed down.

She might be pushing thirty but she still had it, she told herself as she smoothed down the front of her skirt. Sort of. Too bad she'd never taken gymnastics. Training like that would have really helped to convince her son that she was Wonder Mom—a mom with amazing powers—practically a comic-book hero.

She turned to the window and waved at the two

boys, then walked toward the house. Tiger ran ahead of her, all bushy and annoyed at her part in the drama.

"We need to work on your motivation," Kerri told the cat. "We need more fear and less annoyance. Mrs. Barclay's cat is always willing to work with me if you're not interested."

Tiger ignored her and raced into the house. Michelle held open the back door and grinned. "Not bad, Wonder Mom."

CHAPTER TWO

"I HEARD ABOUT the cat rescue," Kerri's friend Linda said that evening after the dinner dishes were done and Kerri had tucked Cody into bed. "Half the town thinks you're a saint and the other half thinks you should be institutionalized."

"I'm not a saint," Kerri said as she leaned back against the sofa. "I'm just trying to do the best I can."

She'd already told Linda about her disastrous meeting with Nathan King.

"I don't know what else to do," Kerri admitted, which wasn't her style. She never allowed herself to even think about failing. After all, she was Wonder Mom.

The idea for the crazy name and costume had popped into her brain four years ago, shortly after Cody had been diagnosed with Gilliar's Disease. He'd been five and in a lot of pain. He'd gotten so down, he refused to go to school or hang out with his friends.

In a move that many would consider too bizarre for words, Kerri had come up with the idea of being

Wonder Mom. If she had secret powers, they would also be passed on to her son. And if Cody had secret powers, then he could certainly conquer his disease.

With the help of some neighbors and a hydraulic jack, she'd arranged for her son to "see" her lift a car with one hand. He'd been so impressed he'd begged her to let him sign up for T-ball. Over the years she'd figured out a costume, a logo and had made regular appearances doing the seemingly impossible.

She didn't know if it was the whole Wonder Mom persona or just good luck, but Cody's disease had progressed more slowly than expected. If looking like an idiot was helping, she was happy to do it every day.

"What about what Tim mentioned?" Linda reached for her glass of wine. "Say it's happened and maybe it will."

"A little clarity would have been nice," Kerri murmured. "All I can come up with is that he was suggesting I announce Nathan King agreed to give the money."

"Why not?"

Linda was an attractive brunette in her late forties. She'd spent twenty years working with Abram Wallace in the research facility in town and Kerri had come to rely on her intelligence and practical sense. She had met her when Linda had come to her with a hair emergency.

"Would it work?" Kerri asked more to herself than Linda. "Can I do that? Lie?"

Linda smiled. "It won't be the first time. It's not like you actually had the references you claimed to have to get that restaurant job."

"I know, but the reference thing would fall in the white-lie category. Is announcing a donation that hasn't been made illegal? I'm all Cody has. If I were to go to jail…" She opened her mouth, then closed it. Somewhere deep inside her brain a light went on.

She straightened. "I'm having an Oprah 'aha' moment," she said, hardly daring to think the whole thing through. Was it possible? Could she pull it off?

"I have letters," she told her friend. "Form letters from King's company. So I could scan in the letterhead and then write a different letter saying he's giving us the money. I give that to the local paper. They get all excited, word goes out to the wire service and voilà, the whole world knows."

Linda grinned. "It could work. And the jail threat?"

"That's the great part. Do you really think a big-time developer is going to put the mother of a sick kid in jail? If he tried, there has to be some sleazy lawyer willing to take on my case. Think of the publicity. Worst-case scenario, Nathan King backs out of the donation, then someone else may step forward."

Linda leaned forward and pulled a folder out of her purse. "I don't think he'll be backing out. I did a little research of my own. Nathan King is trying to build those luxury high-rise towers on Puget Sound."

Kerri wrinkled her nose. "Yeah, yeah. Million-plus-dollar condos and upscale shopping and restaurants. In my next life I'll buy one."

"He's getting a lot of resistance from city government. You've only been living here a few months, but I've been in the Seattle area all my life. Nathan King has made a lot of enemies. He's not well liked. Really bad publicity could ruin his chances of getting his project through."

Hope burned hot and bright in Kerri's chest. "He couldn't afford to put me in jail."

"Probably not."

"I would represent every little person he's ever stepped on in his quest to amass his fortune."

"Exactly."

"I like it."

The two women clinked wineglasses.

AFTER FINISHING his breakfast, Nathan King put down the *Wall Street Journal* and opened the folder of clippings that had been left with his paper. Every morning he reviewed what the newspapers had said about him the previous day.

In his current battle for zoning and funding, press reports were a necessary evil.

He flipped through copies of articles about his various businesses, an op-ed piece on the horrors of luxury high-rise construction, a short report on the wire about his plans to contribute fifteen million toward research on Gilliar's Disease and an interview with a pro-environment reporter who had twisted his every response to make him sound both cruel and stupid. If they—

He carefully set his coffee on the table, then flipped back to the previous page.

There weren't many details. Just a statement about the donation and a couple of sentences that research would resume at the facility in Songwood, Washington.

Nathan already had out his cell phone. He hit the speed dial for Jason Hardy.

"You're getting an early start," Jason said when he answered. "What's up?"

"Someone is trying to blackmail me into giving her fifteen million dollars."

"What? Who?"

"I don't know her name. Some psychotic waitress who ambushed me at lunch last week. She wants me to donate to some cause." There was no point in telling Jason what cause. Nathan never discussed his son's illness and subsequent death with anyone. Not even his closest friend and attorney. "She even tried bribing my chauffeur to get to me. She's crazy. I want her stopped."

"And people think being incredibly rich is trouble free," Jason said easily. "Was she working at The Grill?"

"As a server. A bad one."

"I'll start there. Give me until the end of the day

and I'll get you a full profile. So how's she black-mailing you?"

"She issued a press release on our letterhead say-ing that I would personally be donating the money to some research facility in Songwood."

"The money goes there rather than to her?" Jason asked.

"She's got a sick kid. The head guy there is work-ing on the kid's disease. She wants a miracle."

"Well, sure. Is it fatal?"

Nathan refused to think about the slow and pain-ful death that claimed children with Gilliar's Disease. "Is that compassion I hear in your voice?"

Jason chuckled. "Sorry. I forgot myself. You'd think law school would have beaten that out of me. I'll call you later."

THE HAIR BARN WAS like any one of a thousand small-town beauty salons. It was bright, cheerful, and the source of all the local gossip.

As Kerri wove the pointed end of her comb through Amber Whitney's dark blond hair, she listened care-fully to the talk all around.

"My Frank says they'll have to hire at least fifty new scientists," Millie of the dry cleaning store was saying. "That will take some time. But they're going to be well paid, so if you want to sell, this is the time. All those research people will need housing. Sure, a few of them will live in Seattle or North Bend and

drive up the mountain, but plenty will settle here."
She sighed. "It'll be like it was, when the town was
thriving. It's good for business."

"I wonder how many other people they'll be hiring,"
Millie's friend said. "Secretaries, janitorial staff, office
workers. Maybe some basic lab techs. My Denny
would much rather work there than go back to logging."

The town buzzed with news of the donation. It was
all anyone had talked about ever since the press release
had hit the wire. Kerri swallowed back the knot of
guilt in her throat and kept weaving Amber's hair.

Lying to the town was a repercussion she hadn't
thought through. Everyone was so excited by the
prospect of the lab opening up again.

She didn't want to hurt these people. She didn't
want to hurt anyone. She'd been so intent on simply
getting the funding for Dr. Wallace that she hadn't
considered there were other lives on the line. If
Nathan King didn't come through…

He had to, she reminded herself. Just that morning
there'd been an article in the Seattle paper about how
Nathan's charity work should be considered when it
came to giving him the zoning he wanted. If he was
exposed as a man who went back on his word, maybe
he wouldn't get his towers. Of course, if she were
exposed as a liar and a fraud, he might get the
sympathy vote.

"Hey, Mom."

She turned and saw Cody at the front of the salon.

Most days she tried to be done before he got out of school, but Thursdays she worked late.

"Hey, kiddo. How was your day?"

"Okay."

Cody balanced on his crutches. Kerri was pleased to see that the new style, with the bracing around his forearm, seemed to be helping his balance. That and the fact that she'd finally cleaned out his backpack. It had gotten so heavy, she'd been afraid he would fall on his back like a turtle and be unable to get up.

"Be right back," Kerri told Amber, then crossed to her son.

Cody was on the short side for his age group— not a surprise, considering his condition—but smart, with that emotionally mature edge sick kids seem to get. At nine, he'd reached the point where he was un-comfortable being kissed by his mom in public. Kerri had yet to reach the point where she didn't care.

"Math test," she said as she pulled him close and dropped a quick kiss on the top of his head. "Tell me you kicked fraction butt."

"They're all totally kicked," he said as he squirmed away, then smiled at her. "I missed one."

"One? One? Oh, man. I have to disown you now."

"Leave me on the curb for some stranger to take me away?" he asked with a grin.

"Absolutely. Someone who doesn't care about kids who aren't perfect. You missed one. I may never recover from the disappointment."

"Spaghetti with garlic bread."

She opened her eyes wide. "Excuse me? Young men who miss one question on their math tests do not get to demand things like spaghetti with garlic bread for dinner."

"It was an A, Mom. You know missing one is still an A."

"Are you kidding? An A? What is this world coming to? I'm appalled. And you know how I get when I'm appalled."

She reached for him. He ducked away, but the crutches hindered him. Kerri dove in and began tickling him. She was careful to stay away from his ribs. Like all his bones, they were fragile.

He giggled and squirmed, then relaxed in her arms.

"I'll make spaghetti," she murmured into his hair. "Then we'll tackle the spelling words. You'll wait for me at Brandon's?"

"Uh-huh."

"Good. Try to keep Tiger out of that tree, okay? I'm on a Wonder Mom break for the next couple of days."

Cody looked up at her. "I will, Mom. See you later."

She was supposed to let him go and she would…in a second. But staring into his eyes like that, she was reminded of Cody's father. Cody was so much like her late husband. It was a unique combination of pleasure and heartbreaking pain.

"Be good," she said.

He nodded and left the salon.

"DON'T BE STUPID," Jason Hardy said. "I'm telling you this based on my personal experience as your lawyer. You pay me three hundred dollars an hour for that experience, Nathan. So listen."

"I'm listening."

"No, you're not. If you were still listening, you'd be back in the city. Instead you're driving up I90 by yourself. I don't want you confronting that woman alone."

"That woman" was one Kerri Sullivan. A single mom and hairdresser. Nearly every detail of her insignificant life was listed in the folder next to him on the passenger seat of his Mercedes.

She'd been an average student in high school, a cheerleader. Her parents had been killed when she'd been fairly young and she'd been raised by her maternal grandmother. She'd gone to community college, but had dropped out after less than a year to go to beauty school. She'd met and married Brian Sullivan. Brian had been in the army and died when his truck had overturned. Eight and a half months later, she'd given birth to her only child.

Cody Sullivan, age nine. His Gilliar's Disease had been diagnosed when he'd been five. He'd lived longer than most and was only now entering the truly degenerative stage.

In the past four years Kerri had lived in Texas and Minnesota. She supported them by working in beauty salons. Her location choices weren't random.

She moved to where the research was being done. She'd run out of options, until she discovered Dr. Abram Wallace's work in Songwood. She'd moved there three months ago.

"I won't let her blackmail me," he told Jason. The built-in speakerphone in his car picked up his low voice.

"So what are you going to do? Threaten her? That's *my* job, and let me say, for the record, I resent you trying to take the fun out of it." Jason sighed. "I mean it, Nathan. You're going to get angry and say some things you shouldn't."

"She thinks she's trapped me. She thinks I can't back out because I'll look bad. Who the hell does she think she is?"

"A desperate mom?" Jason asked. "You have nothing to say to her."

"I'm going to make her stop. No one holds me hostage."

"You're going to make the situation worse. You have a very competent staff. We want to do our job. Let us deal with her. You don't need any more negative publicity."

"I want her ass in jail," Nathan muttered.

"Not going to happen. Let's imagine that headline. She's got the sympathy factor. I don't like what she's doing, either, but let's be logical."

Logic? Nathan wasn't interested. Whether it was a well thought-out plan or just dumb luck, Kerri

Sullivan had gotten plenty of play from her bogus statement. He'd actually been contacted by someone at the research facility in Songwood, asking about the particulars for the donation. They were, she'd informed him, ready to begin hiring. Two other parents of kids with Gilliar's Disease had also tried to get through to him. Just to thank him, their messages had said.

"How the hell does one hairdresser get all this done?" he demanded.

"She's got balls," Jason said, a hint of admiration in his voice.

"Remember whose side you're on," Nathan told him.

"You don't have to remind me. Being on your side is the reason I'm telling you to turn around and come home. Let me handle her."

Nathan grimaced. "You're breaking up," he said into the perfectly clear connection. "I'll call back when I'm on my way down the mountain."

"Dammit, Nathan. Don't you hang up. And don't do anything either of us will regret."

Nathan disconnected the call.

Thirty minutes later he was in downtown Songwood, letting his GPS system direct him to the Hair Barn. When he found it, he parked and walked directly inside.

The place was filled with women. Conversation stopped the second the glass door closed behind him.

A dozen or so pairs of eyes settled on him, but he ignored everyone except the blonde he remembered from the restaurant.

Last week he'd been too pissed off to notice anything about her. Now he compared the real, live Kerri Sullivan to the picture in her folder.

She was fairly average. Blond hair, blue eyes, medium height. Pretty enough, in a corn-fed kind of way. There were a million women just like her in the Midwest, which wasn't a good thing. If he had her arrested and she got the kind of press coverage he knew she was more than capable of generating, every one of those million women would relate to her. She'd come off as pure as Snow White and he'd be the damned evil stepmother.

He ignored everyone else in the place and walked directly to her.

"We have to talk."

She paused in the act of sweeping up hair from the floor and glanced at him. "I don't think so."

"Maybe I'm here to tell you what you want to hear."

"You look way too angry for that to be true. I'm guessing you want to threaten me. I don't accept threats during work hours and I'm on the clock for another hour."

He swore silently. Jason was right—she had balls. Giant ones.

"Ms. Sullivan," he began, aware of every other person in the place listening to their conversation.

"I said no," she told him, squaring her shoulders and trying to stare him down. "I make minimum wage plus tips. The fact that you know who I am and where I work tells me that you've done your research. That probably included a copy of my last couple of tax returns. You know what I make. I'm a single mom. I can't afford to miss time off work because you're in the mood to talk."

He wanted to crush her like the insignificant insect she was. But he also respected her ability to negotiate like a pro. Under other circumstances, he might find himself respecting *her*.

"Fine," he said, pulling out his wallet. "How much do you want?"

"About fifteen million. I thought that was pretty clear."

"I meant for our conversation."

"I'm not taking your money for that."

He glanced around, then returned his attention to her and lowered his voice. "What if I just tell them the truth? That you made it all up."

Her blue gaze never wavered. "I'll burst into tears and demand to know how you could be so cruel as to crush the hopes of an entire town."

He swore. "We're going to talk."

She nodded slowly. "Fine. Have a seat. I'll cut your hair."

"You mean scalp me. No thanks."

She leaned the broom against the wall and put her

hands on her hips. She was trying to look tough, he thought, and failing miserably.

"Look," she said. "I'm good at what I do. I'm relatively new in town and I'm still building my clientele. I'm also interested in convincing you to donate fifteen million dollars to save my son's life. Why on earth would I want to risk all of that by scalping you?"

"You know I don't want to give you the money and I'm willing to do just about anything to stop you. That doesn't make us friends."

"Maybe not, but whoever's been doing your hair isn't doing a very good job." She patted her chair. "Come on. I'll turn you into a chick magnet."

"I'm already a chick magnet." But he reluctantly lowered himself into the seat.

Behind him, conversation resumed in the salon. Several women pulled out cell phones. Great. Soon he'd have an audience.

She covered him in a black plastic cape, then reached for a spray bottle and wet down his hair.

"How'd you do your research?" he asked.

"Internet. I can only type about twenty words a minute, but I'm tenacious."

"And talented. The letter from my company looks authentic."

She smiled at him in the mirror and reached for scissors. He held in a wince when she made her first cut.

"It is authentic. You agreed to pay the money."

"And if I hadn't?"

"Someone who had nothing to lose might have a form letter from your office. Form letters, although rude and thoughtless, do come with letterhead. A good scanner, a little creativity, the right software and there we are."

"You contacted me before?" he asked, knowing he shouldn't be surprised.

"Of course. I sent in a grant proposal. Your committee didn't even consider it. Evil bastards."

"We get a lot of requests," he said absently, wondering why she'd been turned down. The report in his car also contained some information on Wallace's lab. According to all accounts, he'd been close to a cure before the explosion.

"How old was your son when he died?" she asked.

The unexpected question cut through him like a laser. He stiffened, then consciously forced himself to relax.

She wanted them to connect over shared pain, he reminded himself. To convince him to give her the money.

He said nothing.

She combed several strands together, then trimmed the ends.

"Cody's nine. In the fourth grade. He's bright, which helps, because sometimes he has to miss school. You remember what that was like. He likes all sports, but baseball is his favorite. I swear, we've seen every televised baseball game since he was three. Now that we're in Washington, he's a Mariners fan."

Daniel had liked football, Nathan thought, then pushed the memory away. Damn Kerri Sullivan.

"I have a very expensive team of lawyers," he said, his voice as conversational as hers had been. "They're going to take care of you. You can go away quietly or with a lot of noise, but you will go away."

She stepped back to study the cut, then moved in close again and picked up her scissors. "What are you going to do? Throw me in jail?"

"If necessary."

She leaned closer. "Coldhearted billionaire throws mother of dying child in jail. Zoning commission refuses zoning petition. They kind of go together, huh?"

"Blackmail is illegal."

She stepped back and smiled. "Blackmail. Oh, right. Because I have the power. I couldn't even sleep with your chauffeur when I tried."

"Tim is gay."

"I found that out. But he was very nice about it, which I appreciated. The man has style. You could learn a lot from him." She trimmed more hair. "Face it, Mr. King. I've already won. You can't go back on your word. You'll look like the villain most people think you are. Write the check and walk away. Consider it your good deed for the month."

"I will not be manipulated by some hairdresser."

"Of course you will. You got to the top by doing

what has to be done. Think of me as an unexpected expense."

He narrowed his gaze. "You don't care what you do, as long as you get your money."

The chair spun so fast he started to slip. He grabbed the arms and found himself facing Kerri directly. Her blue eyes were the color of the ocean during a storm.

"You want to build your fancy-assed condos, have at it. I don't care. But let me be completely clear. I am fighting for my son's life. So you're right. I will stop at nothing. I will march into that zoning commission, place my hand on a Bible and lie. I will tell everyone who asked that you promised the research facility the money and now you're trying to get out of it. I don't care if I go to hell, Mr. King. I care if my son lives."

He recognized her desperation. He'd felt it once. He'd been just as determined and it had all been for nothing. He'd lost and the morning he'd buried his seven-year-old son, he'd vowed he would never care about anyone ever again.

The door of the Hair Barn opened and a teenager with a camera walked in. He marched over to Kerri's station, aimed and took a picture.

"The local paper?" Nathan asked when the kid left.

"Uh-huh. I'm guessing one of the other customers called the paper to say you were here. I'm doing this for Cody, but there are other lives on the line.

This town is dying, and opening the research facility again will bring it back to life."

He swore under his breath. He didn't give a damn about the town or her or her kid. He just wanted his permit to build his towers. The ones with his name on them so he could show the world what he'd done and who he was.

Kerri turned him back to the mirror, rubbed something sticky into her hands, then through his hair. She smoothed and squished and then whipped off the cape and stepped back.

"I'm done."

He studied himself. The cut was good. Damn good. Unless the crap she'd put on his head gave him a rash, she'd been totally professional.

He stood and reached for his wallet. "How much do I owe you?"

"Seventy dollars, plus tip." She smiled as she spoke.

His gaze strayed to the sign hanging over the mirrors. The one that said a man's haircut was seventeen-fifty.

He handed her a hundred-dollar bill. "Keep the change."

She took the money without blinking. "I will."

"I can sue you," he said. "Drag you into court."

"Interesting. There is the problem of perception," she told him. "And oral agreements. I'm not a lawyer, of course, but for all intents and purposes, you're here to firm up the final details. We have a picture to prove it. Do you think after all the promises you made, if you back out and the town takes *you* to court, we can get punitive damages?"

Shit. Who was this woman?

He sucked in a breath. "You use me, I use you."

It was as if someone had turned a light on inside of her. Her eyes brightened, her skin flushed and he half expected her to glow.

"Use away," she said. "Pictures, interviews. I'll tell the world you're a god. I'll even sleep with you if you want."

He looked her up and down, then smiled slowly. "I just might take you up on that."

CHAPTER THREE

KERRI PULLED into the driveway in front of her tiny garage and wondered if maybe offering to sleep with Nathan King had been a mistake. He was just cold-blooded enough to take her up on the idea, if only to prove her determination had limits. Which meant she was going to have to prove him wrong by saying yes.

The man was good-looking enough to be appealing under other circumstances, assuming she was into tall, dark and ruthless. But he wasn't her type. She preferred a man who had a heart. Like Brian, she thought as she got out of her car and waited for Nathan to pull up behind her and do the same.

Her late husband had been perfect—or at least perfect for her. Funny, caring, giving, loyal. Oh, sure, he'd been male, so there were times when he'd made her crazy, but not crazy enough to ever regret marrying him. She knew she'd gotten lucky when they'd met and fallen in love—something she wasn't expecting to happen again. Lightning didn't strike twice. Besides, all she cared about these days was getting Cody better. There was no time or energy left over for anything else.

"A strange man in the middle of the day. What will the neighbors think?" Nathan asked as he followed her up the steps and into her small two-bedroom house.

The rental was much like all the other places she'd found over the past few years. Run-down and cheap. The latter was her only requirement. Unfortunately, it usually came attached to the former.

Kerri smiled at him, then led the way into her kitchen. "The neighbors all know who you are. They're going to think the truth—that you're here to talk about the money you're giving to Dr. Wallace's research facility."

"I'm here to talk about our deal."

"Same thing."

She motioned to the chairs flanking the narrow table in the corner. "I'll make coffee. It's that or water. I save the milk for Cody. He needs it more than you do."

"I didn't realize there was a milk shortage." He shrugged out of his jacket and sat at her table.

"There isn't. Have you priced milk lately? Do you know how much a boy Cody's age can drink in one sitting?"

"No—to both."

Right. Because it would never occur to him to check the price of anything. She would bet that he had someone to do his grocery shopping for him. She focused on that because it was a whole lot easier to think about than to remember that Nathan had already been through what she was desperate to avoid—the loss of a child.

"Coffee is fine," he told her.

She nodded, then dumped the old grounds in the trash, put in a filter, new ground beans, water and flipped the on switch. Unable to put off the inevitable, she turned to face him.

Even sitting, Nathan was a big guy in a relatively small room. She had a feeling he was one of those people who used up an unfair amount of air. He had to be, because it was oddly stuffy in here.

"I'll have my lawyer draw up the paperwork," he told her, his expression determined. "Everything will be explained in detail, including the fact that you won't tell anyone about our deal. You and your son will be available whenever I ask, to do whatever I ask. Charity events, press functions. From now until the zoning commission meets in six weeks. In return, I'll give Dr. Wallace and his lab fifteen million dollars."

She crossed her arms over her chest. "I have terms."

He glared at her. "No, you don't. This is not negotiable, Ms. Sullivan."

"Of course it is. Everything is. And if you're going to use your money to get me to sleep with you, you should probably call me Kerri. It makes things more special."

He stood. There was no mistaking his temper. Anger burned hot and bright in the room, making her think that if she could harness a little of that energy, she could cut down on her electric bill.

"I am not using my money to get you to sleep with me."

"That's what you said. Before. At the salon."

"You offered."

"I was making a point. I will do whatever it takes to get Cody better. Even deal with the devil."

"You mean me?"

"You're not the devil." She tilted her head and stared at him. "You're a powerful, egotistical man who is too used to getting his way and doesn't care about other people very much, but you're not the devil."

The anger turned icy. "How flattering. Have you considered that you may want to hold off on insulting me until after the money has been transferred?"

She smiled. "You're not going to change your mind. For what it's worth, I *am* grateful."

"That's not immediately obvious."

"Would you be more comfortable if I fawned?"

"No."

"Then think of me as refreshing."

"Is that what you call it?"

She smiled. "Some people find me very charming."

"They see you as a steamroller and move fast to get out of your way."

"I'm a mother on a mission."

"The same thing."

He wasn't going to back down and she could get a serious cramp in her neck if he continued to loom over her like some annoyed, threatening, tall person.

"I can't totally be at your beck and call," she said, changing the subject. "I have a job and a life."

"You have a job and now *I'm* your life. I'll respect your work hours."

"Why do I doubt that?" She walked to the cupboard and pulled down two mugs. They were both chipped. She looked through her selection, but none of them were in great shape.

Nearly as bad as the chips were the gaudy logos on the front. Every one of them had been a freebie. Billionaire Nathan was just going to have to work around that, she thought as she poured coffee and handed it to him.

"I'll take it black," he told her, "what with milk being so scarce."

"Don't mock me. I'm poor."

"Don't assume about me. I'm rich."

She sighed. "You're not going to make this easy, are you?"

"You're blackmailing me. Why should I?"

"It's the gentlemanly thing to do."

He put down the coffee untasted. "I'm not interested in being a gentleman, Kerri. I'm interested in winning. I will honor my part of the bargain—see that you do the same. If you don't, I promise you'll regret screwing with me."

She set her mug next to his. "You can't do anything to me that's worse than what's already happening."

Something dark and painful flashed in his eyes. "I can still make your life hell. I'll have my secretary phone you and set up an appointment. We'll meet in my lawyer's office."

She wanted to snap at him, but the truth was, he could have ignored everything she'd done and not given her the money. Because of him, her son had a chance. Annoying or not, the man deserved to have her meet him at least halfway.

"Okay. Look, I'll try to help when I can, but I have Cody to think about. So at least give me some notice?"

"I'll do my best."

"Are you going to want me to show up at fancy stuff? If so, wardrobe could be an issue."

"I don't know." He pulled a business card out of his wallet and put it on the counter. "This is my direct number at work and my cell number. If you need to get in touch with me."

She picked up the card and waved it. "How much would a tabloid give me for these phone numbers?" she teased.

His eyes narrowed. "That is confidential information."

"So I can call whenever I want, right?"

He picked up his jacket and walked to the front door without speaking.

"Okay, fine. I won't play fast and loose with your personal info. Do you need *my* phone number?"

He turned back to her. "I have a file on you, remember?"

"I try not to." She glanced at the clock on the wall. "Cody will be home in a few minutes. You could stay and meet him."

"No, thank you. I have to be back in Seattle."

Translation—he wasn't interested in her son. She reminded herself he'd given her the money and she owed him. "Then I'll just be here, quivering in anticipation of your phone call."

One corner of his mouth twitched. "If only that were true."

DR. ABRAM WALLACE SLAMMED shut the door to his truck and walked into Bill's Food and Feed to pick up his weekly order. Bales of hay topped by bags of dog food stood to the left of the open double wood doors. On the right a galvanized tub held ice chilling imported asparagus and a basket of hothouse tomatoes. Bill catered to everything that ate—human and animal alike.

Abram stuck his hands in his coat pockets as he walked and kept his head down. He nodded as he passed a couple of women talking, then moved straight to the counter.

"Hey, Professor," Bill, a large man in his fifties, called out. "I got your order all ready. Looks like Linda's making you meat loaf. Lucky guy."

Linda, Abram's assistant, hadn't mentioned making dinner, but it was something she took on once or twice a week. He didn't pay attention to food and only ate because it allowed him to keep working. If it was up to him, he'd eat the same thing day after day. But Linda insisted on variety and making homemade meals so he wasn't always heating up something from a can.

"You must be excited," Bill said as he passed over a large box containing Abram's order. "About the money for the research facility. Nathan King's giving you fifteen million dollars."

Abram gave him a blank look.

"You haven't heard?" Bill paused. "You know, so you can start up again. Healing those sick kids."

Abram avoided newspapers and he didn't own a television. Linda kept him informed of any major events and reminded him to vote every few years.

"I don't know what you're talking about," he grumbled. Money? For research? He'd closed down the lab years ago. After the fire, he'd had to. There was no going back. He couldn't do that again. Couldn't take the chance.

"You're going to open the lab," Bill insisted. "With the money. Everyone's talking about how it will save the town."

Abram took his order and left. Fool, he thought as he retraced his steps to his car.

There was no saving Songwood. It was too late for both of them. Linda had asked him once why he stayed. He hadn't answered her, but he knew the reason. He'd killed the town. The least he could do was stick around and die with it.

"YOU'RE AN IDIOT," Jason Hardy said as he led the way into a small conference room.

"So you've said."

"Just trying to do my job. You shouldn't have gone up to Songwood by yourself."

"You're repeating yourself," Nathan told him as he walked over to the table against the far wall and poured himself a cup of coffee. "At what you make an hour, you should be more original."

"You're not cooperating," Jason muttered. "I have a bad feeling about all this."

Nathan reached for the container of cream, then paused as he remembered Kerri Sullivan hoarding milk for her son. As if milk was hard to come by. Although given her paycheck and her medical expenses, perhaps it *was* a luxury.

He remembered his mother complaining about the amount of food he'd put away when he'd been a teenager. But there had been affection, at least from her. His father was another story.

Involuntarily he turned to look out the window.

The conference room offered a sweeping view of Puget Sound, including the spot where Nathan's towers would go. Too bad his old man wasn't around to see them built. Not that the dead could ever admit they were wrong.

"If word of this gets out, you're screwed," Jason said.

Nathan shrugged. "It's a calculated risk. There's a confidentiality clause in the paperwork. Kerri and I will keep silent. And you're bound by client privilege. Who else is going to know?"

"I don't like it," Jason told him. "You should have let me handle this."

"It'll be worth it." Nathan sipped his coffee. "The fifteen million means nothing to me. If using Kerri Sullivan and her kid gets me my permits, I'm happy. If I'm happy—"

"I'm happy," Jason said with a shrug. "You're the boss. I just worry you're getting in over your head with her."

"Kerri? No way. She's nobody. A hairdresser."

"She was capable of getting you to back down and hand over fifteen million. Just be careful."

Nathan appreciated the sentiment, even as he found the idea of Kerri having any impact on him laughable.

"How long have you known me?" he asked Jason.

"Seven years. Close to eight."

"How many times have I screwed up?"

"None." His attorney nodded. "I agree with what you're saying. Just be careful."

"You're paranoid."

Jason grinned. "That's why I make the big bucks."

There was a knock at the conference door and then Kerri stepped inside.

She wore a dress and high heels, surprising Nathan. Her hair hung loose and she'd put on make-up. She was still farm-girl pretty. Not his type. But she would make a good impression on the people who mattered.

Nathan ignored her and glanced at Tim, who stood behind her.

"Any trouble?" he asked his driver.

Kerri sighed. "I was a very good girl. I was ready on time and I told funny stories nearly the whole ride here."

Tim's face remained impassive as he said, "No, sir."

"We shouldn't be more than an hour. Then you can take Ms. Sullivan home."

"Yes, sir."

Kerri smiled at Tim. "You should call him Nathan. I think he'd like that."

One corner of Tim's mouth twitched. "I appreciate the advice, Ms. Sullivan."

"Oh, sure. *Now* it's Ms. Sullivan. And we were so close just a short time ago."

Tim closed the door. Kerri glanced around, then walked toward Jason.

"Hi. I'm Kerri Sullivan. You don't look like a lawyer. Nice haircut, by the way. So, are you going to protect my rights, too? Should I call legal aid and get my own representation?"

Jason shook her hand. "Everything is very straight-forward, Ms. Sullivan."

"You are so lying."

Jason grinned. "Not as much as you'd think. I kept things simple. Mr. King provides the money to the research facility, you allow yourself and your son to be—"

"Exploited?" she asked sweetly.

Jason ignored that. "You and your son allow Mr. King to present himself in a more favorable light."

"Lucky us."

Nathan stayed by the window, watching rather than participating. He admired Kerri's bravado when it was obvious, at least to him, that she was terrified. Her hands trembled slightly and she kept inhaling deeply, as if consciously telling herself to breathe. None of the indicators were blatant, but he knew what to look for. It always paid to know what the enemy was thinking and feeling.

Not that she was his enemy. She was too far out of her league for that. He kept thinking he could squash her like a bug, if he took the time.

Except he couldn't—he needed her. He, who prided himself on needing no one.

Jason led her to the conference table and set a

folder in front of her. "Here's the paperwork. If you would please look it over before you sign."

She opened her purse and pulled out a sheet of paper. "I have a few requests of my own, first," she said.

"Excuse me?" Jason asked.

Nathan ignored him and turned his attention to Kerri. "The hell you do."

"I mentioned it when you were at my house."

"You were kidding."

"I was at the time, but when else am I going to be able to negotiate with the great and powerful Nathan King?" She fluttered her lashes at him. "I've been reading about you online. You're even richer than I thought. So I'm going to need a little bit more to cooperate."

"Did I mention the money hasn't been transferred yet?" She was bluffing, he thought. She had to be, but damn, she was good.

"You'll do it." She pushed the list toward Jason. "The top two are not negotiable."

Nathan took another sip of coffee. "Read it," he said, intrigued even as he prepared himself to be taken.

He could guess what she would want. A new car. Hers was a piece of crap. Some dented, rusting import with an engine that missed and bad tires. Maybe some cash. He eyed her cheap handbag. A shopping spree. The women he knew always wanted to go shopping.

"New baseball uniforms for the Songwood high school baseball team." Jason looked up at him. "Apparently their old ones were destroyed in a flood."

"They store their equipment in the basement," Kerri said. "A pipe broke last week and everything was ruined. They've been fund-raising and they're doing pretty well, but they aren't going to have enough for new jerseys. The pants, too. And before you ask, you don't get to put your name on the back or anything. This isn't about you."

If he'd been drinking, he would have choked. Baseball uniforms?

"Ah, a commitment to provide all the turkeys needed by the First Baptist Church of Songwood for their Thanksgiving and Christmas dinners," Jason continued. "Two thousand tulip bulbs for the Songwood community center to plant in the fall. A new fence for the elementary school playground and five thousand dollars for the local library."

She had to be playing him, Nathan thought. No one got him alone with what they thought was a blank checkbook and asked for tulip bulbs. That, or she was an idiot.

"What about for yourself?" he asked.

She looked at him. "I have what I want. Money for research. I wish I could just buy a cure, but I can't. This is the next best thing. You made that possible and I appreciate it."

"I can tell," he said drily.

"No, I mean it. You're paying for a miracle. How often does that happen?"

Nathan shifted uncomfortably. He looked at Jason and nodded. "Fine."

Kerri beamed. "Seriously? All of them? I should have asked for low-cost housing for the needy."

She didn't mean herself, he thought, amazed when he would have assumed he was beyond amazement. She had nothing but her current paycheck in the bank. No savings, no IRA, no nothing.

It was a game. A strategy. She would reveal herself soon enough.

"There's just one more thing," she said, smoothing her skirt. "It's personal."

He put down his coffee and folded his arms over his chest. Here we go, he thought. Now they were going to see the real Kerri Sullivan.

"I need help with something." She stared at Jason, rather than Nathan. "Something big. I need to fly."

"You want a plane ticket?" Nathan asked.

"No." She sighed.

"You're not getting a private jet."

She turned to him. "I don't want a private jet. I want to fly. By myself." She held out her arms, as if they were wings. "Or maybe walk on water, although that could be more problematic."

Great. He was making a deal with someone insane. That would help his stress level.

She looked back at Jason. "When my son was diagnosed, he got depressed and I was terrified he was going to give up. He was only five. I decided that I needed to give him a reason to live. A reason to think he would make it when other kids couldn't. I told him I had superpowers and because he was my son, he had them, too."

Jason was good, Nathan thought. His lawyer barely blinked.

"Superpowers?" Jason asked.

"I have a costume and I do tricks. I'm Wonder Mom. I arranged for Cody to see me lift a car, which was pretty cool. But he's older now and honestly, my last stunt was with a cat and I don't think he believed me. So I was thinking if I could do something special, that would be good."

Jason cleared his throat. "Do you have an idea how you want to make this happen?"

"Fairy dust?" Nathan asked.

Kerri ignored him. "A harness and a crane for the flying. A platform just under the water for that. I don't know and I don't have the resources." She looked at Nathan. "You do."

He held up both hands. "You're Wonder Mom. How can a mere mortal possibly help?"

Kerri narrowed her gaze. "Is he always an ass?"

Jason started to choke on his coffee. Nathan waited patiently until the other man managed to croak, "No. Not at all."

"You should make that sound more convincing," Nathan murmured.

Kerri faced him. "What does it matter to you? You'll assign some secretary to find me what I need and be done with it. It's nothing to you and it's everything to my son. Do you get that?"

Nathan had been called a lot of names in the past eighteen or twenty years, starting when he was in college and taking rich kids for their allowance at high-stakes poker games. He'd been written up in newspapers and magazines as a heartless, money-hungry bastard who would rather rape the environment than spend an extra buck on saving whatever microscopic insect he was displacing with his buildings.

He'd been told he was heartless, soulless, lacking in morals, and he'd felt nothing. But when some corn-fed, blond *hairdresser* looked at him like he was slime, he felt…guilty.

What the hell was up with that?

He felt awkward and uncomfortable—emotions he didn't allow himself. This was *his* meeting. He was in charge. Who did she think she was?

"Kerri, you're asking a lot," Jason said. "Maybe if there was—"

"Do it," Nathan told him.

Kerri's eyes widened. "Just like that?"

"Like you said, I'll assign some secretary to take care of it. What do I care?" He made it a point to never care. That's why he was the best.

"Okay. Thank you. It means a lot to me."

She frowned slightly, as if not sure what was up with him or what he had in mind. Good. He liked her off balance.

"Then we have a deal," Jason said.

Kerri nodded and reached for the pen. She added the "Wonder Mom" clause to her list, then started to sign the documents already prepared.

Jason grabbed them. "You have to read them first."

"Why?" she asked, taking them back and signing them. "We all know I don't have a choice. Mr. King gets what he wants and I get what I want."

Nathan still wasn't sure he liked her, but he was beginning to respect her. "Still not a deal with the devil?"

"Still not."

"Then maybe you should call me Nathan. What with us doing business together."

Her eyes widened, as if she remembered their conversation from a few days ago during which she'd told him to call her by her first name because sleeping together otherwise would be awkward. Only he wasn't going to sleep with her.

Yet as she stood, he found himself looking her over, taking in the curves underneath her loose dress.

She shook hands with Jason, then looked at him. "I guess I'll go find Tim."

"I'll walk you down."

She smiled. "Still don't trust me?"

"I want to keep an eye on you."

"Because I might run off with a stapler? It's a law office, Nathan. What possible trouble could I make here?"

"You'd be surprised."

He led her to the elevator, then pushed the Down button. "Jason will mail you a copy of the documents you signed."

"I know he will. He seems very efficient. And nice. I didn't expect that from a lawyer."

"Have a lot of experience with them?"

"Not really. Is he married?"

Annoyance exploded hard and hot inside of Nathan. "Is that the game? You can't get me, so you want Jason? He makes a lot of money, but unfortunately he does have a wife. They just had a baby."

Kerri patted his arm. "You have quite the temper. Do you know what all that built-up anger is doing to your cardiovascular system? It's not healthy."

The elevator arrived. She stepped on, then looked expectant. He put out a hand to hold the door.

"You didn't answer the question."

"That's because I thought it was rude." She sighed. "I saw a sign in one of the big corner offices on the way in—It's A Boy. I wondered if it was his. I was going to send a card. Nothing more."

Nathan couldn't remember the last time he'd felt like an idiot. He was confident he'd been a lot younger and somehow his father had been involved.

He got on the elevator. "I'm sorry," he said, the words unfamiliar and hard to form.

"You should be."

"That's gracious."

"You assume the worst about me."

How was this his fault?

He was a master of negotiation. He didn't get flustered or confused or run out of things to say. But this woman made him crazy.

He turned to tell her that, then realized he couldn't admit the weakness. She looked up at him expectantly, so he did the only thing he could think of.

He kissed her.

CHAPTER FOUR

NATHAN'S MOUTH WAS warm and firm, but not demanding, which surprised Kerri. She'd expected to be ravished, not kissed. He didn't grab her. Instead he let his lips handle all the action, and they did a fine job.

Her eyes fluttered shut as she gave herself up to the kiss, enjoying the heat, the pressure, the little tingles that shot down her arms. Without meaning to, she tilted her head slightly, in silent invitation.

One he ignored, she thought sadly. His touch was fleeting, more heat than substance, and left her wanting more. Something she wouldn't have guessed. When he pulled back, she felt an unexpected whisper of hunger. Probably because she hadn't kissed a man since Brian had died…before Cody had been born. How sad was that?

He looked stunned, as if he hadn't planned to kiss her. She quickly reassured him.

"It's okay," she told him. "I don't mind."

His expression hardened. "Is this about sleeping with me for the money?"

"What? No. Besides, *you* kissed *me*."

"It's your fault it happened."

"That's mature." Why was he making this so difficult? "I don't mind. It's fine. I owe you."

"So you'll have sex with me?"

"Not the most subtle come-on." She considered the question, then answered honestly. "If it's important to you." She touched his arm. "You came through for me. That means a lot."

"Fifteen million dollars' worth of meaning."

She smiled. "At least I'm not cheap." Her smile faded. "Don't make this more than it is. I was grateful and I spoke in a moment without thinking. I offered Tim a kidney. That doesn't mean I'm scheduling surgery."

"So you won't sleep with me."

"Are you asking me to?"

"No. I'm looking for clarification. Is sex on the table?"

"Do you want it to be?"

"This isn't about me." He sounded frustrated.

"But you're the one asking."

"I'm not asking. I'm not interested."

"Then we don't have a problem."

"But if I was, you'd say yes?" he asked, sounding as if he really wanted to know.

"I don't know. Maybe." She eyed his mouth. Maybe with a little more kissing.

Then she jerked her head away. No, she reminded herself. She had to put all her energy into Cody. If she turned her attention from him for even a second, something bad might happen.

"You don't want me, so it's not an issue," she said. "Right?"

The elevator doors opened and she stepped out into the parking garage. Tim was waiting by the limo. She sighed. It had been a lovely ride. She looked forward to the return trip. Maybe they could stop by Kidd Valley for burgers before they headed up I90. She was starved.

She turned back to Nathan. "I'll see you soon," she called.

He muttered something she couldn't hear and pushed a button. The elevator doors closed.

"Strange, strange man," she said to herself, and walked toward Tim.

FRANKIE TYPED frantically on her computer keyboard. Even when she wasn't sure what to say, she kept typing because the rhythm was as important as the words. Her to-do list hovered in the periphery of her mind, but most of her attention was on her article for the monthly newsletter. She had the lead.

Damage to the Puget Sound continued at a devastating pace. So many species of plants and animals had already disappeared. Many more were on the verge of becoming extinct. Sometimes, when she wrote, she felt as if the fate of the planet rested on her shoulders. That if she could just find the right combination of words and sentences, she could change everything.

"Frankie, got a sec?"

Frankie looked up at her boss and nodded, not showing her irritation at being interrupted. She hated to be interrupted before she was finished. It broke her rhythm. But she'd learned that most people didn't understand that.

She finished her sentence, saved her file, then pumped some hand sanitizer onto her palms and began rubbing her hands together.

One, two, three, four. One, two, three, four. Exactly eighteen times the groups of four, because seventy-two was her favorite number.

She followed Owen into his crowded office. There were reports and books and office supplies stacked everywhere. The room seemed to close in on itself. Sometimes Frankie couldn't stand to be in there—she needed order—but today she was strong.

She looked at her boss. "What's up?"

He sighed heavily. "We're not going to make it, Frankie. We don't have the funding. I've been fighting them for nearly two years and it's a battle that can't be won. We're shutting down."

"No," she breathed, unable to believe him. "No, no. This is where I belong. We have to stay in business. We have to make a difference. We're needed."

Owen, a thirtysomething, heavyset man, shrugged. "We've let most of the staff go already. The truth is we're too radical to get mainstream funding and the fringe element that agrees with us is generally lacking in funds. Right now the only thing that keeps us from going under is the money you put in. I can't keep taking that from you."

"I don't mind," she said quickly. She didn't need the money. Blood money, she thought as she closed her eyes and saw the blood on the living room walls. It wasn't like in the movies. It wasn't clean or neat or organized. When someone got shot in real life, it was messy. It smelled and it stayed inside your brain forever.

"It's not right," Owen told her. "You need that money yourself."

"I don't." For what? This place was her life. "We need publicity," she said. "Something big."

Owen's eyes were kind. "Frankie, let it alone. I figure we've got a month left. I'll understand if you want to leave now and look for something else. Or hell, take a vacation now that you're not spending every penny here. Check out the endangered plant life in Hawaii."

"We can get him," Frankie told Owen. "He wants those towers and there's going to be a lot of protesting. We can use that. We can get him."

It was what she wanted more than anything. To destroy Nathan King. To punish him in every way possible. To leave him weak and alone and afraid.

"You can't keeping doing this, Frankie."

"I can. I will. I'll find a way."

"It's time to put the past behind you."

She'd trusted Owen enough to tell him the truth about what had happened—she'd never thought he would use it against her.

She stood. "It will never be time. I'll never forgive him. I'll get him, then people will listen and we'll have enough money."

Owen rose to his feet. "Frankie, he's your brother. He's the one who gives you the money. You can't use it to destroy him."

"Sure I can. That's what makes it a perfect plan."

She walked back to her desk and returned to her typing. But her mind wasn't on the article anymore. It was on how she was going to destroy Nathan once and for all.

"BUT I DON'T WANNA," Cody whined. "It'll be boring."

"Probably," Kerri said as she smiled at her son. "Long and boring."

"So we could stay home."

"You're right. Why should we worry about all the kids in the world who don't have food or a home or toys? I mean, they should just have to put up with that. It's way more important than you being bored."

Cody sighed heavily. "You're trying to make me feel bad."

"I know. Is it working?"

"Kinda."

"Look at it this way. I'll bet the food will be really good. And it's a charity for kids, so there might be some fun stuff for you to do. Either way, we're helping and that matters."

"Okay."

The consent was grudgingly given. Kerri could have just told him they were going and he didn't have a choice, but she preferred to have him a willing partner. Besides, he had to learn about the importance of giving to others. Although technically they were attending the charity because Nathan King had e-mailed her that her presence, along with her son's, was expected. But she preferred to put a happier spin on things.

"Can we have some of the charity?" Cody asked.

"Not this week."

"But what if there's really cool stuff there?"

"Then you'll know what to put on your birthday list."

Although if it was too expensive, she wasn't going to be able to afford it. Something to worry about later, she told herself. Fortunately, Cody's wants had been fairly manageable to date. Although he'd asked for a video game system at Christmas last year, it hadn't been one of the really pricey ones and she'd been able to swing it…barely.

"Tell you what," she said. "Events like this usually have a raffle. If it's for something really cool, I'll give you five dollars for tickets."

"Sweet." He grinned. "Think we'll get lucky?"

"If it's a car, I really hope so."

"Me, too. But don't buy any tickets if it's weird, okay, Mom? Remember that year's supply of soup you won a couple of years ago? They were really bad."

"I know."

It had seemed like a great prize until they'd sampled the first can. The soups had been inedible.

"You wouldn't even give some of them away," he grumbled. "We had to eat them all."

"I didn't want to make anyone else suffer."

"But it was okay to make me suffer?"

"Of course," she told him with a grin. "You're my child. I can do all kinds of horrible things to you. Like make you eat vegetables."

He laughed. "And clean my room."

"And do homework. Or like now, when I tell you to go pick out something nice to wear."

He grumbled under his breath as he turned on his crutches and moved out of the kitchen. She watched him go, seeing so much of her late husband in her son. Every day Cody reminded her more and more of Brian. She treasured the similarities, even as they continued to break her heart.

Someone knocked on the front door. She walked through the living room and let in her friend Linda.

"I come bearing basic black," Linda said. "Along with a couple of blazers and accessories."

"Thank you. You're saving me here. I don't have

a charity-worthy wardrobe. It's just an afternoon thing, but I know all those rich people are going to be really well dressed and I need to fit in."

"You'll do great," Linda told her. "Now let's get you dressed."

Kerri led the way into her small bedroom. She'd already curled her hair and put on makeup. After Linda closed the bedroom door, Kerri slipped out of her robe, then studied the selection her friend had brought.

"I like the black skirt," she said, picking it up and holding it in front of her. "Basic, but a good simple style. I bought some black pumps at the thrift store last week. They've barely been used and they're Stuart Weitzman. Who gives those away? I figure somebody must have died or something and the family had no idea what they were donating."

"Lucky you." Linda held up a cobalt-blue blouse. "What about this? I have a black tweed blazer. You'll look coordinated without being too matchy. With some earrings and maybe a bracelet, you'll be good to go."

"It's perfect."

Kerri quickly tried everything on. The blouse and blazer were a touch long but otherwise fit great. The shoes were two kinds of heaven. Stylish but comfortable. She shrugged out of the blazer, then went into the bathroom where she began removing the curlers.

"Tell me you've received the money," Kerri called. "I'm not stepping one foot into that limo if it hasn't been transferred yet."

She looked in the mirror as she spoke, making sure she got all the curlers. Linda was still in the bedroom.

"It's been transferred," the other woman said.

"Good. So you're going to be hiring more researchers?"

"It takes time to pull it all together."

That didn't sound right. Kerri dropped an electric curler into the sink, then stuck her head in the bedroom. "Is there a problem?"

Linda shook her head. "It's fine. Things are moving along."

All the right words, so why did Kerri suddenly have a knot in her stomach? "The money got into the bank, right?"

"All fifteen million. Apparently it came from Nathan King's personal account."

If only, Kerri thought ruefully. "Yeah, I'll have that much when I get paid on Friday."

"Oh, me, too."

They laughed.

"So what's he like?" Linda asked. "Are you enjoying him?"

"I haven't tied him up and asked him to call me his love poodle yet."

"Good to know. You'll want to save that for your second week together."

"We're not *together.* I have to admit he's good-looking, but his attitude could use an adjustment."

"It's not in your nature to be totally grateful, is it?"

"I'm grateful, but I won't crawl. I think I bug him, which is just an added bonus. He's a little strait-laced." She returned to the bathroom and pulled out the rest of her curlers, then smiled in anticipation as she said, "Not a bad kisser."

There was a moment of silence followed by Linda's appearance in the small bathroom.

"You kissed him?"

"He kissed me, but it was still good. Lots of tingles. It made me realize I haven't seriously kissed a guy since Brian died. I miss kissing and touching." But not with just any guy. If she had the choice, she would like to be doing all that with Brian.

"Now you can do both," Linda said. "Although I'm not sure about Nathan King. Be careful. He's a dangerous guy."

"Not to me. I'm not interested in him or anyone that way."

"How did you come to be kissing?"

Kerri tried to remember. "I'm not sure. We were talking about whether or not his giving up the fifteen million meant he could sleep with me."

"What? He expects to get sex?"

"I'm not sure. I think it was more an intellectual discussion, then he kissed me. Probably to shut me up."

Kerri bent over at the waist and brushed her hair. Then she fluffed it with her fingers, straightened and reached for the can of hair spray.

It took a couple of good passes to get all the

curls to stay in place. "I'll do another spray right before we leave."

She put on fake pearl earrings and a gold-tone watch, then slipped into her fabulous shoes and pulled on the blazer. Then she stared at herself in the mirror.

"I still look like me," she said. "I was hoping for better."

"You look great."

Kerri knew that on a good day she could pass for pretty, but no one would ever describe her as elegant or sophisticated.

"This isn't my world. I won't know what to say to anyone."

"Just smile and if someone gets bitchy, remember she gets cramps and bloats, just like the rest of us."

There was another knock on the front door. "That'll be Tim," Kerri said as she walked through the living room to answer it. "I suddenly feel so popular."

"It's because you're a special person," Linda teased.

"I'm getting that." Kerri opened the front door and smiled as she saw both Tim and Lance on her tiny porch. "Two for one," she said. "It's my lucky day."

"Isn't that the truth," Lance said as he walked inside, then kissed her on the cheek. "You're looking very ladies-who-lunch. Love the shoes."

"Aren't they great? Less than ten dollars."

Lance winced. "You're not going to want to mention that today."

"I know. Hi, Tim."

"Kerri."

Tim nodded slightly as he, too, walked into her living room. The space had never been big, but with four adults, one of whom was the size of a small mountain, the space shrank even more.

Kerri introduced Linda.

"I've heard all about you," her friend said. "You got Kerri the job at The Grill so she could attack Nathan King."

Tim shifted slightly. On anyone else, Kerri would call it a wince.

Lance grinned. "Did I tell you? I'm a hero at work. They're all talking about how I handled the crazy woman. Nathan came in to the restaurant last week and personally thanked the manager for my quick action. I got a raise."

"Impressive," Kerri told him. "So what did Nathan get out of it?"

"Nothing," Lance told her. He glanced at Tim, then lowered his voice. "There are untold depths to our Mr. King, sweetie."

"That's what they say about Antarctica, but those depths are chilly."

"He's not all darkly evil," Lance said. "He gave you the money."

"I know, I know." She looked at Tim. "Want to chime in here and defend your boss?"

"No."

"Tim is very tight-lipped about his work." Lance

winked. "A loyal employee. The only kind our Mr. King hires."

"You should call him Nathan," Kerri said.

"Using his last name makes him all the more mysterious."

"Because you like the guy?"

"Tim likes him," Lance said. "I trust Tim."

As Tim had been the one to come up with the idea of announcing the fifteen-million-dollar grant, Kerri liked him, too. But that didn't mean she trusted his judgment when it came to Nathan.

"We should go," Tim said.

"I'll get Cody."

Five minutes later, Linda was waving goodbye as they climbed into the waiting limo.

"I want details," her friend called. "Take notes."

"Promise."

Cody maneuvered into the car. Kerri grabbed his crutches and followed him into the vehicle.

"Sweet ride," her nine-year-old said with a grin as he slid onto the long bench on the side. "When I grow up, I want one of these to take me everywhere."

"I thought you wanted a sports car that goes really fast."

"Oh. Right."

"Get both," Lance said as he settled next to Kerri and closed the door.

"Yeah," Cody breathed as he rubbed the leather seat. "I'll get both."

His words made Kerri's chest tighten. Please, God, let him live long enough to make that decision, she thought, knowing that, without a miracle, odds were Cody wouldn't see his twelfth birthday, let alone reach sixteen and learn to drive.

"We should buy a lottery ticket, Mom," he told her. "If we won big, we could get one of these now."

"And hire Tim."

"Tim would never leave Nathan, but you could hire me," Lance told her.

"It's a deal."

Cody looked at Lance. "Mr. King is, like, really rich, right?"

"We're talking billions."

"Cool."

He'd come from nothing, Kerri thought, remembering her research on the man. He'd grown up in Bremerton, a navy town across the sound. He'd left for college and then had managed to amass an impressive fortune.

Maybe that's what she'd done wrong, she thought humorously. She'd never graduated from college, and apparently beauty school didn't count.

"Is the charity thing going to be boring?" Cody asked Lance.

"There are a lot of kids there, and games and the food is excellent," Lance said. "You'll have fun. There's a huge arcade set up and all the games are free."

"Yeah?"

Lance nodded, then turned his attention to Kerri. "I hate your lipstick. Do you have a different one?"

She dug in her purse and found two at the bottom. Lance studied them both, then handed her the pink one.

"Put this one on top."

As she did, she looked at Cody, who rolled his eyes.

"Not your thing?" she asked with a grin.

He sighed heavily. "Does this limo have a TV?"

NATHAN KEPT a mental list of people he tried to avoid. Carol Mansfield was one of them. She was the tall, thin ex-wife of a high-powered executive and a successful boutique owner in her own right. She was the right age and had the right pedigree—she should have been someone he wanted to date. But there was something about Carol that made him think of a bird of prey coming in for the kill.

"You don't usually attend these sorts of things," Carol said as she put her hand on his arm. "You're more the send-a-check type. Not that it isn't lovely to see you."

"I think this is an important cause."

"Children's charities?" She raised her eyebrows. "How charmingly unexpected. Are you meeting someone?"

"What?"

"You keep looking around. Either you're meeting someone or I'm boring you." She laughed as if the idea of her boring anyone was impossible to imagine.

"A friend."

"I see. A female friend?"

"Just someone I know."

"Which means a woman. I didn't know you were seeing someone."

"I'm not. It's not like that."

He told himself he didn't owe Carol an explanation, even as he wondered why he felt it necessary to make it clear he wasn't dating Kerri. Maybe because she'd made it clear she wasn't interested in him.

If she'd wanted to make sure nothing ever happened between them, she'd done a hell of a job, he thought grimly. Not knowing if her response was genuine or her twisted way of paying him back for the money put him in an impossible situation. Damn her.

He heard the sound of laughter and turned. The sun poked through the clouds just in time to light the entrance to the hotel and cast Kerri in a golden glow.

Maybe it was a trick of the light, but she looked good. Pretty and dressed to fit in. Her hair was curly, which was different but still appealing. She glanced behind her and he saw her kid moving easily on his crutches.

Nathan felt a subtle shift beneath his feet, as if there'd been an earthquake. He blinked and, instead of Cody, he saw his own son. Daniel on crutches, then Daniel in a wheelchair, because that was next. He blinked again and his son was gone, but the reality of what would happen to Cody remained.

Nathan knew what it was like at the end. How the body weakened, how he would go from the chair to bed. How at the end, the drugs didn't work and all the boy could do was scream from the pain.

He wanted to walk away, to be anywhere but here. What the hell had he been thinking when he'd agreed to the deal?

"You sent me an e-mail," Kerri said by way of greeting.

"Yes. I needed to tell you where we'd be meeting and what time."

"I know, but jeez. How did you get my e-mail address?"

"I have a file on you."

"Sure, but my e-mail address? Isn't that private?"

"Not in my world."

She considered that for a second. "You could have just called."

"E-mail is more efficient."

"A phone call is more personal."

"We don't need to be personal."

She smiled. "You say that now."

Was she bringing up the kiss? Annoyance flared, but he ignored it. Emotions weren't productive.

"So what's the deal with this place?" Kerri asked. "Is there anything specific I should be doing?"

"Walk around with me and pretend you're enjoying yourself."

"Should I carry a sign telling the world I think you're a god?"

"You're a lot less reverent now that you have your money."

"I know. Isn't it fun?"

"Don't talk about the money," he said, ignoring her question.

"Promise."

"Just be friendly. Don't give out personal information, don't volunteer anything. If someone asks if we're dating, say no, but don't use a facial expression."

"What? How can I know what my face is doing?"

"You know what I mean."

"You're giving me way too much credit." She waved Cody forward. "Cody, this is Mr. King. Nathan, my son."

Trapped, Nathan shook hands with the kid without really looking at him.

"Nice to meet you," Cody mumbled.

"You'd rather be anywhere but here, right?" Nathan asked. He pointed to the far corner, where a multicolored balloon arch beckoned. "All the kid stuff is there, including the free arcade."

Cody grinned. "Sweet."

"I'll take him," Lance said. "Make sure he doesn't get lost."

"Thanks," Kerri told him. "I think I have to stay with Nathan and play grateful supplicant."

"And here I thought you were sincere," Lance said.

"I am." Kerri's eyes sparkled. "Have fun, Cody. Be good. Stay in the kids' section until I come to get you."

"Oh, Mo-om."

She looked at Nathan. "That's boy speak for 'Why, yes, Mother. Of course I will. I would never give you a moment's trouble because you are so loving and kind.'"

Cody grumbled something under his breath as he went off with Lance. Nathan watched them go, wondering if his relationship with Daniel had been so comfortable. He'd loved his son more than he'd ever loved any other person, but sometimes he hadn't known what to do or say.

"He's having a good day," Kerri said happily. "I love the good days. They make me believe in miracles."

"You have to be realistic," Nathan said, oddly annoyed by her faith and optimism.

"No way." She looked at him, her blue eyes narrowed. "If I was realistic, Cody would have been dead a long time ago. Faith matters. My grandmother was diagnosed with liver cancer and given six months to live. She refused to believe it. She thought her doctor was an idiot. She lived six years because she wanted to see me graduate from high school." Some of the fight went out of her. "She did. She lasted until the following summer."

Kerri crossed her arms over her chest and stared at him. "So I'm a big believer in cheating death and I'll take on anyone who says otherwise."

She radiated strength and power and an inner beauty he'd never noticed before. In that moment, he almost believed her. But he had a grave marker for a little boy that reminded him that miracles were a cheap trick and faith was for suckers.

CHAPTER FIVE

"I WANT THEM ALL to go away," Abram said angrily. "There are too many people. They're disturbing my concentration."

In the past few years he'd learned to work in silence. While the progress was slow, it was safer that way—if it was just him. If no one got involved. No one got hurt.

"It's difficult to start up a lab without having people," Linda teased. "We could try using something quieter, like mice, but without the opposable thumb…"

She paused, as if waiting for him to smile. He didn't. Nothing about this was funny.

"They need to go away," he insisted. "They can go back where they came from and take their money with them."

"No, they can't," she said. "Abram, this is a second chance for all of us. Not only for the sick children you'll save, but for you and your work."

"I don't want a second chance. I want to be left alone." He stood and walked into the lab, the one place he could lose himself in his theories and find peace.

"It's not going to happen," she said. "You have to look at the résumés and choose the best people for the research. Time is precious. Children are sick."

He didn't ever think about the children. Not thinking about them allowed him to go through the slow, methodical process that led to discoveries. He didn't hurry, he didn't push. He went one step at a time, as he should, following promising leads when they appeared, but always returning to the original premise.

"I can't do this again," he told her, sitting at his computer, staring at a blank screen. "You can't ask me to."

"What are you talking about? You always said that with just a little more funding, you could find a way to control the disease."

"That was before." Before the nightmare that had ruined everything.

"Nothing bad is going to happen," she assured him.

He turned on her. "Do you remember? Do you remember the explosion, the fire? People died. Good people died. Everything was destroyed. We were left with nothing and now the town is dying, too, and I can't stop it. I won't do it again. I won't take the risk."

She walked toward him. "Abram, no. You can't mean that. You have the money. You need to find a cure."

"At what price? I killed them, Linda. Me. I'm

supposed to heal people, to make the world better, but I didn't. I put off the repairs and in the end, they were dead. I won't destroy anyone else. I will live out here, doing my work and when I'm gone someone else can take the money and continue."

"No," she said firmly. "You'll do it. No one blames you for what happened. But you have to move forward. If you don't, more children will die. Don't you think the people who lost their lives would want you to continue?"

He stared at her. "No, they wouldn't."

"You're wrong."

He turned away. "It doesn't matter. I want you to send them all away. Return the money, if you can. Otherwise, leave it for whoever comes after me."

He reached for his lab coat, but before he could slip it on, he heard her say, "No."

He glanced at her. His usually calm, pleasant assistant stared at him with a look of fury in her eyes. Abram wasn't one to guess at other people's emotions—when he tried he usually got it wrong. His ex-wife had said it was because he didn't care enough to pay attention and she'd mostly been right. But there was no escaping Linda's rage as she glared at him.

"You can't refuse to do this," she said.

"I already have."

"No."

"Tell them to take back the money."

"Tell them yourself."

"What?"

She'd never spoken back to him before. Never been anything but supportive.

"Tell them yourself, you selfish bastard. This is wrong, Abram. It's bone wrong and you know it. You're brilliant and with that great mind comes an obligation to the world. You have always believed that. God has expectations. Isn't that what you said?"

"This is different," he muttered, feeling strangely small and embarrassed.

"It's exactly the same and you know it. I won't be part of this." She raised her hands and let them fall back to her sides. "I can't believe it. I've given my life to you because I believed in your greatness, but you're just afraid. You're terrified to lose again, so you've stopped trying. You're not a great man. Greatness is measured by how one faces adversity. Everyone can be committed when things are going well. I'm so ashamed of you right now. I expected better of you, Abram. So much better."

And then she was gone. With her stinging words still echoing in the lab, she walked away from him. Something, in the twenty years they'd been together, she'd never done.

She would be back, he told himself. Of course she would. Linda took her obligations seriously. She cared about him. She'd always been there for him. He couldn't imagine a world without her.

Determined to wait her out, he settled down in

front of his computer to study the results of his latest experiment. He believed in his gut that the disease was a defective autoimmune response. If he could isolate the…

He pushed away from the computer. It was too quiet. The silence seemed a living thing that pressed down upon him, pulling the air from his chest.

He usually enjoyed the quiet, but that was before. When he knew Linda would be in her office, or showing up later. Before she'd said he was nothing and that she was ashamed of him.

He tried to tell himself she didn't mean it, but he wasn't sure. And with that quiet doubt came unexpected pain.

"YOUR TWO-O'CLOCK IS HERE," Nathan's secretary told him.

"Send him in," Nathan said, then regretted the invitation when Grant Pryor walked into the office.

Nathan leaned back in his chair and studied the man. "And here I thought I had an appointment with a reporter."

Grant crossed the room and sank down into one of the leather chairs without being asked. He was short and balding, pushing forty, with a forgettable face. He worked for the Seattle tabloid that passed itself off as an independent press. In truth, the rag was nothing more than an excuse for poor journalism. Grant Pryor had joined their staff about five years ago and had decided that Nathan King was his ticket to the big time. He made it a point to cover Nathan's doings, always putting a spin on them that made Nathan look like the devil trying to destroy the fair and innocent citizens of the Emerald City.

"I was at the charity event on Saturday," Grant said. "Always a good time. I saw the lady you were with." He consulted his notes. "Kerri Sullivan. Not your usual type."

"Maybe I'm stepping up to the next level."

"We all know that's unlikely," Grant said. He pulled a pen out of his inner jacket pocket. "So who is she? I mean, you can tell me now and save me the research. Not that I expect you to do me any favors."

"Kerri and I are friends."

"Bullshit. You, friends with a hairdresser from Songwood? No way."

Grant had a point, but Nathan wasn't going to concede it. "Have you ever stopped to consider that in all the years you've been doing stories on me, you've never found anything out of the ordinary? I'm just a businessman, Grant. Nothing more."

Grant ignored that. "So what's the deal with her? You're workin' something. I just have to figure out what it is."

Nathan wished briefly for a legal system that made it easier to get a restraining order against the press. But as Grant hadn't committed any crimes, Nathan was left with the pain in his ass and little he could do about it.

"No matter how hard you try," he said, "you'll never get into real journalism. Not now. You've been a hack for too long. The *New York Times* won't come calling."

"That depends on what you're hiding."

"I'm not hiding anything."

Grant stood and grinned. "That's what they all say. But none of them are telling the truth. Neither are you, Nathan, and I'm going to find out what's really going on."

KERRI HUMMED as she dropped spoonfuls of chocolate-chip batter onto the baking sheet. She always tried to be a positive person, but these days it was actually easy. For once, everything was going well.

Cody's string of good days continued, making her secretly dream about an unexpected remission. Gilliar's Disease wasn't especially kind to its victims, but there had been rumors, more urban legend than documented medical fact, about remissions. Sometimes for months.

Please God, let it be so, she thought, knowing time was what she needed the most. Time for Dr. Wallace and his team to find a way to, if not cure the disease, then at least stall it.

In her battle against time, she felt like Captain Hook, of Peter Pan fame, constantly hearing the steady approach of the end. But for the first time in years, the ticking wasn't quite so loud.

She finished with the first pan and put it in her

oven, then set the timer. She'd just started dropping batter onto the second pan when someone knocked on her front door.

For a moment, Kerri wondered if it could be Nathan and found herself excited at the thought of seeing him again. She wouldn't mind another round of tweaking the tiger's tail and if he wanted to kiss her just to prove something, she wouldn't object, even though she should.

She was still grinning at the thought when she opened the door and saw Linda standing there. But her normally well dressed, pretty, calm friend looked disheveled and blotchy.

"What's wrong?" Kerri asked as she pulled her inside. "You're not okay, so don't pretend you are."

Tears filled Linda's eyes. "I'm sorry," she whispered. "Desperately sorry. I didn't know. I knew there were problems, that he blamed himself for what happened, but I never thought it would matter. That it would get in the way. I didn't know. I swear, I didn't know."

Kerri went cold without even knowing why. "What are we talking about? What's wrong?"

Linda swallowed a sob, then wiped her face. "Abram. At the lab. He says he won't hire the researchers, won't open the lab up again. He says he's the reason those people died before, when it exploded. That he killed the town and he won't risk hurting anyone again. I told him no one blames him, but he doesn't believe me. I don't think I can change his mind, Kerri. I walked out. I don't know what to do."

Kerri went cold. It was as if her body temperature dropped fifty degrees. She expected to see chilly clouds when she exhaled.

Pain was everywhere, starting at her heart and radiating out to her fingers and down her legs. The death of hope was excruciating.

Then she turned her head and stared down the stubby hallway to the closed door of her son's room. Cody was finishing his homework in anticipation of a Mariners game on TV that night. She saw his happy smile, his trusting gaze. She remembered her promise to his late father.

"I'll talk to him," she told Linda. "I'll go see him and convince him. He's going to get that lab up to speed again and they're going to find a cure."

She would buy a gun and threaten Abram Wallace's life if she had to, she thought grimly. Because they were too close to a cure to stop now.

ABRAM WALKED through the quiet office as he headed for his lab. Normally he enjoyed the silence, but not today. Nothing had felt right since Linda had left that morning. He tried to tell himself that it didn't matter, that she would be back later to scold him about how he wasn't eating or make him walk out in the sun. But he couldn't quite bring himself to believe it.

She'd never been anything but supportive, anything but caring. She'd kept him going through the darkest hours of his life after the explosion. After he'd found out people had died because of him.

Solace, he thought grimly. All he wanted was solace. A chance to forget, even for a minute. But he never forgot. He couldn't.

A soft chime caught his attention. He glanced at the security monitor and saw a woman had entered the lab. She wasn't alone. There was a boy with her. A boy on crutches.

Abram wanted to bolt for freedom, but something kept him in place. He watched the different cameras as she made her way down the long corridor, following the wide path to the only room with lights on. Then she pushed open the double swinging doors.

"Dr. Wallace?"

She didn't look like any of the people who had died in the explosion, yet there was something about her. It was as if all their ghosts had taken up residence in her and returned to look him in the eye.

He thought about how some of his colleagues would be surprised that he believed in ghosts. He was a man of science, after all. But he'd learned that there were many things in the world he would never understand and for which explanations would never be found.

"I'm Dr. Wallace," he said slowly, willing to accept the punishment in any form.

"I'm Kerri Sullivan. This is my son, Cody."

Cody looked at his mother, who nodded, then the boy moved forward and held out his right hand.

Abram didn't want to touch him. He didn't want to feel his skin or look at him. Because Abram knew what was going to happen to him in excruciating detail.

Then the scientist in him took over. He shook Cody's hand, then walked around him, noting the way he stood, the weight he put on his feet and how he used his crutches.

"He's old," Abram said.

"Nine."

"So the disease has progressed slowly."

"So far."

He turned to Cody. "How do you feel?"

Cody rolled his eyes. "Mo-om, do I have to do this?"

Kerri shook her head. "You want to wait back in the reception area?"

"Uh-huh."

The boy went out into the corridor. Kerri turned to Abram.

"He's having a lot of good days, lately. Not so much pain. He's not on anything strong. Yet."

But he would be, Abram thought. Soon. Very soon. Then he would be in a wheelchair, then a hospital bed and then he would die.

Kerri grabbed his arm. "You could save him."

Abram took a step back. "No. I can't."

"You can and you will. You have a gift. God

decided to make you brilliant and with that comes responsibility."

Linda had said much the same thing, he mused, again telling himself she wouldn't stay away permanently. She would forgive him and return. She had to.

Kerri shook his arm. "Listen to me," she said harshly. "You have to fix this. You have no right not to try. It's your job." She looked at him more closely. "It's more than that. It's your calling. You have the power to save him and you're not trying. How dare you not have a thousand scientists working day and night to solve this. You have the answers within you. Linda told me you were close before. She said you could do it. We're talking about children, damn you. My child. My son. He deserves this."

She spoke with conviction and power. He wanted to turn away, but he couldn't bring himself to move. Maybe he needed this, he thought. Maybe it was his punishment.

"Save him," she ordered.

"I can't."

"You have to. I won't let him die. And if you don't care about him, what about the other children who will die because you can't be bothered? I pray there's a special place in hell for you. I swear, if there is, I'll be there, putting more wood on the fire and watching you burn."

"You don't understand."

"You're right," she said angrily. "I don't and I don't want to. If I had the power to fix my son, I would, but I don't. So I did the next best thing. I found you. Last I heard you needed twelve million dollars to fund the rest of your research and find a cure. I got you fifteen million, in case the price of miracles had gone up. I will do anything to make this happen. I will sell my soul to the devil or I will stand here and put a gun to your head. I don't care which. You are going to do this."

What he remembered most about the explosion was the heat of the fire that followed. Maybe it had been the fires of hell she'd talked about. He'd never experienced such raw power—so uncontrolled and destructive. Much like the disease that ravaged Cody Sullivan's body.

He looked down at his hands…they were shaking. He looked at the woman standing in front of him, felt her need, her pain and knew he could do nothing.

"I'm sorry," he whispered. "I can't."

He braced himself for the next attack, for the barrage of words. Instead, all the color drained from her face and she swayed slightly as if she were going to faint.

Before he could reach for her to catch her, she turned and ran. He was finally alone.

Feeling very old and so very useless, Abram sank into his chair and cradled his head in his hands.

CHAPTER SIX

FRANKIE TOOK her latte to a table in the corner. Starbucks was one of the few crowded places where she felt comfortable. She'd never figured out why. Maybe it was the smooth coffee and the jolt of caffeine. Maybe it was the warm motif or the way people who sat in Starbucks were always so calm and sophisticated. Reading the paper, working, listening to music. It made her feel good to be a part of what was happening, even if it was just on the periphery. The Bell Square Starbucks was her favorite.

She sipped her latte and watched the people around her. She was early for her appointment, a habit of hers. She wanted to be able to pick the table, pick the seat. Safety first, she told herself.

She saw Grant come in. He paused, looked around, then walked over to her without getting a coffee. That bugged her. He should get a coffee—that's what the store was about.

She'd known Grant about two years. They'd met at a rally, when he'd come up and introduced himself. He'd talked about her brother, asking her general questions. Right away she'd figured out that he wanted to take Nathan down. Grant believed Nathan was his ticket to a real newspaper.

It had taken Frankie a couple of months to decide whether she could trust Grant. It was one thing for her to destroy her brother, but it was another for the world to know about it. People wouldn't understand—they would think because they were family, she shouldn't want Nathan punished. But those people hadn't seen the blood...hadn't lived through it all.

Once she'd decided to trust him, she'd given him whatever information she could. It hadn't been much. He'd always pressed her to go see her brother, to find out what was happening in his life, but she'd resisted. She didn't want to see Nathan or talk to him. She wanted him punished. A few months ago, she'd broken off contact with Grant.

But now things were different. With the newsletter shutting down, she felt pressure. To lose everything and have nothing to show for it wasn't right. It wasn't fair. Nathan had everything and she had nothing.

It hadn't always been that way, she thought, remembering the time before he'd left. He'd taken care of her. She'd depended on him, but then he'd been gone and she'd been alone.

"Hey, Frankie," Grant said as he slid into the chair opposite hers. "What's up?"

She'd phoned him and arranged the meeting. He'd

been surprised to hear from her but more than willing to get together.

His eyes were pale. He was about her height, which made her feel more safe with him. He wasn't big, like Nathan.

"We're being shut down," she told him. "In about a month."

Grant leaned back in his chair. "So you want to go out with a bang?"

He always used clichés. Not her favorite thing about him. "I want to do something. I don't know where to look. I thought you would."

Grant looked at her for a long time. "You know about the towers he wants to build."

She wrinkled her nose. "They're awful. Like the rich need more places to live. Do you know how many species will be displaced by his buildings? All so he can have his name fifty stories up."

She pressed her lips together. If she said much more, she would start to lose control. That was never good. She clenched her hands together on her lap and began counting. One, two, three, four. One, two, three, four.

She kept it up, counting steadily, until she'd downed eighteen sets of four. She inhaled as a calm washed over her.

Grant nodded slowly. "That's them," he said. "He wasn't getting much support, so it didn't look like he would get the zoning permission he needed. Then he made this donation."

"To what?"

"Some lab up in Songwood. A scientist there is working on the cure for Gilliar's Disease."

"That's what Daniel died of," Frankie murmured, not wanting to think about the boy. She'd liked Daniel. It wasn't his fault that Nathan was his father.

"The timing is suspicious," Grant told her. "Plus Nathan's hanging out with this woman. Kerri Sullivan. She's got a kid with the same problem. He paraded both of them around at a charity event last weekend. There's something going on. Something that isn't right. Maybe you could find out what it is."

"No." She shook her head. "No. I can't find that out."

"You could try."

"No. I don't want to see him."

"It's the only way."

"He won't tell me anything," she insisted.

"Maybe he doesn't have to. Maybe you can just look around."

Nathan's office? Grant was an idiot. Nathan wasn't going to leave her alone in his office.

"You can do things I can't," Grant continued. "He trusts you."

Did Nathan? Frankie wondered. Was he that stupid? Probably, she thought. He certainly didn't see her as a threat.

"Okay," she told him. "I'll try to find out something. I'll go see him."

"Good."

"You can stop the towers?"

"I can try," Grant told her.

"I want them brought down."

"They haven't been built yet."

Maybe not but she pictured them falling and falling. Thinking about the structures crumbling in a pile of dust made her smile.

"Maybe your brother's involved with that Kerri woman."

"I don't think so," she said absently. "He doesn't get involved. Doesn't care."

He had once, years ago. But then he'd gone away. He'd changed. Nothing touched him. Except maybe Daniel.

Frankie blinked the memories away. All of them. Nathan deserved everything bad he got. He didn't have the dreams. He didn't know what it had been like. He'd left her.

"I'll go to see him," Frankie told Grant. "I'll find out what I can and call you."

She stood and grabbed her coffee, then walked out onto the sidewalk.

It was nearly seventy, on a rare clear day. Frankie let her eyes adjust to the bright light, then she started down the sidewalk, careful to step where she always stepped, not looking left or right, counting, always counting.

Without meaning to, she remembered teaching Daniel to count, first to ten, then to twenty. He'd been smart. A fast learner. He'd smiled. She remembered that most. How he'd always smiled when he'd seen her. He would run up to her, his arms open. He'd wanted hugs and she'd been happy to give them.

She had loved him. But when Nathan had told her his son was dying, a part of her had been happy. She'd been ashamed then, ashamed of feeling pleasure. But as much as she loved Daniel, she wanted his father to suffer. Daniel's death had nearly brought her brother to his knees.

She'd gone to the hospital at the end, and had sat with the boy. She had felt her own heart break with the realization that he would be gone soon. Sadness and pleasure.

They had confused her then and they confused her now.

She waited at her bus stop, then boarded and saw her favorite seat was open. She sat exactly in the middle, looking at no one, willing the trip to be over quickly.

Fortunately there wasn't a lot of traffic. When she was back across the bridge, she got off at her stop and headed for her small apartment.

Once there, she threw out her coffee and walked to the sink. She pumped the smooth, creamy soap onto her hands and began to wash. One, two, three, four. Over and over, eighteen times.

The ritual relaxed her, eased the tightness in her chest until she could breathe again. Until she was clean.

When she was done, she dried her hands on one of her special towels, then walked to the window and looked up at the sky.

It was a beautiful day, she thought wistfully. The kind of day that made her recall what it was like to be normal.

She wasn't anymore. She knew that. She needed help. A doctor, medication. Someday, she told herself. But not just yet.

She let her gaze drift lower until it landed on another building Nathan owned. Seeing it and the shadow it cast made her angry again. Better to be driven than cured, she told herself. She would destroy Nathan. When he had nothing, maybe she would feel better. Maybe then the blood would go away.

NATHAN PARKED in front of Kerri's small house. He still didn't know what the hell he was doing here. He'd gotten a call from Dr. Wallace's assistant saying there was a problem with the funding, but nothing more. When he'd tried to reach Kerri at work, he'd been told she'd called in sick. A first for her. But she wasn't answering her phone at home.

Was she sick? Injured? And what had happened to the money he'd sent to the research facility?

He looked at the beat-up car in the driveway. She was home at least. Had something happened with Cody?

If it was the latter, he wanted to be anywhere but here. He was not getting involved with that kid. The smartest thing to do would be to turn around and head back to Seattle. Or maybe the smartest thing would have been not to drive here at all.

"Dammit all to hell," he muttered as he climbed out of his car and headed up the front walk. He pounded on her door and waited.

Seconds later it opened. Kerri stood in front of him, but not the Kerri he knew.

Her blue eyes were red and swollen, her skin blotchy. She blinked at him, said, "Go away. I can't do this now," and started to close the door.

He put a hand up to stop her, then pushed his way inside. "Can't do what?"

"Whatever it is you want. Go somewhere. Do something. I can't. This is a bad time."

He stared at her, taking in the oversize and stained T-shirt and baggy sweats. "You look like crap."

"Whatever."

Worse, she looked…broken. He didn't like the word, but it fit.

"What's wrong?" he asked.

She walked to the sofa and collapsed on a flat cushion. "He won't do it. Dr. Wallace. Linda told me there was a problem, so I went to see him myself. He won't continue the research. He blames himself for the explosion."

Nathan must have looked blank because she continued with, "Remember? He was working on a cure and the lab exploded. Something about an electrical problem. I don't know the exact details but people were killed. The lab was closed and as it was Song-wood's biggest industry, the town began to die." Tears filled her eyes before spilling down her cheeks. "He was my last hope. I don't have anywhere else to go. He was going to be my miracle for Cody."

She hunched over, as if in pain. "I can't let my son die, but I'm out of options. I spent all last night on the Internet, looking for someone else working on the disease, but there's nothing new. No hope. It's the death of hope. Do you know what that feels like?"

He hadn't realized how much life and power Kerri's optimism gave her until it was gone.

"How do I tell him?" Kerri asked, not looking at Nathan. "What am I supposed to say? Just kidding about that cure thing, kid? It's so unfair. It's wrong. All of it."

Without thinking, he pulled her to her feet and into his arms.

"Don't give up," he murmured, holding her close. "You're stronger than this."

"I'm not. I'm having a breakdown. There's a difference." She sighed. "It's hard to be strong. I'm faking it every minute. We've been living on borrowed time for years now, and I've always known it. I'm not giving up," she repeated. "I just need a break."

She didn't hug him back, but that was okay. He

wanted to offer comfort—something unusual for him, but he was going with it. When she rested her forehead on his shoulder, he felt the hot dampness of her tears.

"I've been willing him to stay alive, but I'm afraid I don't have anything left. I've begged, I've pleaded, I've prayed, I've made bargains with God that will get me sent to hell, but I don't care. I never cared about anything but keeping Cody going. Giving him the strength to hang on."

She continued to talk, but he couldn't listen. Not to this. He put his hands on her shoulders and eased her away, then took a step back.

Cody was her life and without him she would have nothing. She would never give up the way he had.

Nathan pushed the ugly truth away, but it refused to budge. It sat there, round and squat, daring him to deny what had happened. That he'd given up. He'd taken the easy road and he'd never been able to forgive himself for it.

"I'll fix this," he told her. "I'll make Dr. Wallace get back to work on finding a cure."

She wiped her face with her fingers. "How?" she asked, her voice shaking. "Stand over him with a gun pointed at his head? I already thought of that one. It's not practical on a lot of levels. For one, your arm will get tired. For another, you can't make someone care. It doesn't work that way."

"I'll beat the crap out of him if necessary," he

muttered, knowing he would if he had to. "He can't do this. He took the money."

She looked at him. "It was a wire transfer, Nathan. You can't refuse those. But I would suggest you watch your mailbox. I'll bet he sends it back. Or gives it to someone else."

"He can't."

"How are you going to stop him?"

"I'll have Jason talk to him."

"Lawyers can be scary," she said. "But not scary enough. Besides, Dr. Wallace is old. You can't beat up an old scientist."

"If he's old, it makes my job easier."

Her mouth quivered slightly. For a second, he thought she was going to smile and started at his sudden need to see her spirits lift.

"I could have Tim do it, but he would be insulted by the lack of challenge," he said.

She nodded, then began to cry again. She collapsed back on the sofa, sobbing as if her heart would break.

He stood there awkwardly, not sure what he should do. He'd tried hugging and that hadn't worked. He was out of ideas and desperate.

He went into the kitchen and started opening cupboards. He found plates, glasses and food, but nothing to drink.

"Don't you have anything to drink?" he yelled. "Vodka? Scotch? Cooking sherry?"

"Stop raiding my kitchen," she said from the doorway. "No, I don't have any alcohol."

"Is it a religious thing?"

Despite the tears, her mouth turned up at the corner. He felt like a hero.

"I can't afford it," she said. "Nathan, this is the real world. I think milk is expensive. I'm not going to waste my money on something like vodka."

"We have to talk about your priorities." He crossed to the phone and picked it up, then dialed directory assistance. "Yeah. Songwood. The liquor store."

He pulled a pen out of his pocket and wrote on a scrap of paper on the counter. "I'll have something sent over," he told her. "You have any preferences?"

"I don't think they deliver."

"They do now. I'll get some food in here, too. What do you want?"

WHEN NATHAN KING DECIDED to take charge, he did it in a big way, Kerri thought as she watched him talk to the manager of her local Albertsons. He'd already persuaded the local liquor store clerk to drop off his order and now was negotiating the same treatment with the grocery store.

She knew she should have protested the gallons of milk, the jumbo laundry detergent and the pounds of meat and chicken he'd requested, but that would take more effort than she had. What did it matter if

Nathan bought her and Cody some food? When the sky was falling, it was hard to worry about the little things.

After he'd hung up the phone, he put down his pen. "I got fried chicken for tonight. I didn't think you'd want to cook."

"That was thoughtful. Thank you. For all of it."

He shrugged. "No big deal."

"I'll never get through all that liquor."

"The Scotch is for me."

"What about the rest of it?"

"One day you'll want to celebrate. And you'll be ready."

"For a whole party?" She studied him, the hard lines of his face, his dark eyes. She never would have thought of him as a kind man, yet it was there…in him.

She glanced at the clock. "Cody will be home soon." She was going to have to pull herself together. Make sure he didn't know she'd been crying. "You can't say anything."

"I won't," Nathan told her.

"It's better if he doesn't know. If he believes everything will be fine, then maybe it will."

"I agree."

Did he? Really?

"Why are you here?" she asked. "What made you come over today?"

"Linda called and told me there was a problem. You weren't at work and you didn't answer your phone at home. I wanted to make sure you were all right."

Checking up on her? No one had done that in years. Not since Brian—a lifetime ago.

"Don't get too excited," he told her. "This isn't going to happen again."

But it had happened now. She had someone to lean on, even for a moment. It felt good.

"I need to get cleaned up," she said, and retreated to her small bedroom with its even tinier bathroom.

When she looked at herself in the mirror, she nearly shrieked. She looked like an extra from a cheap horror movie. Her skin was blotchy, her eyes and mouth swollen.

After washing her face, she put a cold, wet wash-cloth on her eyes for a couple of minutes, then went for a lot of concealer and mascara.

When she was sure she wouldn't frighten her son, she returned to the living room, just as Cody walked in the front door.

"Do I know you?" Kerri asked.

Her son grinned at her. "I'm your only kid."

"I don't think so. I'm sure I would have remembered giving birth."

"You're really weird, you know that, right?" Then he dropped his backpack on the floor and moved toward her.

She let him hug her so she wouldn't squeeze too hard, even though she wanted to hang on forever and never let go. When he stepped back, she pointed to Nathan.

"You remember Mr. King," she said.

"Hi, Mr. King," Cody said.

"Call me Nathan."

"Okay."

There was an awkward silence. Kerri picked up her son's backpack. "Do you have any homework?"

"Just some reading. I did it at lunch. I'm hungry. Are there any cookies left?"

She pointed to the cracked, twice-glued cookie jar in the shape of a football and tried not to think about the fact that her son could do his reading at lunch because he couldn't run around and play like the other kids.

"We're having fried chicken for dinner," she said to distract herself. "Nathan is having it delivered."

Cody spun around. "Really? Takeout?"

"You bet. Mashed potatoes and gravy, along with coleslaw and rolls."

"Sweet!"

"Because there's something wrong with my cooking?" Kerri asked, pretending to glare at her son.

"No, Mom. It's great. But sometimes, you know, a change is good. I like takeout. And restaurants." He made a fist and pretend-punched her in the arm. "But your cooking is the best."

"I know a pity compliment when I hear one."

Cody grinned. "Can Brandon come over after dinner?" he asked.

"Sure."

"I'm going to my room." He took his backpack from her and maneuvered down the short hallway.

Kerri turned back to Nathan and found him watching her son. She tried to read his expression and couldn't. Hardly a surprise.

"Are you okay?" she asked quietly.

Nathan turned to her. "Of course. Why wouldn't I be?"

"I didn't know if this was hard for you. Being around Cody."

"Your son has nothing to do with me," he told her.

"I'm trying to be sympathetic."

"Not required or welcome. We aren't all emotional basket cases."

"What?" She glared at him. "Excuse me? I'm a rock. Considering the setback, I think a small but tasteful breakdown was in order. Who do you think you are, judging me?"

She felt like backing the car over him. She wanted to be intimidating enough to make him cringe.

He stunned her by smiling slowly. "That's the Kerri I want around. Anger is a lot more useful than self-pity."

It took a couple of seconds for his words to sink in. "You are so not allowed to play me."

"Whatever works. Besides, you played me first."

"It was for a worthy cause."

"So is this."

Which meant what? she wondered. "You're not easy," she murmured.

"I don't try to be." Nathan shoved his hands in his front slacks pocket. "You trust the world and I trust no one."

"I'm the optimist."

"Which one of us is going to end up being disappointed?"

He was right about that. "But there's more to life than being right," she said.

"There's winning."

"Is that what matters most?" she asked, already knowing the answer.

"It beats losing."

NATHAN HUNG UP the phone and reached for his wine. Kerri sat across from him at the table littered with the remains of their dinner. Cody had inhaled fried chicken like he hadn't eaten in a week and then excused himself to go off to his room. Kerri was flushed from a single glass of wine, which fit with what he knew of her. She was a good girl, from the top of her glossy hair down to what he would guess were sensibly unpolished toes.

"You're scary," she told him. "Dr. Wallace is in big trouble."

"Nobody screws with me," Nathan said. "Jason

will find out Wallace's weakness and use it against him."

"You could just sue him."

"That would take too long."

He waited for her reaction to his words, but there wasn't one. The fact that her son was living on borrowed time wasn't news to Kerri.

Laughter and a few shouts drifted back from Cody's bedroom, where he'd retreated with his friend Brandon. Kerri shrugged.

"Video games. Apparently it's very intense."

"You don't play?"

"I've tried a few times. I always get my butt kicked. I don't have the time to devote to becoming an expert. I limit his access to the games, but not by much. He's a good student. If he enjoys them, why not let him?"

Nathan knew enough to read between the lines. Cody should get in as much fun now as possible, because there wasn't going to be a later.

He remembered having the same thoughts about Daniel. His son had—

He drew in a breath as an unexpected pain shot through his chest. It was emotional rather than phys-ical, but breath stealing nonetheless.

After all this time, he thought, surprised the ache still existed. He would have said he was over it. But maybe one never recovered from the death of a child.

She picked up her wine and took a sip. "So,

Nathan King, tell me about yourself. I only know business stuff. Do you have family?"

"There's no need to discuss my personal life."

"Ooh, doesn't that sound pompous. Does that stick up your butt make it painful to sit down?"

As soon as she spoke, her eyes widened and she set down the glass.

"Did I say that out loud?" she asked, sounding horrified.

"Yes."

"I am so sorry. That was rude. This is my house and you're a guest and I should keep comments like that to myself." She took another drink. "But if you don't tell me, I'll just go to Google and get the info that way."

"I'm surprised you haven't."

"I know some things from my research. There's a reporter who really hates you. Grant Somebody."

"Grant Pryor. I know him."

"What's his deal?"

"He wants to work for a real paper. He thinks the right story about me can get him there."

"That's a lot of pressure. For you, I mean. Holding someone's career in the palm of your hand."

He smiled. "Now you're playing *me*."

"I know. It's fun, isn't it? So why you? Why not some other rich guy?"

"Because I'm a coldhearted bastard and that makes me interesting."

"Do you really see yourself as a bastard?"

"We're not having that conversation."

"All right, but now you have to tell me something about your family."

"You don't want to know."

"Yes, I do." She smiled. "Come on, Nathan. We're practically friends. Who's around still? I know you have an ex-wife, but is that it? Mother? Father? Siblings?"

"One sister."

"There. Was that so hard?"

Not for her, he thought. But maybe for him. He didn't like thinking about Frankie, about how she blamed him for what had happened.

"I was pretty young when my parents died," she told him. "It was a car accident. My grandmother raised me. What about you?"

He supposed in her world the exchange of personal information was natural and expected. It wasn't in his.

"My mother shot my father, then turned the gun on herself the second year I was in college," he said flatly. "My sister was seventeen and at home at the time. She walked in on them after the first gunshot."

Kerri's face froze in horror. "Oh my God. That's terrible. For all of you. Nathan, I'm sorry." She reached across the table and rested her fingers on his hand, as if her touch would help.

"I'm fine," he told her. "It was a long time ago."

"Where's your sister now?"

"Here. In Seattle."

"Are you close?"

"She blames me for what happened," he said. "Because when I left, things got worse. My dad was a drunk. A mean drunk. He beat the crap out of my mom and me. Although he never touched Frankie, he wasn't an easy man to live with. I got out—a football scholarship to USC. That left Frankie by herself to deal with it. Dad picked on her verbally because she wasn't…" He hesitated. "She has some problems."

Kerri frowned. "Like what?"

"OCD, mostly. She gets something in her head and it doesn't go away."

"Is she seeing a doctor or psychologist?"

"I have no idea."

Kerri's eyes widened. "How come?"

"We have nothing to do with each other. I've tried to talk to her, get her help, but she won't have any part of me."

He'd done more than try. He'd practically kidnapped her to get her into a place that was supposed to be cutting-edge, but Frankie wasn't sick enough to be committed. She'd simply walked out. Sometimes he was convinced she didn't want to change. That she was happy being on the fringe.

"I support her," he added, knowing it was stupid— both the mention and the reality of it. She used most of her salary to fund that idiotic out-there ecology group she belonged to, and looked for ways to punish him.

"I'm sorry," Kerri murmured.

"Don't be."

"I can't help it. I'm very softhearted."

"You're wasting your energy on something that doesn't matter."

"We're talking about your family."

"Mine, not yours," he reminded her.

"You're a total cynic."

"You're a softhearted fool who assumes the world is a good place."

She fluttered her eyelashes at him. "I'm also really, really cute."

She was that, he admitted. More than cute. Sexy. There was something about the way she moved, the openness of her smile. He'd known a lot of beautiful women, but no one like her. Her combination of innocence and determination baffled him. How could she have blackmailed him into giving up fifteen million and yet still be so damn trusting?

Unexpected heat surged within him, making him want to pull her close and kiss her again. He'd liked kissing her before and wouldn't turn down a repeat performance. There was only one thing standing in his way—he couldn't know if she was responding because she enjoyed what he was doing or if it was because she owed him.

His ego said of course she liked kissing him, but his brain was less sure, which put him in a damned uncomfortable position.

He stood. "I need to get back to the city."

"Okay. Want to take some leftovers? There are still a couple of pieces of chicken."

"I have a full-time housekeeper who cooks for me."

"Then never mind. We'll keep them."

She rose and followed him to the door. "Thanks for coming to check on me," she said. "You made me feel better, which I didn't think was possible."

Unable to help himself, he touched her cheek. "Don't worry. We'll get Wallace back into his lab and digging for the answers. Trust me."

"You just spent a lot of time telling me I was really dumb for trusting people."

"I'm different."

She smiled. "Why did I know you were going to say that?"

CHAPTER SEVEN

LINDA WAS GONE. Abram felt it as soon as he walked into the lab the next morning. There was something in the air, something dank and moldy, as if the roof had started to leak. Only there hadn't been any rain and there was no reason to suspect the structure.

He found proof on his desk, in the form of a letter. The contents were painfully specific. He was not the man she'd thought he was. She had devoted her life to him, assuming he was dedicated and honorable. Instead, she'd discovered he was little more than a quitter who would rather let the world suffer than deal with the past and move on. She could accept the rest of his flaws, but leaving children to die when he could prevent their demise was unforgivable. She regretted every minute she'd spent with him.

The last statement was the worst. He could handle her accusations by telling himself she simply didn't understand. But knowing she had regrets made the darkness inside him grow until he knew there would be no escape from the shadows.

Still holding the letter, he moved toward his computer and sat down without turning on the machine. He stared at nothing and remembered another time and another woman leaving him. His wife.

She had seemed to admire his devotion to his work, until the day they married. Then she'd said he was too involved, that his lab took all his time and energy, leaving neither for her. They had argued. In the end, what she said had proved to be true—she wasn't his passion. When she left, he barely noticed.

Her leaving hadn't been more than a ripple in his life. He had his research and Linda. Always Linda. While there had never been anything romantic between them, she was the one constant he could count on. She was always there, looking after him, encouraging him, making sure he ate right and slept. She understood what the breakthroughs meant, how he got discouraged when there was no progress. She believed in him. He couldn't imagine life without her.

He stiffened. No. That wasn't possible. She was a convenience, like a coffeemaker, nothing more. Except…except…

He missed her. Missed the sound of her footsteps, her calm voice, the way she organized his desk, brought him lunch and listened while he talked about his work. She understood what he was trying to do and always had suggestions and encouragement.

He missed talking to her. He missed her quirky movie reviews, her attempts to be a vegetarian that always failed within twenty-four hours, the way they did Sudoku together over coffee.

Which meant what? That he had feelings for her? For Linda?

Abram considered the possibility and knew, while he might have great affection for her, what bothered him the most was losing her respect. Because she had always believed in him, he had been able to believe in himself, even through the dark times. He could probably recover from her leaving, but knowing she did so while thinking less of him was impossible to bear.

Fifteen minutes later he parked in front of her small house and hurried to the front door. He opened it without knocking, knowing she rarely locked it no matter how he lectured her on her personal safety.

He heard noises coming from the rear of the house and walked down the hall, only to stop in shock as he saw open boxes scattered around the room. Boxes she was filling with her belongings.

"You're leaving me," he said, his voice low and harsh.

She didn't bother looking up as she emptied her dresser. "You were right. I should always remember to lock my front door. You never know who is going to break in."

"Linda, no."

She ignored him. After finishing with the dresser, she started on her nightstands. Item after item was tossed in the boxes.

When his wife had left him, he'd come home to an empty house and had barely noticed. She had been right—their marriage had been a mistake and he had never loved her. But Linda was different. Linda mattered.

He wanted to physically reach out and stop her. To unpack the boxes himself.

"You can't leave," he told her. "I need you."

"Ask me if I care."

He'd never seen her like this. Distant and cold. His chest tightened.

"I'll do it," he said. "I'll open the lab, hire the scientists. Whatever you want. Just don't leave."

She straightened and stared at him. "Not good enough, Abram. You can't do this for me. You have to do it for yourself—because you believe—and for the children, because they deserve a chance."

"I'll do it because it's what I'm meant for," he said slowly, praying the words were enough. "Because I've been blessed and because it's both my responsibility and my passion."

She stared at him as if she didn't believe him. Disbelief thinned her mouth.

"Please," he said, begging for the first time in his life. "Please."

He took a step toward her and gently removed the T-shirt from her hand.

"We will find a cure," he said. "For Cody. For the other children. Together. I will do it, Linda. Even if you leave, I will move forward with this work." He meant the words, even if he wasn't sure how he would work without her at his side. "But I'll work faster if you are with me. Please stay."

"I don't know," she admitted. "Everything is different."

"I'm not. I can be the man you thought I was. One chance. Just one."

She stared at him for a long time. "Just one, Abram. Don't press me. I *will* leave if you screw this up."

"I know. I won't. You'll see."

He would prove himself to her. He had no choice. Without her, he was nothing.

TIM SHIFTED his weight from foot to foot, looking uneasy and making Nathan feel they were both on a boat in restless seas.

"It's, ah, ten days," Tim said, then swallowed.

"No problem," Nathan told him. "You have plenty of time on the books. You should take a couple of weeks off."

"No. Just the ten days is fine. I'll make sure the substitute driver is filled in. The transition will be seamless."

"I appreciate that." Nathan studied his driver. "You don't take a lot of time off."

"I know. But Lance wants to go on a cruise. To Alaska. He booked the trip and gave it to me as a surprise."

From his tone, Nathan guessed Tim would have been more excited by a box of scorpions.

"You'll have fun," Nathan told him.

"I guess. Okay, boss. That's all."

Tim left. Nathan watched him leave and tried to imagine Tim in a tropical shirt, sunbathing on deck. Although in Alaska, there wouldn't be a lot of warm weather. Still, the image eluded him.

His secretary knocked on his door and entered. "Hey, Mr. K. Just reminding you I'm leaving early today. My granddaughter is in her school spring play." Ellie grinned. "She's lead tree."

"You wouldn't want to miss that."

"I know. So I'll be leaving about one-thirty."

He nodded and she backed out of the room.

It occurred to him that everyone he knew had someone else and he didn't. It wasn't a new situation. He preferred to be alone. It was cleaner that way, with less complications. He'd been married once and little about his relationship with Paige was something he wanted to repeat.

Still, he felt a restlessness that had him reaching for the phone.

"Hair Barn," a female voice said.

"Kerri Sullivan."

"Hold on."

Seconds later he heard, "This is Kerri."

"It's Nathan. I want us to have dinner tomorrow night here in town. Somewhere people will notice. I'll have my assistant drop a few hints to local media. Tim will come pick you up about five and you can spend the night in a hotel. He'll take you home in the morning."

"Aren't you all imperious," she said. "Sorry, I can't."

He frowned. "I own you."

"I said I would do my best to cooperate. There's a difference."

"Which you're not doing."

"Oh, please. I'm not just dropping everything for you. What about Cody? He's nine. I can't leave him alone for the night."

"He can stay with his friend."

"I have to work."

"Reschedule. I'm sure the old ladies of Songwood can wait to get their hair dyed blue."

"You're incredibly disrespectful," she told him, not sounding amused. "For your information, tomorrow is prom Saturday. I'll be working all day, at least until six-thirty, because there's always one emergency that requires a quick fix."

"You're saying no?"

"I'm saying this isn't your finest hour, then I'm saying no."

Before he could respond, she hung up on him.

NATHAN WAS STILL pissed off the next day. Kerri obviously didn't understand the finer points of their arrangement. Determined to explain them to her, he drove to Songwood, arriving a little after four in the afternoon.

He went directly to the Hair Barn and found he had to park more than three blocks away. There were dozens of cars and when he walked into the salon, he understood why.

Teenage girls filled every available chair and most of the open space. They were in groups, laughing, shrieking, running around with curlers in their hair. They didn't seem to notice him and as he wasn't into jailbait, he ignored them.

He walked directly to Kerri's station, where she worked on a girl's hair, spraying strands, curling them into long ringlets, then spraying them again.

"What were you thinking?" she asked, meeting his gaze in the mirror. "You don't want to be here today."

"I came to check out my competition."

She handed him the can of hair spray, then smoothed a curl into place. "This is girl central. Teenagers come in from all over the mountain. They travel in packs and don't leave until they're all done. There's enough estrogen in this place today to turn you into a woman."

"Not possible."

She grinned. "Want to bet?"

"Absolutely."

She grabbed the can and sprayed again, then thrust it back at him. "You're just crabby because I wouldn't change my plans for you."

"It isn't a behavior I want repeated."

Her eyes sparkled with amusement. "Will you want to spank me later?"

She was teasing him, which should have bugged him, but instead he found her almost charming.

"You'll be done at six-thirty?" he asked.

"Yes, but I'm not driving into the city with you, so don't even think about it. I'll be exhausted." She finished the last ringlet. "Okay, Brittany, now do you want it all up with the curls falling down the back of your neck?"

"Uh-huh. I brought ribbon." The teenager smiled at Nathan. "It matches my dress."

The kid was an uncomfortable combination of all grown-up and little girl. "How old are you?" he asked.

"Sixteen, but my boyfriend's a senior."

"She could be your daughter," Kerri said sweetly.

The girl looked at him. "You do kind of look like my dad."

"How flattering." He put the can of hair spray on the counter in front of him. "I'll pick you up at seven. We'll eat locally."

"I can't decide if it's your charm or your graciousness that I like the best," Kerri told him.

"You have the next couple of hours to figure it out."

"YOU'RE THE WORST," April said as she grabbed the eyeliner from Kerri. "Close your eye. You're all squiggly. You're supposed to be the adult here."

"I *am* the adult here," Kerri muttered.

"You're not acting like it," the fifteen-year-old told her. "You can't even do eyeliner right."

"I never wear it."

"You won't get a boyfriend if you don't make the effort."

"Words to live by," Kerri muttered. "I don't want a boyfriend."

April's mouth dropped open. "But then you'll be *alone.*"

"There are worse fates."

"I can't think of any." The teenager stepped back. "Okay. That's better."

Kerri looked at herself in the mirror. Her eyes looked bigger, darker and possibly mysterious. She turned slowly, checking out the black wrap dress she'd borrowed from Michelle. Her hair was still in curlers and her feet hurt from standing all day, but otherwise, she thought she just might be pretty enough to get a boyfriend.

She checked her watch. It was five to seven. "I'm late," she murmured as she began pulling the curlers out of her hair. "Nathan is always on time."

April leaned against the door frame. "Is he that rich guy I read about in the paper?"

"Yes."

"Cool. Think he'll pay me extra? You could tell him my family is really poor and I'm saving for college."

"Your father is a doctor and you're an only child. Money is hardly tight."

"I don't get a lot of allowance. My dad says I have to come up with half the insurance money or I won't get a car next year when I turn sixteen. He says I need to learn responsibility."

Which explained her availability to babysit at the last minute on a Saturday night.

"I'll be paying you the usual amount," Kerri said firmly.

"Bummer. But if he offers, don't tell him no. I mean, it wouldn't hurt for me to inflate my prices just a little. He can afford it."

"Just because he can afford it doesn't make it right to charge him more," Kerri said, then remembered that she'd charged Nathan seventy-five dollars for a haircut.

An entirely different circumstance, she told herself, ignoring the sliver of guilt sliding down her spine.

April sighed heavily. "Okay. Fine. My regular amount."

"I made cookies, if that helps."

"It does. Besides, watching Cody is no big deal. He just wants to play games or watch TV. Not like some of the families I work for. I hate it when there are babies. I always get the poopy diapers. It's gross."

Someone knocked at the front door. Kerri shrieked and went to work on her hair.

April grinned. "You look nervous."

"I'm fine. Please answer the door. I'll be right out."

The teenager left. Kerri fluffed her hair, then sprayed it. She applied a last coat of lip gloss, grabbed her purse and walked out to the living room.

Nathan stood talking to April. At the sight of the tall, good-looking man, she felt a distinct tightening in her chest. Anticipation, she thought absently. She was looking forward to their evening together.

She came to a stop. Anticipation? Over seeing Nathan? Going out with him was about paying him back for the fifteen million. She was practically selling herself. Well, without the sex. She shouldn't feel anything except obligation.

Only Nathan wasn't the stuffy, boring guy she'd thought he would be. He was interesting and funny and charming, in his own way. Who would have thought?

Had his hair always been that thick? she wondered absently. Had he always had that tiny scar by his lower lip? He'd shaved and changed his shirt, which shouldn't have mattered, but suddenly did.

He glanced up and saw her. "Hello."

Kerri suddenly felt flustered. As if she didn't know what to say. "Ah, hi. I'm ready." She turned to April. "We won't be late."

"That's fine. Cody and I have already picked out a movie. Is it okay for us to have microwave popcorn?"

"Sure. He knows where everything is. You have my cell number?"

April rolled her eyes. "Yes, Mrs. Sullivan. You know I took that CPR class, right? I'm totally certified."

April had been babysitting for them since they moved to Songwood. She was one of the best around. Kerri knew April had everything under control. The question had been more about her unexpected nervousness around Nathan than anything else.

"I can't help asking," Kerri told her.

"It's okay." April leaned in close. "He's kinda hot for an old guy."

"He'd be thrilled to hear you say that."

"Look." April held out a fifty-dollar bill. "He paid me."

"You're one step closer to wheels."

"How cool is that?"

Kerri smiled at Nathan. "You driving?"

"You have to ask?"

"I guess not."

They left the house. Kerri slid onto the cool leather of the passenger seat of Nathan's car. When he was next to her, she said, "You seriously overpaid the babysitter."

"I know, but now she likes me."

"Do you have to buy your way into all of your relationships?" she asked before she could stop herself. "Sorry. I shouldn't have said that."

"It works on staff."

"I never thought of April as staff. She's my babysitter. Well, technically she's Cody's."

"When she has a choice of working for you, knowing you're doing something with me, or sitting for another family, who is she going to pick?"

"Interesting point. So life is very smooth for you."

"Most of the time. Every now and then someone like you comes along."

"Someone who refuses to be staff?"

"Someone unexpected."

Silly, useless words, she told herself. But they still made her feel all tingly inside.

She told herself it was nothing more than exhaustion. A reaction to all the stress in her life. She was tired and discouraged and wishing things were better. That was the only reason she reacted to what Nathan said.

"Jason has already drawn up the papers to serve Wallace with a lawsuit. We're asking for an injunction, preventing him from working on anything if he won't do the research. I have two detectives digging into his background, looking for ex-wives, kids, anything we can use against him. I give it two, three days, tops. He'll be back in his lab."

She hoped he was right. Because when she thought about Cody's disease progressing, she found it impossible to breathe.

"I appreciate all you're doing, but can we talk about something else?" she asked.

"Sure. Do you know how hard it is to get a reservation at a restaurant in town?"

That made her smile. "Here in Songwood? No one takes reservations."

"Which is my point."

"There are only diners and burger places. They don't take reservations."

"The guy at the Dynasty Palace was nearly convinced, but then I called Vern's Bar and Grill and Vern himself promised us the best table in the house."

She laughed. "I hope you're not expecting much. Vern runs a roadside bar that serves casual food."

"He promised live entertainment and dancing."

"I know there's a stage, so I guess that's possible. I've never been to Vern's on a Saturday night."

"You've been missing a classic experience."

She looked at him and found him smiling at her. Something about that smile made her feel that anything was possible.

They got to Vern's and parked. Sure enough, the hostess led them to a corner booth with a small Reserved sign in the middle. The hand lettering on a piece of cardboard told Kerri that Vern didn't usually reserve tables. As he'd said before, money made Nathan's life flow very smoothly.

The place had been built when Songwood was still a logging town. Heavy beams supported the ceiling and the walls were paneled. Booths outlined the dining area with a small dance floor in front of the stage at the far end of the room. Tables filled the rest of the space.

While there was no live entertainment yet, a couple of guys were setting up and country music drifted from hidden speakers.

When they'd been seated, a waitress appeared with a bottle of Dom Pérignon in an ice bucket. Kerri shook her head.

"You had to have dropped that off earlier," she told him. "There's no way I'll believe Vern just happened to have this sitting in the back room."

"It's pretty fancy," the waitress said as she popped the cork. "Did you know you can buy it at Costco?" She looked at Nathan. "One of those big warehouse stores."

"I know what Costco is," Nathan told her.

"Let me guess," Kerri said. "You have their stock in your portfolio."

Nathan shrugged. "Some."

The champagne was poured and their waitress left them alone. He picked up his glass.

"Thank you for joining me this evening. A beautiful woman makes everything brighter."

It was a line, she told herself. One he probably used all the time. But still, it flustered her.

"I, ah, thank you." She sipped the champagne. "It's nice. I'm really tired from working today, but I'm glad you invited me out to dinner. I don't do this very much. Go out. With men. Not that we're dating. I know this isn't a date. But it's still, you know…"

"Nice?" he offered.

"Right." She knew she was talking too much but

didn't know how to stop. "It's tough, with Cody. Dating, I mean. Not that I'm interested. Which is good. Single moms aren't exactly hunk magnets."

He'd been drinking as she spoke and choked slightly. After coughing, he asked, "You're looking for a hunk?"

"No. I didn't mean it that way. I have no idea what I'd want. I had someone great once. Brian— Cody's father. He was a good guy. The kind of man who makes everything better just by being in the room."

Nathan leaned back in the booth. His expression was unreadable. "Tell me about him."

"You don't mean that."

"Sure. What was he like?"

Kerri warmed to the topic. "Funny. Kind. He wasn't a big guy—he was only a few inches taller than me. But he was such a presence. People just wanted to be close to him. We met at a mutual friend's barbecue. It was like in a movie. We saw each other from across the room and just knew we were meant to be together. He died before I even knew I was pregnant." She rubbed her fingers up and down on the stem of her glass. "That's the worst part. He never knew he was going to be a father."

She took a sip. "Okay, this is really a bad topic. We shouldn't talk about Brian."

"He was a large part of your life."

Except for Cody, the best part. "He was."

"Since then?" Nathan asked. "Have you gotten involved with anyone?"

"No. I couldn't. When Cody was a baby I didn't have the time or the interest. After he got sick…I guess I still don't have the time or interest. I need to take care of him, be there for him."

"You get to have a life, too."

"No, I don't. I know it probably sounds stupid to you, but I made a deal with God. I would give Cody a hundred percent and He would keep my son alive."

"Giving up your life for his?"

"Something like that. It's working. That's all I care about."

"You can't believe you're required to give up everything or Cody will die."

She wondered if what he really wanted to say was that Cody was going to die anyway.

Nathan leaned toward her. "You could be so much more."

"You mean more than a hairdresser? No, thanks."

"You should have gone to college."

"How do you know I didn't?"

Nathan only looked at her, which reminded her of the file he'd no doubt prepared on her. The one that most likely mentioned her single semester at community college.

"There are so many opportunities," he said. "You're smart, driven. You gave up too easily."

"Don't be judgmental. I was just starting to like you."

"I'm telling the truth."

"Your version of it. I like my work."

"There are people who can't be more. Leave that type of work to them."

"You're a snob and an elitist."

"You're selling yourself short."

She should be annoyed with him and start telling him off, but she sensed he meant to be helpful. That he wanted more for her, which was kind of sweet.

"You could have the world," he told her.

Maybe, but all she wanted was for her child to get better. Compared to that dream, the world seemed pretty small.

She glanced at the tiny dance floor. There were two couples swaying to the music. Suddenly she wanted to join them.

"You could ask me to dance," she told him.

He slid off the seat and reached for her hand. "Yes, I could."

CHAPTER EIGHT

KERRI LET HERSELF relax in Nathan's arms. They drifted more than danced, one of his hands holding hers, the other at the small of her back. She tried to remember the last time she'd danced with a man and realized she didn't care. It simply felt good to be doing it now.

One of the advantages of being with Nathan was that she knew it would never go anywhere. They had nothing in common and if she hadn't been trying to blackmail him into supporting her cause, they would never have met. So she was free to enjoy the moment for what it was—a dance with a handsome man.

She closed her eyes and breathed in the scent of him. He smelled clean and sexy. Heat from his body warmed her, making long-dormant places wake up and take notice. She felt a heaviness in her breasts and a distinct clenching between her thighs.

Sex, she thought, not sure the awakening was a good idea. She wanted sex. She had no intention of getting involved, even casually. Which meant the only intimate relationship she could consider was with her shower massager.

But for now, this was enough. Her head on his shoulder, their thighs brushing, his heartbeat making her feel connected to someone, if only for that moment.

"Are you enjoying this or is this part of what you owe me?" he asked, his voice rumbling against her ear.

"You have to get off the money thing. You didn't write *me* a check. I'm getting no immediate benefit. I'm hoping for a more long-term miracle, but until that happens, you're pretty useless to me."

He chuckled. "I liked it better when I intimidated you."

"That never happened."

"You called me Mr. King the first time we met."

"I was being polite and you nearly had me arrested. I think you called me a bad name. I know you swore."

"You were way out of line."

"It worked."

"That it did."

The song ended and they moved back to their table. The waitress appeared. They gave their orders, then Kerri reached for her glass of champagne.

"So how did you get from where you started to here?" she asked. "I remember something about a college football scholarship. What position did you play?"

"Do you know anything about football?"

"Not really."

"Then does it matter?"

She laughed. "I guess not. Were you good?"

He smiled slowly. "What do you think?"

"That you didn't go pro."

"I was good but not that good," he admitted. "I wasn't too disappointed. I had other plans."

"To make your first billion and take over the world?"

"It was a goal."

"So how did you go from being a scholarship student to that first billion?"

"I played poker with rich kids and won." His expression was self-satisfied. "I started in my freshman year. They had money to burn and very little card sense. I built up enough money by April to buy a small house in South Central L.A. I fixed it up and sold it for a profit. The following summer, I bought two houses. The next, an apartment building."

She'd barely finished a semester of community college. As she'd thought before, worlds apart.

"I took on a partner in my senior year and we started buying property seriously. We made our first million that year. I bought him out five years later."

"Did he want to be bought out?"

Nathan looked at her. "Most people don't bother to ask that question."

"I'm insightful."

"He wasn't as happy as he could have been, but I wasn't interested in having a partner anymore."

"You used him to get what you wanted, then tossed him aside."

His gaze never wavered. "Yes."

"Just checking."

The information didn't surprise her. The Nathan King who danced with her was a charming, hand-some, sexy man, but underneath, he was and would always be a ruthless bastard. She knew it should frighten her, but, somehow, it didn't.

"THE OTHER DAY I counted how many Mario games Cody has," Kerri said as she and Nathan walked toward her front door. "It's incredible what those video-game people have done with one short guy. I think he was a plumber once. I can't remember. But he's all over the place. There was a gorilla before, wasn't there?"

They stopped in front of her door. Nathan smiled. "You're nervous."

"I'm not."

"You're talking about video games, and not mak-ing any sense."

He'd been standing a step below her. Now he moved onto the same one, so he was taller and, oddly, much more male. Not that he hadn't been male before, but it was more obvious now and she…

She held in a groan. It was one thing to babble to

someone else, but it was a real problem when she started babbling to herself.

It was the circumstances. They'd just been out to dinner, they'd danced, talked, laughed. It was practically a date which meant, at the end, kissing. Maybe lots of kissing.

Except this wasn't a date and they weren't involved. Despite her claims that he hadn't directly given her money, she was in his debt. Or as he liked to phrase it—he owned her ass. And if it was his, she could hardly keep him from touching it, could she?

"What are you thinking?" he asked. "Your eyes are flashing something, but I can't figure out what."

"Nothing important."

"Liar."

Then he bent down and pressed his mouth to hers.

They'd kissed before, briefly, powerfully. So she should have been prepared for the impact of his lips against hers. But she wasn't. The heat caught her off guard, as did the electrical thrills that shot through her.

They darted through her body, giving off little charges in her breasts and between her legs. She went from intellectually interested in the exercise to "take me hard" in about an eighth of a second.

All this before he even got serious, she thought hazily as he moved his mouth against hers. He eased a little closer, then touched her bottom lip with his tongue.

It was all the invitation she needed. She parted for

him, then sighed heavily as he claimed her with a sweeping stroke that stole her ability to breathe.

He put his hands on her waist, resting them there. She liked the warm weight but would have preferred them moving. Roving, exploring, touching. Her nipples were hard and hungry, her skin drawn tight in anticipation of a man's touch. She'd been without so long, she'd forgotten what it was like to ache with every cell in her body.

She wrapped her arms around his neck, clinging because she felt herself shaking. Just a little. Just enough to be embarrassing.

She tried to tell herself it was just a kiss. No big deal. But where before she'd been able to keep control, now she felt driven by need.

It was time, she told herself. Too much time without sex. Or circumstances. She owed Nathan, so she was being grateful. It wasn't specifically him— it couldn't be. Oh, but could he kiss.

He moved his tongue easily, exploring her with the patience of a man who loves his work. She kissed him back, dancing with him, stroking him, nipping slightly as he retreated.

He chuckled then and moved his hands to her butt. He cupped her curves, then squeezed. Her insides clenched. It took every ounce of willpower she possessed not to arch forward until she pressed against him in an age-old invitation.

But two things stopped her. First, her terror that

this was a party for one and that he wouldn't be hard.
Second, that they weren't going anywhere, not even
to bed. She didn't get involved, no matter that the
man in question made her wet, weak and willing.

He pulled back and stared into her eyes. "I wish
I knew what you were thinking," he told her. "I don't
know if you're really enjoying this or if you're in
payback mode." He grimaced. "I don't generally
have to question myself."

"I know," she murmured, aware that if he slipped
his hands between her legs he would find out exactly
what he was doing to her. She was swollen and ready
and she had a feeling it was going to be a long night.

Part of her wanted to reassure him and part of her
knew it was better if he thought she was playing
with him. Safer—for her, at least.

She stepped back and reached for the door handle.
"Good night, Nathan."

"You're not going to tell me?"

She shook her head and slipped into the house.

SUNDAY MORNING Kerri threw herself into house-
cleaning. Cody was with Brandon, so she cranked up
the radio and sang along as she scrubbed floors and
tile. She was just about to plunge the soapy brush
into the toilet when someone rang the doorbell.

Her first thought was that it was Nathan, and
with that thought came a distinct shiver of anticipation. She told herself there was no reason he

should stop by. He wasn't going to make the hour-long drive just to say hi. If he wanted to see her, he would call first.

But none of the logic did anything to make her insides stop quivering. She pulled open the door, then froze when she saw Dr. Wallace standing on her tiny porch.

Reality crashed in on her. Fear and anger combined until she wanted to reach across the small space separating them and pull out his still-beating heart.

She wanted him dead. No, that wasn't right. She wanted him suffering. Writhing in pain for an endless eternity. Maybe after a few hundred years she would be willing to feel a little compassion. But not until then. Certainly not now.

He twisted his hands together in front of his mid-section. "I'm sorry," he told her. "That's why I'm here. To tell you I'm sorry and that I was wrong. I'm already back to work. We're hiring more scientists. This is my life's mission—finding a cure. I won't rest until there is one. We need a treatment, as well, something to slow the progression until we can isolate the cause. I still believe the enzymes hold the answer. I'm looking there."

He stopped and stared at her. "Why are you crying? This is happy news."

She reached up and touched her cheek, only to find it was wet. "I didn't know I was."

She'd felt nothing but a down-to-her-bones wash

of relief. Her legs ached, as if she'd run for miles. It was difficult to breathe, but all in a happy way.

"I won't give up," Dr. Wallace told her. "I want you to know that. What I said before…" He shook his head. "I was wrong. I know I put you through hell. I can only apologize. You can forgive me later, when we save your son."

Kerri dropped the toilet brush and lunged at Dr. Wallace. She wrapped her arms around his neck and hugged him and cried and hugged him some more.

"Thank you," she breathed. "Thank you."

"Don't thank me yet. I still have so much work to do." He gently pulled her arms free and stepped back. "We'll celebrate later."

She nodded, because she was still crying and it was tough to speak. She wanted to ask what had changed his mind, then decided it didn't matter. There was hope again. Hope where there had been none.

"We should have something experimental soon," he continued. "Something your son can try." He hesitated. "It will be dangerous, before the medical trials."

"I don't care," she said quickly. She and Cody didn't have time to wait for years of medical trials. "I'll sign whatever you want. Just get him something soon."

"I will do my best." Dr. Wallace nodded and left. After closing the door behind him, she sank to the floor and tried to catch her breath.

She wanted to shout her happiness. They had a reprieve. Pray God, it was enough.

The phone rang. She stretched out her arm and grabbed it.

"Hello?"

"Kerri, it's Nathan. I just had a call from Jason. Wallace is back in the lab and they're ramping up to work at full capacity."

She nodded, still fighting tears.

"Kerri? Are you there? This is good news."

"I know."

"Are you crying?" His voice was sharp. "What's wrong?"

"Nothing. I'm happy. He was just here. You did this. You made him start up his research again."

"As much as I would enjoy taking credit, it wasn't me, and Jason had barely started to squeeze. He did this on his own. Maybe you got to him."

"Maybe. The truth is, I don't care why. I just want a cure."

"I know."

She drew in a breath. "Sometimes it's hard to keep going," she said, voicing the thought for the first time. "Sometimes it seems like it's just me and Cody against the world."

"You're not alone. You have a whole team now."

Did she? She'd been carrying the burden herself for so long that it was difficult to imagine being in a place where she could set it down for a while.

"Dr. Wallace is the best," he continued. "He'll find something."

"I know."

She believed, because she had to.

"While I'm glad this got resolved," Nathan said with a smile in his voice, "it puts me in a hell of a situation. I was all geared up to fight. I have to walk away without the thrill of victory."

She gave a strangled laugh, then wiped her cheeks. "You'll get over it."

"I like going to battle."

"Of course you do. You like to win. To take, to pillage."

"I haven't pillaged in a long time. I miss it."

She had the sudden thought they weren't talking about battles anymore. She remembered how she'd felt the previous night, standing on the porch, in his arms.

She'd forgotten what it felt like to be held by a man, kissed by a man. She'd forgotten what it felt like to want. Now that she remembered, she didn't know how to make the need go away.

But she would figure it out, she reminded herself. Nothing mattered but Cody—especially now that they were back on track.

"I appreciate your letting me know about Dr. Wallace," she said. "I'm relieved it all worked out."

"Me, too. You still owe me for prom night. You blew me off."

"I was busy, and I don't owe you."

"Sure you do. You can come to Seattle and we'll have lunch. I'll show you the mock-ups for the towers I want to build. You can be impressed."

It wasn't that she didn't want to see him, it was that being around him made her feel uneasy. Nathan had gone from being a means to an end to something that might be dangerous.

But he was right—she did owe him.

"I'm off tomorrow."

"Tim will pick you up at ten-thirty."

"Tim and I are getting really close. It's touching."

Nathan chuckled. "Thanks for letting me know. See you tomorrow."

"THAT WAS UNCOMFORTABLE," Kerri muttered as they left the restaurant. "Did you see the manager glaring at me?"

"He wasn't glaring," Nathan said. "He hid out in his office."

"Can you blame him? That was a hideously bad idea. I should never have let you talk me into going there." She glanced up at Tim, who held open the back of the limo. "You're smiling. You think this is funny."

"No, ma'am."

"Ma'am? You're going to pay for that. I'm singing with the radio the whole way home."

As she had a voice that made cats howl in protest, she was threatening him with a lot. Tim winced, then stepped back to let Nathan into the car.

"Don't torture him," Nathan told her. "I don't want to lose him."

"I blame you both. I can't believe we went to The Grill for lunch. I was fired from that restaurant."

"You said you were fine with the idea."

"Before we went there. I had no idea what I was getting into. Talk about humiliating."

Actually, she hadn't minded eating in the fancy place. She'd never had much of a chance to taste the food during her brief employment. For reasons that weren't clear, she felt nervous around Nathan. The babbling had started with the entrée and didn't show any signs of stopping.

She pressed her lips together in an effort to keep from talking, then said, "Are we going to your office now? We don't have to. Tim could take me home."

"You should see the towers. You're a part of them now."

"Not unless you plan to give me a two-bedroom condo. I'd prefer a water view, please. I don't need an especially high floor. Something in the middle would be fine."

"Good to know."

He seemed perfectly relaxed, which she resented. Why couldn't *she* relax? Why did she have to be aware of every little thing about him?

Like now, in the car. They weren't sitting all that close together on the leather seat, yet she could feel the heat from his body. She caught any movement he made, was aware of the tone of his voice, the rhythm of his breathing, the fact that he'd gotten his hair cut.

If she didn't keep her attention firmly on the conversation, she started to think about kissing him, touching him, having him touch her.

When she got home, she was going to give herself a stern talking-to and maybe even think about punishment. She had to get herself mentally focused. If she allowed her energies to stray for even a second, Cody would suffer. She believed that as surely as she believed air was necessary for life.

"Is your office bigger than Jason's?" she asked.

"You're obsessed with my attorney."

"Not at all. He seems nice. It was a great office. Maybe I missed my calling. Maybe I should have gone into corporate America and had a great office with a view."

"It's not too late."

It was for her, she thought. Nathan wanted to talk about her future, but until Cody was cured, he was all she cared about.

They pulled up in front of a high-rise. Nathan led the way to the elevator then pushed the button for the top floor.

"You're going to be hating life if there's ever a really big earthquake," she told him. "Just remember that."

He smiled and escorted her into the elevator.

An impressively smooth ride later, they exited on the executive floor of the King Investment Group. A receptionist sat behind a desk that was more tower than writing surface.

"Good afternoon, Mr. King."

"Gypsy."

Kerri eyed the pretty brunette. "Gypsy? Seriously? That's her name?"

"It says so on her paycheck."

"Who does that to a child?"

They passed lots of big offices filled with busy-looking people.

"Not a lot of women on the executive floor," she murmured.

"Over thirty percent at senior levels. I don't care about gender. I don't care if they're extraterrestrials. I want people who do a good job."

The desk in front of the double doors was empty. Nathan opened the door on the right, then stepped back to let her go first.

Kerri braced herself to be impressed and walked into Nathan's sanctuary.

His office was about three times the size of her whole house. It was a corner space, with plate-glass windows. To the west was the sound, to the south, Safeco Field and beyond. The colors were muted, and the furniture looked expensive, with lots of wood. The sofa area in the corner would seat at least eight people; the conference table had room for twelve.

"It looks just like our break room at the Hair Barn," she said with a grin. "Except we have more phones."

He ignored her and crossed to a freestanding easel. After flipping over the top sheet, he stepped back. "What do you think?"

The architectural rendering showed two staggered towers in a garden setting. There were huge windows, balconies, and what looked like a park on each roof.

They were large, imposing and beautiful, in a stark sort of way. Not anyplace she would want to live, she thought, not sure what it was about them that she didn't like. The sheer size? The lack of personality, although she had no idea how one built a high-rise with personality.

"They're great," she said at last.

"You hate them."

"What? Of course not. Your name is big." She pointed to the lettering—*King Towers*—on the side. "I thought only Donald Trump did that."

"I'm not sure about the name," he admitted. "It might be better without that."

"Not my area of expertise."

She tilted her head as she studied first the building, then the man. "So this is it?" she asked. "This is the pinnacle of your career. The towers on the sound and then you've won."

He shrugged. "I'll have other goals."

"But this is the big one?"

"It is for me."

"Because of how you grew up?"

"Because every day my old man told me I wouldn't amount to shit, and he's wrong."

Recognition from the dead couldn't be easy to get, she thought, wondering if the towers would be enough. Or if Nathan would need something bigger and more impressive next time. He had billions. At what point was it enough?

"Are you happy, Nathan?" she asked.

He looked at her. "Hell of a question."

"I know. Are you?"

He was silent a long time, then he grabbed her arm, pulled her close and kissed her.

When his firm lips claimed her, she decided she might be willing to let the question go. When he nipped at her lower lip, then eased the spot with his tongue, she decided that conversation was a total waste of time. When he put his hand on the curve of her rear and squeezed, she forgot what they'd been talking about.

The man knew how to kiss, she thought hazily as their tongues circled and teased and aroused. He knew how to do a lot of things. All that intense focus. What would he be like in bed?

Even though she wasn't going to go there, she allowed herself a moment of speculation. A moment of imagining his hands…everywhere.

He broke the kiss to nibble his way along her jaw. She held in a moan, but it was tough. Long-sleeping nerves awoke to find there was a party going on and they liked it. He licked the skin below her ear, then nipped at her lobe. Shivers raced through her body, making her tremble.

She clung to him because the alternative was to collapse on the floor. When he squeezed her rear again, she couldn't help arching against him. Her belly came into contact with his arousal and she had to hold in a scream.

He was hard and thick and she wanted to rub against him like a cat. In that moment, nothing mattered but the man and how he made her feel. She wanted to rip off her clothes and have him touch her everywhere. She wanted to feel all the melty, tingly, moany things in all the parts of her body she'd ignored for years and years. She wanted him rubbing and teasing until she had no choice but to lose herself in her release. She wanted to feel him inside, stretching her, taking her, making her scream with the power of what he was—

"Take Me Out to the Ball Game" suddenly filled the relative silence of his office. It took Kerri a second to realize that it was her phone and that it was the ring tone she used for Cody's school.

She jerked free of Nathan's touch, found her purse and pushed the talk button on her phone.

"What happened?" she asked breathlessly.

"Kerri, I'm sorry. It's Cody. He fell. There was some water in the hallway. His crutch slipped. They're taking him to the hospital. You need to hurry."

CHAPTER NINE

"I'LL COME WITH YOU," Nathan said as Kerri hurried to the elevator.

"No. I don't want that." She had to get out of here and fast. All of this was her fault, she knew that. Now she could only pray for forgiveness and a miracle.

Be okay, she prayed. *Be okay. Be okay.* The words played over and over in her mind.

"Kerri." He sounded impatient.

She ignored him. "You can't help. I need to get there. Is Tim waiting?"

"That will take too long. I'll have you flown up by helicopter. You'll be there in less than half the time."

"Okay. Fine. Thank you."

She supposed she should protest, but hiring a helicopter would mean nothing to Nathan and if it got her to Cody's side more quickly, all the better.

"Kerri, it's going to be all right."

She knew he meant well. She knew it was exactly

what people said at a time like this. But she wasn't in the mood to be socially graceful.

"You don't know that," she told him. "And neither do I."

KERRI WAS AT THE HOSPITAL in less than a half hour. She walked into the emergency room, wishing the bright halls weren't quite so familiar. She'd been here too many times with Cody. No child should have to be in a hospital this often. It just wasn't right.

She hurried to the nurses' station, then smiled at the familiar face. "Hi, Sharon."

"Hey, Kerri. He's in room four. Go on back." Sharon, a pretty nurse in her midthirties, touched her arm. "He's okay."

Kerri nodded because she didn't know what to say, then she made her way back to the room, where Cody lay on a narrow bed, looking pale and far too small.

"Anything for attention," she said as she entered. "I thought we'd talked about this."

He tried to smile, then winced. "Sorry, Mom. Don't be mad, okay?"

"When am I mad?"

"When I don't clean up my room or I flip channels on the remote. That really gets you all parental."

"It's totally annoying. Pick something to watch. Anything."

Then she was holding him, desperate to squeeze

and knowing she couldn't. He felt solid in her embrace. Familiar. Her son. Brian's son.

She wanted to curl up and cry at the pain her child suffered, at the unfairness of it all. But tears weren't allowed. Not with him and rarely when she was alone. They were a weakness. Besides, she'd already given in once this month, when she'd thought Dr. Wallace had walked away from the research. There would be no more tears for a long time.

She waited until he released her, then she straightened. But she kept stroking his hair and held his hand in hers.

"So what happened?" she asked, her voice deliberately calm. "They said you slipped?"

"It was totally dumb. I turned and then I went down. Everybody saw me."

Which probably mattered more to him than injuring himself, she reminded herself. He was growing up. What his friends thought would soon matter more and more.

"Nothing's broken," Cody told her. "There's not even a fracture. I'm bruised, though."

"I'll bet it hurts."

"Some."

More than some, but he always tried to be brave.

"Did they give you anything?"

Cody waved his other arm, the one with the IV. "Saline and a painkiller. Dr. Vinton did a bunch of X-rays. You should probably go find him."

"I probably should." She kissed Cody's cheek. "You'll be okay by yourself for a minute?"

He rolled his eyes. "Mo-om, I'm nine. I'm not a baby."

"Don't flirt with all the nurses. You know how they take that seriously and then you break their hearts."

"Can I help it if I'm so good-looking?"

She smiled, then kissed his cheek. "You're right— you can't. I'll be back."

She stepped out of Cody's room and paused to catch her breath. It hurt to breathe. There were no words to describe how much she hated this. How much she hated seeing him in pain, broken and weak. She needed a miracle. What were the odds of that?

She walked slowly back to the nurses' station. Dr. Vinton stood there with a chart in his hands. He looked up and saw her.

"Kerri. You're here. Good."

"If it were good, I wouldn't be here. Nothing's broken, right? That's what Cody said."

Dr. Vinton, a kind man in his late forties, nodded slowly. "Nothing's broken. We thought it might be, but the X-rays are fine."

"Okay, so why don't you look happier?"

Dr. Vinton put his arm around her and led her to a small sitting area at the end of the hall. Kerri knew from experience that wasn't a good sign.

"Cody didn't slip because there was water on the

floor," the doctor told her when they were seated. "It may have contributed, but it wasn't the reason. He fell because he can't support his own weight anymore. He doesn't have the strength. We're doing some tests to be sure. This is the normal progression of the disease, it's what we expect to find." He paused. "I'm sorry, Kerri. It's time to put him in a wheelchair."

Her throat tightened as her body clenched in protest. She wanted to jump up and shriek out her complaints to the universe. This couldn't be happening. It was so wrong. No! She wouldn't believe it.

"He can't," she whispered, knowing the wheelchair was a symbol of the end. It meant the disease was winning, that Cody would get worse, probably more quickly now. The pain would increase, as would the need for drugs to control the agony of his bones dissolving.

Dr. Vinton didn't speak. What was there to say? The disease progressed. Cody had had a good run. Blah, blah, blah.

Her eyes burned but she wouldn't give in to the weakness. It served no one.

"I don't want a timetable," she told him. "I want to believe that it's all going to work out. Don't tell me otherwise."

"I won't."

"Maybe with physical therapy he could get strong enough to compensate."

Dr. Vinton studied her. "Kerri, it's not going to help and the exercises will only make him hurt more."

"I know. I'm sorry. I'm reaching."

"Me, too. I want to find something, anything, that will stop this. I'm out of things to try. I won't give you a timetable, but you need to be prepared for what's going to happen."

Prepared for her son to die? How did that happen? Was there a class? An article? No one could help her deal with that impending loss.

"I wish you could just cut me open and take what you need from me," she told him. "My bones, my heart, any part of me."

"I know."

But there was nothing any of them could do except wait for a miracle that might or might not come in time.

"Dr. Wallace, thank you for inviting me to join you in your work."

"Ah, yes. You're welcome. Your work is most impressive."

His colleague, a tiny woman with bright red hair and green eyes, smiled. "I've studied all your experiments. In graduate school, I duplicated several of them. It's quite an honor for me to be here."

Abram swallowed nervously. "Yes. Good. We'll get going right away."

"I know we can do this," the young woman told

him. She clutched a clipboard to her chest and walked purposefully away.

"Looking at them makes me feel old," he said.

Linda rose and collected her notes. "She's brilliant. We were lucky to get her. The fact that she's a fan helps." His assistant smiled at him. "You have a lot of fans. We've been overwhelmed by the number of researchers wanting to work with you."

While he appreciated the fact that staffing would be easy, he was more interested by the respect and happiness he saw in Linda's eyes.

"We will make this happen," he told her.

"I know you will. Everything is different now."

He considered her words. "Yes. You are right. This is a new beginning."

One he hadn't expected. He had a feeling of belonging, which he'd never felt before. A whisper of promise. The sense that perhaps he should have done this long ago.

"We are doing this now," he told both Linda and himself. He only hoped he had not left the work too late.

"HOW ARE YOU holding up?" Linda asked from her corner of the sofa in the hospital's waiting room.

Kerri sipped her herbal tea, then shrugged. "Okay. They're keeping Cody until morning, then letting him go. I've ordered a temporary wheelchair that will fit in the trunk of my car and I'm trying to figure out how I'm going to afford a motorized one."

Linda opened her mouth, then closed it. Kerri had a feeling she was going to offer money.

"Don't go there," she told her friend.

"I can't help it," Linda said. "I want to help."

"You are. You got Dr. Wallace back on track. He's working on a cure. I'm still holding out for something amazing."

"Not just him." Linda gripped her mug of tea tightly. "There's a team. Brilliant minds are focused on Gilliar's Disease. Hold on a little longer. We can beat this."

"I know. At least, I tell myself that. I'm a little short on faith right now, but it will come back." Kerri drew her knees to her chest. "I hate this. I hate that he's here. I hate that it's only going to get worse. I hate how much pain he's going to deal with. And that I can't fix it. I'm his mother. I should be able to make him better."

Linda reached across the sofa and squeezed her shoulder. "You love him and you're there for him. That means everything."

Maybe, but it wasn't enough. It didn't *fix* anything.

"It's my fault," Kerri admitted. "I did this to him."

Linda frowned. "You did what?"

"I broke the deal. The rules are simple—I know them, but I pretended it didn't matter." She swallowed and looked at her friend. "I let myself get involved with Nathan. For just a couple of days, but I know better. I promised I'd give up my life for Cody's and when I stop, even for a moment, bad things happen."

"You don't really believe that."

"It's worked until now. He's defied all the odds. The disease slowed, and he's been able to live a relatively normal life. Then I get sucked into Nathan King's pretty world and it all goes to hell. Do you know what I was doing while Cody fell in school? I was kissing Nathan and hoping for a whole lot more."

Linda's mouth twisted. "I'm going to let that pass for now, but later, when you're thinking straight, I'm going to want details." She set her feet on the floor and leaned forward. "Kerri, you're my friend and I love you, but you're crazy. You don't have that much power. You can't will Cody to be all right and having a few minutes of fun isn't something you'll be punished for."

"You're wrong. I know it sounds unlikely, but I believe down to my bone marrow that the reason he got a break was that I was willing to make the ultimate sacrifice. My life for his. And I broke my part of the deal."

"God doesn't work that way."

"Are you sure? Maybe there's some twisted sense of balance in the universe. A life for a life. I'm ready to give up mine."

"You're allowed to be happy."

"Why? Why should I get something I want when he has nothing?"

"Because your sacrificing doesn't make him better."

"Are you sure? Are you a hundred percent, swear-on-Cody's-life sure?"

Linda opened her mouth and closed it. "I won't swear on his life."

"Me, neither. I blew it. I can't change the past, but I can keep it from happening again."

"Because your son is sick, you're not allowed to care about a man?"

Kerri considered the question. "It's not just Cody. What about Brian? I promised to love him forever."

"You do love him. But that doesn't mean you stop living. I hate being a cliché, but he wouldn't have wanted that. You know he wouldn't."

"He would want me to do whatever it takes to keep his son safe. And if that means giving up everything for Cody, he would have expected me to do it."

"From what I've heard about him, he was a much better man than that. And if you've found some happiness with Nathan—and I still want details—you're a fool if you walk away."

"Because he's rich?" Kerri asked bitterly, knowing this was one time when money couldn't help.

"Because you smile when you say his name. How long has it been since that happened?"

Not since Brian, Kerri thought, her heart aching. "I can't," she whispered. "I can't do this. I have to live my life for my son. If I don't, he'll die."

Linda didn't answer, but Kerri knew what she was thinking. That Cody was going to die anyway.

NATHAN WALKED THROUGH the hospital, toward the pediatric wing. He did his best to ignore the smell of disinfectant and despair, along with the memories that returned as he stepped off the elevator.

He'd only spoken with Kerri for a few minutes the previous night. She'd told him that Cody hadn't broken anything but that he would now be in a wheelchair. She'd asked him not to come by.

He'd planned on staying in Seattle, but somehow he'd found himself taking the limo up the mountain. If nothing else, he could have Tim drive them home.

He found Kerri talking with a doctor. She looked tired but still beautiful, Nathan thought as he watched her. Shadows darkened her eyes. There were lines by her mouth and a slump to her shoulders.

He waited until the doctor stepped away, then approached.

"Morning."

She turned to him. "Nathan! You didn't have to come. We're fine."

He knew that wasn't true. "I can give you a ride home."

"We have one." She pushed her hair off her face. "I'm sorry. I don't mean that to sound harsh. There's just so much to do. I have to get Cody home, get his assignments from school, then get to work."

"I can help with some of that."

"I don't think so."

He frowned. "Since when?"

She folded her arms across her chest. "Look, you've been really great and we both appreciate everything you've done, but this isn't going to work."

What the hell? "You're giving me the brush-off?" He held back, reminding her that he owned her.

"This isn't a good time. I can't…" She swallowed. "What happened between us before. I can't go there again. It's too dangerous."

It took him a couple of seconds to put the pieces together. "You blame me for what happened to Cody?"

"No. Of course not. I blame myself."

"But I'm a part of it."

"No. It's complicated. Look, we have a deal and I'll be there for whatever you want for the towers. Photo ops and whatever else there is. But nothing else. Nothing personal."

He didn't want her. He'd never wanted her. Okay, maybe she'd turned out to be more interesting than he'd first thought, but she didn't matter. No one mattered.

"That works for me," he told her curtly. "I'll get out of your way."

She reached toward him, as if she were going to touch him, maybe offer comfort. Which was bullshit. He was Nathan King. He played the game and he won. She was nothing.

"Thanks for coming all this way," she said.

He nodded and started walking. Rather than wait for the elevator, he took the stairs and he never once looked back.

FRANKIE HAD TIMED her visit perfectly. She knew exactly when Nathan's secretary left for lunch. Five minutes later, Frankie stepped out of the ladies' room and made her way to her brother's office.

She was shaking, which was better than crying. She'd already cried too much. That morning, she'd gone into work only to find out it was going to be her last day. She'd run out of time. It was over.

Terror gripped her. Without work, she had nowhere to go. It was only the realization that her future was a giant black hole of nothing that had propelled her to her brother's office. Nothing else could have gotten her there.

Now, as she pushed the door open and stepped inside, she felt the fear fade away. There was only the certainty of being right and the knowledge that somehow she would make him pay.

Nathan sat at his desk. He was on the phone and looking out the window. He obviously hadn't heard her enter. She stood on the plush carpet and stared at the man who had once been the person she loved most in the world. Years ago…when they'd been small. When they'd only had each other. Before Nathan had left her.

For a second there was only the blood spatters on the wall, but she pushed them away. She had to stay in the moment. She had to remember why she was here.

She looked around the room, taking in the beautiful oversize furnishings, the big desk, the fancy globe on a stand. It was one of those expensive ones with all the countries done in semiprecious gems. Except this was her brother. Maybe they were all the precious ones.

Carefully, quietly, she took the globe from the stand. It was heavy, but that was okay. She lifted it in her arms and threw it as hard as she could against the wall.

The impact was as loud as an explosion. Nearly as loud as a gunshot. The globe shattered, raining shards onto the carpet and leaving a sizable dent in the wall. Nathan turned slowly in his chair and looked at her.

"I'll have to get back to you," he said into the phone, and hung up. He stood. "Frankie. I wasn't expecting you."

"Doesn't that make this fun?"

He walked around the desk. "How are you?"

"What do you care? You never have. But that's okay. Because you're a terrible man. I'm going to destroy you, Nathan. How does that feel, hearing that? I'm going to destroy you."

"Are you hungry? Do you want something to eat?"

He wasn't taking her seriously. She hated that! "Are you listening? I'm going to sue you. You're not getting the towers. Not ever. You can't have them. You have too much and I'm going to take it away from you."

"Why, Frankie? You never cared about material things before."

"I don't care, but you do. You want your name so big and high. You want to be famous. But you can't be. They won't like it when your own sister sues you. People will talk. The newspapers will say things. You're going to be in trouble."

"You can't hurt me."

"Want to bet?" Anger burst into life. "I can destroy you, Nathan."

He leaned against his desk. "Frankie, I want to help. Maybe if you talked to a doctor."

She laughed. "So you can say you fixed me? I'm not going to give you the pleasure of that."

"I'll be there for you."

"No, you won't. You were never there. It was all a lie. You said everything would be okay and it wasn't. It wasn't and you didn't come home and I was alone."

Her eyes burned with tears she blinked away. She could still remember what it had been like—being so terribly alone and afraid.

He took a step toward her. "I'm sorry. I should have come back."

"You didn't want anyone to know the truth. That's why you stayed away."

He nodded slowly. "You're right. I was a kid and I…"

"I was younger," she screamed, hating him, wanting to destroy him. "I was younger and I was there. I was there."

He took another step toward her. She backed up.

"Stay away," she told him. "Don't touch me. I hate you. I'll always hate you."

"I'm sorry about that, too."

"You don't care about me. You don't care about anyone. But you do care about your stupid tower. Stupid like you."

He studied her for a long time. "Will destroying this make up for anything?" he asked quietly.

"I don't care about that. It doesn't matter."

"Frankie, you need help."

"Not from you. Don't pretend to be nice."

"I'm not nice, but I do want to help you." He hesitated, then said, "You're my sister."

"No," she whispered. "Not anymore. Not for a long time. You're nothing to me, Nathan. Nothing."

"That's not true. If it was true, you wouldn't be here. I can get you help. Please, Frankie, it doesn't have to be like this."

There was something in his voice. Something that made her remember a long-lost summer night. Their father had been drunk and screaming. She'd been afraid, so afraid. Nathan had taken her outside and sat with her while the screaming went on and on. He'd held her, rocking her.

"Make it stop," she'd begged him. "Make it stop."

"I can't do that," he'd told her. "I can't, but I know it doesn't have to be like this. When I get older it won't be like this ever again. You won't have to be afraid. I promise."

She'd believed him because she'd been young and stupid and he'd been her big brother. But he'd been wrong…about everything.

Weariness washed over her. She turned and left his office. In the foyer, she gave in to the tears, only to realize too late that she wasn't alone. A tall, thin man sat on the sofa, flipping through a fashion magazine. He was familiar. She made it a point to know most of the people in Nathan's world. But she couldn't put a name to the face.

The man stood. "Are you all right?"

She nodded as the tears fell. "It's just…" And then she remembered. Lance something. He was dating Tim, Nathan's driver.

She walked over to the chair by the sofa and gave in to the tears. "My brother is unreasonable. He's always thought he knows best and he's wrong. I know he's wrong."

"You're Nathan's sister?" Lance sounded surprised.

Frankie nodded and sniffed loudly. "We've been fighting. About that woman he's seeing. I know she's just in it for the money. He's going to be hurt and I don't know how to stop that from happening. He won't listen to me. I'm just his dumb baby sister. I'm just so worried."

Lance sat across from her and took her hand. She hated being touched and desperately wanted to pull back, but this was for a greater good. If she could just get something on Nathan, anything, she could take it to Grant. She could get what she wanted.

"You don't have to worry," Lance told her. "Kerri's okay."

"She's got you snowed, too."

"Not my type. But I know her. She's adorable. She's got a sick kid—Cody. He has what Nathan's son had."

Gilliar's Disease? Frankie shuddered. "So she's using that to get to Nathan?"

"No. You'd have to know Kerri. She's totally focused on her son. She and Nathan are just friends. She's actually helping him out with a project. He gave money to research and now she's helping him with…" Lance pressed his lips together. "With some things. I can't really say what."

How could someone like Kerri help Nathan? A single mom with a sick kid? And why would her brother have given the money in the first place? It wasn't like Nathan at all. Unless…

There were times when her mind was a dark and scary place and there were times when it was as if a light went on and chased away all the shadows. This was one of those times. She saw exactly what had happened and how Nathan was using the woman, just like he'd always used people.

She smiled at Lance. "You've made me feel a lot better. Thank you."

"I'm happy to help."

He probably was, she thought gleefully. Sucker. She stood and waved, then left the foyer. As she rode the elevator down, she pulled out her cell phone to call Grant at the newspaper office. The destruction of Nathan King had begun.

CHAPTER TEN

KERRI HEARD the rumble of a truck on the street but didn't think anything of it until the vehicle came to a stop in front of her house. She glanced out the window, saw it was a rental and was prepared to ignore it until she caught sight of the driver. As Tim was about the biggest man she'd ever seen, she spotted him right away.

Her focus shifted back to the rear of the truck as she wondered what on earth could be inside. If it was a pony, it was going straight back, she told herself, because making a joke was easier than dealing with the guilt that had flickered at the edge of her consciousness ever since Nathan had shown up at the hospital.

She'd been a total bitch. Nothing that had happened had been his fault. Her deal with God was private and not something that made sense to anyone else. Nathan had come through with the money and she owed him. She needed to remember that.

She walked outside and squinted as Tim walked around to the rear of the truck and pulled the back open.

"Is it alive?" she yelled.

He grinned. "Nope. You plug it in. It's fast, though. I took it for a spin myself."

She knew that it was unlikely Nathan would have bought her a car, knowing her feelings about her old beat-up machine. Which meant whatever it was had to be for Cody. She could only think of one form of transportation that her son needed right now.

As Tim ducked into the truck, she bit her lower lip and debated whether or not she could accept it. Then Tim rode a shiny new electric wheelchair down a ramp and she knew she didn't have a choice.

He stopped in front of her, then stood. "I'm going to build a ramp up the front stairs," he said. "I have all the hardware with me. Nathan said to tell you that refusing the wheelchair is about you and this is about Cody, but judging from the look on your face, I don't think you're going to say no."

"I'm not," she said, eyeing the expensive piece of machinery and knowing what a difference it would make for Cody. But it did make her wish she hadn't got quite so cozy with Nathan. Passion complicated everything.

"He's not a bad guy," Tim told her. "I like working for him."

"I never said he was bad. He's just… I can't deal with him right now."

"You can't control timing."

"I can't control anything."

AN HOUR LATER she and Cody turned onto Song-wood's main street.

"There's already a lot of new construction from the lab opening up again. A developer is bidding for housing projects and the diner is getting a new porch."

"Maybe I could do wheelies off the sidewalk."

"Maybe you couldn't."

Cody grinned up at her. While he'd hated the idea of giving up his crutches, he'd been excited when he'd seen his superpowered, bright blue wheelchair. Tim had shown him the basics, then let him loose in the driveway. Cody had mastered the controls in a matter of seconds. With the little trailer that had come with it, they could take the chair everywhere they needed to go. It was an amazing gift, worth thousands of dollars. Kerri wondered how she was going to pay Nathan back.

"Whoa, look at that!"

Kerri turned to where Cody pointed and saw a large crane at the edge of town.

"They're putting in beams for something," she said. "The crane is a total waste of money. I could have flown those beams up for free. Or maybe just for an order of fries. You know I love my fries."

"Mo-om." Cody rolled his eyes. "You can't fly."

She pressed a hand to her chest and sucked in a breath, pretending hurt. "What? Of course I can fly."

"I don't think so." He patted her arm. "But it's important to have goals."

Having him say what she said was both funny and annoying. He was just so sure. "I could fly if I wanted to." She'd already talked to Nathan about the possibility.

"Uh-huh."

They turned at the next street. Cody put his hands on the control. "I want to go really fast to Brandon's."

"Sure. I'll hang back, just to be polite. Because I could fly there if I wanted."

He rolled his eyes again, then shot forward. The wheelchair raced along the smooth sidewalk, leaving her behind in a matter of seconds. By the time he got to Brandon's, he was laughing.

Kerri closed her eyes and breathed in the sound. Happiness. At least for now. She wanted so much more for Cody, but it was the best she could do at the moment. Find a way to make him laugh. The next step was going to be to make a miracle come true.

"I FEEL SO GUILTY," Kerri said as she clutched her mug of tea. "He was only trying to be nice. And now I want to ask him a favor and I know I shouldn't, but it's for Cody and…" She looked at her friend. "Are you even listening to me?"

Linda smiled. "Of course I am."

"You seem distracted." Kerri covered her eyes with her free hand. "Something's going on in your life and all I'm doing is talking about myself. I'm a terrible friend."

"You're not. You're dealing with a lot of stuff."

Kerri straightened. "Stuff we don't have to talk about right now. What's happening with you? I want details, which is what you're always telling me."

Linda shrugged. "There's nothing to tell. Abram is making great progress at the lab."

"And?"

Linda ducked her head. "He really fell apart when he thought I was leaving. While that's not why I did it, it's nice to know that I matter."

"He would be lost without you."

"I always thought so, but now he knows it, too. He's been different. Attentive, caring."

Kerri knew that Linda stayed with Dr. Wallace because he was brilliant, but also because she loved him.

"You could tell him how you feel," Kerri pointed out.

"That would be mature and sensible," her friend said. "I'm not there yet."

"He's not going to reject you."

"Maybe not. But I want to be sure. I think it's better if the first move comes from him."

Kerri didn't want to push, although she couldn't help thinking that after twenty years, Linda had waited long enough.

"KERRI SULLIVAN ON line two," his secretary said.

Nathan studied the phone before picking it up.

"If you're going to say no, I'm not listening," he told her.

"I can't refuse," she said. Her voice was soft and familiar and hit him right in his groin. "It's for Cody. He needs something like that to get around. I couldn't possibly afford it."

Tension he'd ignored faded. "I figured." He remembered when Daniel had gone into a wheelchair. He'd been horrified, but his son had adjusted quickly, enjoying the speed and freedom. At least until his disease had reached the next stage.

"Thank you," she said.

"You're welcome."

"I didn't expect anything like that, especially after what happened when you came to the hospital."

"You were upset. But, Kerri, none of this is anyone's fault. It just is."

"Don't play the logic card. It won't work on me."

"Kerri—"

"No. Don't, Nathan. I can't believe anything but what I know to be true. Besides, I called to ask for another favor."

"Which is?"

"I want to fly."

It took him a second to remember that conversation in Jason's office. "Wonder Mom?"

"Yes. Cody doesn't believe in me anymore. I want to change that. Can you make me fly?"

He pictured her naked, flushed, writhing as his

hands and mouth took her to another dimension. One beyond the heavens where she would fly in the best way possible. But that wasn't what she was talking about.

"Somewhere in Songwood?" he asked.

"That would be easier, but if you want me soaring across Safeco Field, I won't say no."

"The Mariners might object."

"Those picky baseball players. Okay, Songwood works."

"I'll see what I can do."

"Thank you. I owe you big-time."

She hung up and he replaced the receiver. Before he could turn back to his computer, Tim walked into his office.

"I want you to know I'm sorry," his driver told him. "He didn't mean anything by it. He was trying to do the right thing."

Nathan frowned. "What are you talking about?"

Tim put a single sheet of paper on his desk. "You should read that."

Nathan scanned the short letter, then looked back at the other man. "You're resigning?"

"I'll save you the trouble of firing me." Tim sucked in a breath. "A couple of days ago Lance was here, waiting for me. We had plans to go to lunch." He shifted his feet.

Nathan nodded, still clueless as to the point of all this.

"I got tied up in traffic. He was outside your office, in the waiting area. Your sister was here." Tim shoved his beefy hands into his slacks pockets. "Frankie came out of your office crying and Lance was concerned. She said she was worried about you seeing Kerri. That Kerri was just in it for the money and you would be hurt and you didn't need that."

"My sister would like nothing better than to see me beaten and bleeding."

"Yeah. I know. But Lance doesn't, so he explained that Kerri wasn't in it for the money. That you have an arrangement with her and everything is fine."

Frankie knew about the deal. Nathan stood and crossed to the window. "She'll go to the press." With his luck, she would go straight to Grant Pryor.

"I figured. I just found out this morning."

What were the odds? He'd known the truth would come out eventually—it had a way of surfacing. But like this?

He stared at the view, at the clouds chasing across the sky, and wondered when things had gone so badly with his sister. Stupid question, he told himself. He knew exactly when. The moment he hadn't bothered to take care of her.

She'd always been fragile and close to snapping. What she'd gone through would push a rock over the edge. Frankie hadn't had a chance.

But if he knew where things had gone wrong, he

had no idea how he might have made them better. Had there been times when he could have gotten close to her? Tried to make amends? His gut had always told him what he'd done had been too big to be forgiven, but had he even tried?

More guilt. First about his son's death, now about his sister. He'd failed them both. Most people believed he didn't do relationships because he was a heartless bastard. While that was true, there was more to it than that. He was toxic to everyone he cared about.

He turned back to Tim. "You're not resigning and I'm not firing you. Lance didn't know."

"But he told her."

"I'll deal with it."

Not that he had a choice. In truth, Frankie's attitude was his problem, his fault. He should have handled things differently from the beginning.

"I have a team of expensive lawyers on retainer," Nathan said. "They're about to earn their money."

Tim nodded. "I'm sorry."

"Let it go."

His driver left the office. Nathan moved to the desk and picked up the phone, then dialed a number he'd memorized without meaning to.

"I'm coming up," he said when Kerri said hello.

"Nathan—"

"This is business."

"Then I'll be waiting."

KERRI DELIBERATELY DID nothing to get ready for Nathan's visit. She resisted the need to straighten the living room and reapply her makeup. She put out a plate of cookies because it was polite and warned Cody they'd have a visitor. Her son barely looked up from the book he was reading.

"Okay, Mom. Is he bringing fried chicken again?"

"Probably not."

Without any incentive to join the adults, Cody returned his attention to his book.

On his bed, with his legs stretched out and his stocking feet hanging over the edge, he seemed like any normal kid. As long as she didn't look too closely and notice the electric wheelchair parked at the side of the bed or the crutches in the corner.

She moved back and closed the door behind her.

With nothing else to occupy her, she had plenty of time to get nervous. To worry about seeing Nathan again and tell herself she wasn't going to react to him anymore. There would be no fantasies about him kissing her and her kissing him back. No memories of their bodies pressing and the heat he could generate with the lightest touch. He was nothing more than the man she'd agreed to help in return for fifteen million dollars. Not some hot, single guy who made her blood heat and her thighs whimper.

Fifteen minutes later she'd given herself a second stern talking-to, rearranged the spice rack into an almost alphabetical order and sorted laundry. She was so busy trying *not* to listen for Nathan's car that she actually missed it when he pulled up. A sharp knock on the door startled her so much she dropped all of Cody's socks.

She kicked them behind the door to the small utility room off the kitchen and walked to the front of the house.

"Hi," she said as she let Nathan in. "You made good time."

"Not a lot of traffic."

He looked the same as he always did—dark, dangerous and solitary. He was not a man she would seek out, yet here he was—involved in her world. How had that happened?

"What's wrong?" she asked as she settled on the sofa.

He took the worn club chair on the other side of the battered coffee table.

"The press knows about our deal."

"Not possible. I haven't told anyone."

"The leak came from my end."

"You wouldn't have told anyone, either."

"It was my sister."

The one he didn't have contact with? "How?" she asked. "I thought you never saw her anymore."

"She came to the office." He stared past her, as if remembering the visit. "She was angry. She's been working for a tree-hugging newsletter. They're not even close to legitimate, so they can't get funding.

They can't hang on any longer. She blames me. She wants me punished."

"Did you do anything to deserve that?"

He looked at her, his eyes the color of night. "Not with her newsletter. They're not worth the effort."

Talk about lacking support. "I take it you're not a fan of environmentalists."

"They're fine if they have a point. In her world, punishing me is enough reason. She hates the idea of the towers and wants to stop me. She was angry. When she left, she ran into Lance and convinced him she was terrified that you were out to get me and that I wouldn't listen to reason where you were concerned."

Kerri had been sympathetic right up until that last bit of news. "What? Me? Out to get you?"

"It was her story. Lance played the good guy and told her she had nothing to worry about. That you and I had a deal."

Kerri held in a groan. That was just like Lance. He was sweet and caring. Of course he would reassure Nathan's sister. Especially if he didn't know they weren't exactly close.

"What makes you think she went to the press?"

"I told you—she wants me punished."

An interesting theory that begged a single question. Why? Why would Frankie hate her brother so much? They only had each other. Shouldn't they want to bond together?

Kerri knew better than to voice the question.

She'd been the one to return her relationship with Nathan to a more businesslike footing. Associates didn't get personal.

"So how do we fight this?" she asked instead.

"Legally. Get out some press of our own. We have less than a month until the commission meets. In that time I have to convince them I'm a poster boy for good business, that I love Seattle, its people, and that I would never do anything out of pure self-interest."

"So it's not exactly a challenge," she murmured.

His gaze narrowed. "Are you mocking me?"

"Maybe a little. It's a lot to get done in a short period of time."

"I won't lose my towers."

They were her responsibility, too, she reminded herself. She'd made a deal.

"What do you want me to do?" she asked.

"Nothing."

"Excuse me? I'm on the Nathan King team, remember? I'm the head cheerleader."

"I'll deal with it. You have other things to think about. You may hear from the press. If so, contact Jason. He'll handle them."

Was Nathan passing her off to his lawyer because he was the best person for the job or because he, Nathan, didn't want that much to do with her?

She shouldn't care, she told herself. She should be pleased he was listening to her and doing as she asked. But she wasn't—because life was nothing if not perverse.

"I'm not worried about the press," she said. "I'm tough."

"We might be about to find out just how tough you are."

With that he stood, then walked to the front door. He was gone before she could figure out if she wanted him to stay.

NATHAN OPENED his condo door a little after six in the morning and picked up the paper. For the first time in his career, he'd made it to the front page. Below the fold, but still right there, with a picture and a headline designed to make him look like an ass.

"Billionaire Developer Paying Single Mom and Sick Kid to Win."

CHAPTER ELEVEN

THE DAMAGE CONTROL meeting started with one of the associates at Jason's firm discussing the viability of a lawsuit. Nathan ignored the conversation. Whether or not he sued didn't matter. It was a long-term solution to a short-term problem. With the commission meeting in less than a month, he needed a way to make good in public immediately.

He noticed that everyone attending ignored the irony of the situation—that the newspaper article had printed only the truth. He *had* given the money on the condition that Kerri and her son appear on his behalf. He'd broken no laws, violated no codes. But he'd come out looking like the coldhearted bastard he was—something the public couldn't forgive. A successful man who wasn't humble. They would take him down if they could. His job was to make sure they didn't.

"This is going to play out in the press," Jason said. "We need to give them something else to report. The flip side. We can start with a series of interviews. Kerri Sullivan is—"

"Not involved in this," Nathan said firmly.

"She has to be. She's the catalyst for all this. If we send her out—"

"We're not. She has enough going on. Leave her alone."

His friend's frustration was obvious and Nathan knew why. Without Kerri, there wasn't much of a story to tell. But he wouldn't ask her to speak on his behalf. Not now.

If pressed, he would explain that it was because Cody had gone into a wheelchair, but he knew it was more than that. It was because of what she'd said. Of how she'd blamed him for what had happened to her son.

He knew her accusations were irrational. There was no bargaining with fate or God or any other source of power. Cody had survived because his body had been better equipped to deal with the disease. That was it. But Kerri didn't get that, and he knew there was no way in hell he could change her mind.

"I don't want her involved," he told Jason.

The door to the conference room burst open and Kerri walked inside. "Sorry I'm late. There was traffic."

"Too late," Jason murmured.

Nathan glared at her. "You called her?"

"Yesterday. I assumed you'd want her here."

"I didn't."

Kerri glanced between them. "Don't all welcome

me at once. It goes to my head and then I'm impossible to deal with for the whole rest of the day."

Nathan pushed to his feet. "You should be at work."

"It's Monday. My day off. Why aren't you more excited to see me? I can fix this."

He remembered when she'd first dared to confront him and he'd vowed to crush her like the insignificant bug she was. A hairdresser with no money fighting him?

But she'd won with relative ease and he was a fool if he ignored what she brought to the table now.

"I didn't want you to have to deal with this."

She smiled. "I told you, I'm tough. Don't worry, Nathan. I'll save you."

"I don't need saving."

"We all need saving."

She took her place at the conference table and glanced around expectantly. "So, where are we with this?"

She was a kitten trying to protect a shark. He should have thrown her out. But he didn't. He couldn't. He wanted her there, at his side, defending him. Not because he needed it but because of what it meant.

Ridiculous. Next he would be telling himself he cared about her.

He didn't get involved. He'd learned that lesson a long time ago. He was a soulless bastard who cared for no one more than himself. Winning was everything. At any price.

He would use Kerri because it made sense. Because it would let him get what he wanted. At the end of the day, success was all that mattered.

"IT'S JUST NOT FAIR," Kerri said as she followed Nathan into his condo and gazed out the floor-to-ceiling windows. "Your entire life is one great view after the other. At your office, at your lawyer's office, at home. It must be a serious drag to go to a restaurant or pick up your dry cleaning."

"Maybe the ordinary world makes me appreciate this."

"Do you get used to it?" she asked. "Do you start to take it for granted?"

"Sometimes. Then I remember what I started with."

Nothing. The same as her. Only he'd done a lot more with his time and energy.

She eyed the cream-colored sofa. "I don't suppose that's a nice easy-to-clean microfiber."

"I have no idea."

She touched it. "Nope. Ultrasuede. Very plush." She carefully brushed off her skirt before sitting down. The last thing she wanted was to leave behind a stain.

He took the oversize chair opposite the sofa. There was a glass table in between them—an elegant, almost hard curve in a metal frame. There were abstracts on the wall, a neutral rug over hardwood floors and the view.

The expanse of sky and city dominated the room.

"You live here," she said, gesturing to the room. "I live in my two-bedroom rental. We both started with nothing. What makes where we are so different?"

"I wanted success I could measure in terms of money. You didn't."

He'd spoken quickly, as if he hadn't had to think about the answer.

"As easy as that?" she asked.

"I had a college scholarship. That was an advantage."

"Did you want to go to college?"

"Yes. I knew it was a way out."

"I was never much into school," she admitted.

"What did you want?"

She considered the question. At eighteen she'd been mourning the loss of her grandmother and wrestling with the idea that she was truly alone in the world. The future had seemed dark and scary. She'd been so afraid.

"I wanted to belong," she told him. "I wanted to be a part of something. I wanted a family."

"Which you got."

"What did you want?"

"Money, power, a portfolio."

Which he had. "Is that it?" she asked. "The only difference is our goals?"

"Mostly. Determination and luck play a part. Money isn't important to you."

"It is when I don't have enough to pay the bills. I really appreciate your buying Cody the electric wheelchair, but I wish I'd been able to afford it myself."

"You want enough money to live on and pay the bills. I want it all."

"You don't care that you're alone?"

"No. I don't need people the way you do."

And she didn't need money the way he did.

He leaned forward, resting his forearms on his thighs. His expression was intense. "Kerri, when you decided you wanted fifteen million dollars for Dr. Wallace's research, you got it. How long was it from finding out what was required to get him going again to handing him a check?"

"I don't know. Six weeks, maybe. Seven."

"Fifteen million is a lot of money. You found a way because it was important. You're determined and resourceful. If being rich mattered to you, you'd be rich. You just don't care that much about material things."

He made it sound so simple. She supposed he was right—she didn't need a specific type of car. Just one that worked. She wasn't into designer labels; clothes weren't really her thing.

"I care about Cody," she pointed out. "If you believe I can create fifteen million dollars when it means everything to me, why can't you believe I can will my son to stay alive?"

"It's not the same."

It was to her, but she didn't want to fight about it anymore. "I'm glad Jason's putting a plan together."

"It's going to be a tough fight."

"We'll win."

"You sound confident," he said.

"I am."

"This isn't your battle."

She smiled. "Sure it is. You own me. Remember?"

His dark eyes flared with something she couldn't identify, although she felt a distinct quiver low in her belly.

They weren't going there again, she reminded herself. Look what had happened last time. Was she willing to risk something else awful happening to Cody?

"I'm in this all the way," she said to distract herself from the lingering attraction she felt.

"I'll let Jason know. How's Cody?"

"Fine."

"Is he doing well with the wheelchair?"

"He likes how fast he can go. Tim built a ramp that allows him to get in and out of the house easily. Ironically, our carpet is so ratty and old that it actually helps him move around on it. He zips all through the house."

"How's he doing at school?"

"Why all the questions?" she asked. "You aren't usually this interested in him."

Nothing about Nathan's expression changed, but

she felt him withdraw, as if she'd hurt him. No way, she told herself, guilt fueling annoyance.

"You never ask about him," Kerri pointed out. "Even when he's in the room, you ignore him. You don't talk to him or look him in the eye. I assume it has something to do with your son and I'm sorry if Cody reminds you of him. I don't want you suffering, but I hate it when you pretend he doesn't exist."

"You're exaggerating."

"Am I? I know what you went through. I'm going through it now. Maybe you're angry because I might be able to do something that you couldn't. Or maybe one day I'll be like you. Maybe I won't be able to look at another child without being reminded of Cody. I know you think it's unfair that my son is alive and yours isn't. Maybe that's the real problem. You're trying to pretend it's not true when we both know it is."

Nathan stood. "You're making too much of all of this. That's what you do. You can't know what I'm thinking any more than you can control whether or not your son lives or dies. You think you influence his fate because then you don't have to stand around like every other mortal—living or dying at the whim of circumstances you can't influence. Welcome to the real world, Kerri. Shit happens. You don't get to stop it by being a nun or telling the truth or turning counter-clockwise three times, while facing the sun and clucking like a chicken. It's a crapshoot and sometimes you lose. My son lost. Yours probably will, too. But whether he lives or dies has nothing to do with you."

"You're wrong," she said loudly. "You're so wrong. I have to keep my part of the deal. Faith matters. Faith matters more than anything. There are miracles every day."

"How many of them are deserved and how many of them just happen?"

She hated this. Hated his words and his lack of belief.

"Sometimes we just have to keep moving forward," she told him. "Sometimes it's all about surviving. It's not about deserving. When Brian was killed, I wanted to die, too. I came so close to taking my own life. I knew it was weak, but he was all I had and then he was gone. I was alone and desperate."

She blinked, trying to clear her vision. Nathan had gone all blurry.

"I kept putting it off, mostly because I knew Brian would be disappointed if I took my own life. He would have expected more of me. So I waited. Tomorrow, I told myself. I'll do it tomorrow. Then I found out I was pregnant. That was my miracle. I don't know if I deserved it, I just know it happened."

She wiped her face and was shocked to find tears on her cheeks. She stood and dug deep for the strength to tell the truth.

"If I'd given in to my despair, I would have died without knowing I carried his baby inside of me. I hung on one more day, just one and it changed every-thing. I shouldn't have been pregnant. We were using birth control. It had been the wrong time of the month. But I was. It was a gift—a sign to keep going. To be strong. I vowed I would keep his child safe, no matter what. I will give everything I have to keep my word. *Faith* is everything. It moves mountains. It keeps Cody alive. There's nothing you can say to convince me otherwise."

Nathan looked at her for a long time. She had no idea what he was thinking or feeling.

"Then I'm going to stop trying," he told her. "You can put the blame where you really want it, Kerri. I can handle it."

"I don't understand."

"You don't think it's your fault Cody's in a wheel-chair. You think it's mine. I'm the devil who tempted you down the dark and evil path. I'm the man who wants you in his bed. You can't forgive that."

"It's not about you."

"Isn't it?"

Then, because he was right, she said the only thing she could think of. "I'm sorry."

"Me, too."

"For what it's worth, I don't just blame you. I blame myself."

THAT NIGHT Kerri paced restlessly in her small house. She replayed her conversation with Nathan over and over in her mind, finding dozens of places where she wished she'd said something different.

The guilt was familiar—she was forever feeling guilty about not doing enough—but the shame was new. She'd dragged him to a place he didn't deserve to go. She'd blamed him because then she didn't have to blame herself as much.

I'm the devil who tempted you down the dark and evil path. I'm the man who wants you in his bed. You can't forgive that.

He was right. She couldn't forgive it. She also couldn't forget it.

THE TOWN MEETING DRAGGED on more than two hours, but Kerri didn't mind. There was an energy in the room, an excitement that hadn't been there before. She would guess it had been missing since the explosion that had taken lives and shut down the lab.

It all came down to hope, she thought as she looked at the crowded room. Having it or not having it.

With the lab open, things were good again. The stores were busy, houses were selling, new people moving in. Songwood had been dying, but it had been given a reprieve.

The mayor glanced at her notes. "We have one more order of new business, people. Kerri? Where are you?"

Kerri stood and waved. "Back here."

"Oh, good. Everyone, for those of you who don't know, this is Kerri Sullivan. She's the mastermind behind the lab reopening. Go ahead, Kerri."

Kerri moved to the center aisle where a microphone had been set up. She cleared her throat, suddenly nervous. She'd written some notes, but hadn't actually planned exactly what she wanted to say.

"Hi," she said, hoping her voice wasn't shaking as much as her body. "I'm Kerri Sullivan. I moved to Songwood a few months ago because my son has Gilliar's Disease. I'd heard about Dr. Wallace's research and wanted to talk to him about the progress he was making. But when I got here, I found the lab closed and Dr. Wallace working alone."

She paused to take a breath, hoping it would still the trembling she felt inside. Everyone was looking at her, which was normal, considering she was the one speaking.

It's for a good cause, she reminded herself. It wasn't for her.

"I asked Dr. Wallace what he needed to get started again. He gave me the impossible figure of fifteen million dollars. Now I'm a great hairdresser, but even on my best day, I don't get that in tips."

Several people laughed. A few more smiled. Kerri swallowed, then continued.

"I was determined to get that money, but how? I decided to approach Nathan King for a donation and he agreed." After she'd threatened to blackmail him, she thought with a smile. But there was no reason to share that detail.

"He didn't have to give the money," she said. "He didn't know me from a rock and he'd certainly never heard of Songwood. But he did agree. Just like that. Dr. Wallace got the money and the town will benefit. I know they're saying a lot of terrible things about Nathan King in the paper. As far as I'm concerned, he's funding what may very well turn out to be a miracle. I thought it was just for my son, but now I realize it's a miracle for all of us. So I was thinking we might want to thank him."

"You want to send flowers?" some guy yelled.

"Not exactly. I was thinking more along the lines of Nathan King Day, here in town. We could give him the key to the city, have a parade and invite him to be grand marshal. Nothing too fancy. Maybe with some cars, a couple of floats and the high school marching band."

"He got the high school baseball team new uniforms," a woman said. "They're real nice. They clean up great after a game."

"He gave the library five thousand dollars," someone else said.

"And that fence for the elementary school."

Kerri had forgotten about the items she'd demanded. Apparently Nathan had come through with all of them.

"All of which illustrates my point," she said. "We owe him."

"A parade would be good publicity for him," a man yelled. "For his towers. What do we care about million-dollar housing for the rich?"

"We don't." Kerri shrugged. "At least I don't. I'll never live there. What I do know is that he came through when he didn't have to. I want to thank him for that. If that means helping him, then I'm happy to help. But that's just me."

A woman stood up. "I want to help, too. I really like the new uniforms."

A second woman rose. "My Frank has a new job at the lab. We've been hurtin' bad, what with there not being the same number of logging jobs. We need the money."

"Us, too," a man said. "Give the man his parade. Maybe he'll put up one of them fancy developments here."

The mayor banged her gavel on the podium, then called for a vote. Two minutes later, Nathan King Appreciation Day had been declared, with the promise of a parade and his name featured prominently on banners all around town.

Kerri sank back in her seat. Millie, from the dry cleaners, turned around and patted her hand.

"You did well," the older woman said. "Now Nathan King is going to owe *you*."

"Not exactly, but I'm glad we're going to have the parade." She wasn't sure how the strategy team would react, but it would be positive publicity.

"He's real good-looking, isn't he?" Millie sighed. "I wouldn't mind having a piece of him myself." She smoothed her curls. "If I were a few years younger and not married, of course."

"Of course," Kerri murmured, doing her best not to picture Nathan and Millie together.

When the other woman had left, Linda leaned over. "You did good."

"I was terrified. I don't like the whole speaking-in-public thing."

"You shine when you have a cause."

Kerri winced. "That makes me sound borderline crazy."

"You're not. How did you come up with the idea of the parade?"

"I wanted something visual. Nathan did the right thing and he doesn't deserve to be screwed because some reporter has it out for him. Yes, we have a deal, but it's not like I'm actively campaigning for him. This way is better. The focus will be where it belongs—on Dr. Wallace's work."

"And on Nathan."

"He's used to it."

Linda's expression turned thoughtful. "I find your energy on this really interesting. Whether or not Nathan is getting screwed in the press has nothing to do with you. The money has been transferred. Abram is moving forward with his research. So why the concern about Nathan King?"

Kerri shifted uncomfortably. "I've gotten to know him. He's not the coldhearted shark everyone thinks. He's a real person."

"A real handsome person."

"It's not like that."

"That's not what you said before—when Cody went into the hospital."

"I know. It's complicated. And confusing."

"The man or your feelings for him?"

"I'm not supposed to have feelings for him," Kerri admitted. "And I don't."

"Liar."

Kerri winced, knowing her friend spoke the truth. "I don't have a *lot* of feelings for him. How's that?"

"I don't know. You're the one with issues."

More than issues, Kerri thought. Complications. Concerns and a bunch of other things she didn't want to identify.

"He's nice," she said at last.

"Not a way I've ever heard him described before."

"He's ruthless and driven, but he has a heart. He's caring. He lost a child, too. He's alone and there's something about him…" Something that drew her in even as she knew she had to run in the opposite direction. "I didn't expect to like him, but I do. I hate what the press is doing. So this is my way of fighting back."

"Nothing more?" Linda asked.

"There might be a small element of apology in it.

The last time we were together, we fought. It was mostly me."

"Did you apologize?"

"Not exactly."

"You'll get an entire town to declare Nathan King Appreciation Day and put on a parade rather than say you're sorry?"

"It's not like that. I'll tell him I'm sorry. In the meantime, he has something to work with. It's a big gesture."

"But sometimes the little ones matter more."

Kerri knew that. She also knew the danger of getting involved. "We can't have a relationship. It's not allowed."

"Have you ever considered that you're already in a relationship? That you just don't want to admit it?"

CHAPTER TWELVE

KERRI WAS SO CRABBY she cleaned the bathroom. She decided that if she was already in a bad mood, she might as well do something yucky. So she attacked the toilet with cleanser and a brush, nearly asphyxiating herself in the shower/tub with a combination of confined space and semideadly chemicals, then scrubbed the sink until it shone. When she was finished, she did her best to revel in the satisfaction of a job well done and ignore the constant replay of Linda's claim that she already *had* a relationship with Nathan.

Her friend was wrong, she told herself for the five thousandth time. Liking someone was just friendship. She liked Nathan. Why wouldn't she? He'd been good to her and Cody. Kind, even. And okay, yes, he got her all flustered and wanting when she remembered what it had been like to kiss him, but that wasn't personal. She hadn't had sex, real sex, since before Cody was born. So it made sense that when a hot guy touched her and kissed her she responded. She should be grateful that all her parts were still working. Yay her.

Biology did not make a relationship.

It was simple—she liked a man who had the power to turn her on. An easy explanation. Expected, even. She wasn't involved. She was a friendly, sex-starved woman. Nothing more.

The front door opened and Cody yelled that he was home. After pulling off her gloves, Kerri walked into the living room.

"I was going to come get you," she said.

"Michelle and Brandon walked me home," he told her. He wrinkled his nose. "You cleaned the bathroom. It always smells funny."

"The scent of sanitized. I may move on to your room next."

Cody looked horrified. "I made my bed, Mom. My room is clean."

"I can't remember the last time I vacuumed in there."

"You don't want to start now. How was the town meeting?"

As distractions went, it wasn't a great one, but she decided to give her son a break.

"It went very well. We're going to have Nathan King Appreciation Day in Songwood, with a parade and everything."

"Sweet. Is he going to ride on the fire truck?"

"I was thinking more of an open car."

"Can I ride with him?"

"Ah, sure. If you want to."

"It would be so cool. I've never been in a parade before. And I like Nathan."

With that, Cody rolled down the hallway to his bedroom. Kerri watched him go. She'd never considered that her son would have feelings for Nathan one way or the other.

She hadn't thought they'd spent much time together. Worse, she'd accused Nathan of ignoring her son. Obviously Cody hadn't felt ignored.

Did Cody miss having a father? Dumb question, she told herself. Of course he did. It wasn't that she'd been deliberately trying to keep him away from men—it had just worked out that way.

When Cody had been born, she'd assumed that one day she would heal from Brian's death and start dating again. She'd even thought about remarrying. But once Cody had been diagnosed, she'd lost all interest in a romantic relationship. Every ounce of her emotional energy had gone toward keeping her son alive. She'd made her deal with God and, until the past few weeks, she'd kept it. Her life for Cody's.

She'd been more than willing to make the sacrifice, but somewhere along the way, she'd forgotten that she wasn't the only one involved. That her son might like a say about having a man around.

She'd been doing her best to save Cody, but had she also been selfish, depriving him of an important part of his life?

"Because I need one more thing to feel guilty about," she murmured to herself.

But the idea wouldn't go away. And because what Cody needed mattered more than anything, she thought maybe she should rethink her plan.

"ARE WE BORING YOU?" Jason asked impatiently.

Nathan leaned back in his chair. "Why do you ask?"

"You're not paying attention to anything I've said. I could be talking about elephants."

"As we're planning strategy involving a project worth nearly a billion dollars, I know you weren't talking about elephants."

"You're not listening."

Nathan thought about pointing out that Jason was well compensated for the hours spent on his business, but what was the point? His lawyer was right—he hadn't been listening.

"I have a lot on my mind," he said, by way of explanation.

"Anything you want to share?"

Nathan looked at the six associates in the conference room. "No, thanks."

None of them needed to know that he couldn't get Kerri out of his head. That he thought about her during the day and dreamed about her at night. He didn't do relationships. But somehow she'd crawled inside of him and he didn't know how to get rid of her.

She'd been right, something he hated to admit. He *was* angry that her son was alive and had a chance, while his son was dead. He avoided Cody because the reminders were too painful.

He told himself it didn't matter—that the kid had enough people in his life—but he knew he couldn't let himself off that easily.

Jason's assistant stuck her head into the conference room. "Kerri Sullivan is here. She asked me to let you know."

"Send her in," Jason said.

Nathan looked at him. "We agreed she wasn't part of the strategy."

"You said it. I never agreed. Nathan, she's a good advocate. We need her to win this."

"No, we don't." He didn't want Kerri involved for a whole lot of reasons, most of which he wasn't willing to discuss with his attorney or friend.

"Too late now." Jason rose. "Kerri. Thanks for coming in. I know it's a long drive for you."

"It is. Nathan usually sends Tim to pick me up. You should remember that for next time."

Jason grinned. "Point taken. Have a seat."

"I will shortly." She glanced around the room, her focus settling on Nathan. "Can I talk to you for a second first? Privately?"

She'd dressed for the meeting, wearing a dress and heels. He wondered if the outfit was her attempt to look sensible and businesslike.

She failed on both counts. The dress clung to her curves in a way that made his blood pressure climb to dangerous levels. She'd pulled her hair back in a bun that should have looked scary as hell, but instead made him want to pull out all the pins and run his hands through the soft, silky blond strands. All she needed was a pair of dark-framed glasses to complete the sexy-bombshell-masquerading-as-prim-secretary fantasy.

"Use my office," Jason said.

Nathan's mind immediately went to the comfortable leather sofa and everything he and Kerri could do there. Then he remembered her request to speak to him privately and realized the other man's offer was about responding to that, not giving Nathan a way to fulfill his erotic fantasy. Damn.

He led the way, then closed the door behind them. Kerri glanced at the large windows.

"More great views," she said. "You are blessed that way."

"Not why you're here."

"I know."

She looked at him, her blue eyes wide and filled with emotion.

"I'm sorry," she told him. "About before. About what I said. I have no right to judge you or your grief. I blasted into your life and did what I had to in order to get what I wanted. We have a deal and no part of that is you acting as a surrogate father to my son. If Cody reminds you of Daniel, you have to deal with that. It's not my place to say you shouldn't or you can't."

She was apologizing? "You're giving me too much credit."

"I don't think so. Nathan, you've been nothing but kind to me. You gave Dr. Wallace the money, you came through on all my demands."

"I gave a list to my assistant."

She smiled. "It was more than that. Why aren't you willing to take credit?"

He wasn't sure, but there was a part of him that didn't want her seeing him as a nice guy. It was always safer to be the bastard.

"It's not important," he told her.

"It is to me. You've been there for me in a dozen different ways. No one has been there for me like that in a very long time."

He wanted to change the subject. He wanted them to be somewhere else, doing something else.

"Kerri, don't make me into something I'm not. We had a deal. I'm keeping my part of it. I'll make damn sure you keep yours. It's that simple."

"Is it? What part of our deal included you buying Cody a very expensive wheelchair?"

He didn't want to talk about that, either. "He needs it, you couldn't afford it. End of story."

She tilted her head. "Is it? Why is it so easy for

you to be the bad guy and so hard for you to accept a thank-you?"

"Is there anything else?"

"You mean am I going to continue to torture you emotionally? It's kind of fun, so I'm going to say yes."

She thought she had him trapped. She thought she was winning. He had to remind her who was in charge.

He grabbed her by the shoulders and pulled her close. He moved fast, so she wouldn't have time to resist, then he put his mouth on hers and kissed her the way he'd wanted to since she walked into Jason's office, looking all prim and untouchable.

He used his mouth to mark her, pressing, teasing, moving against her, arousing them both—he hoped. Because being close to her was sure doing a number on him. Just the scent of her was enough to get him hard. Or seeing her or thinking about seeing her, dammit all to hell.

Angry at himself for not being stronger and her for being, well, her, he claimed her with a passion that burned hot and bright, making him hard and hungry and wishing they were somewhere more private than his attorney's office.

He was breaking the rules she'd set up and the promise he'd made to himself. Not that he cared. He was Nathan King—he took whatever he wanted.

Then he felt it—the light stroking of her tongue against his, the pressure of her body straining to get closer. He heard her sharp breathing, the vibration of her silent moan. He eased one hand from her shoulder to her breast and gently cupped the curve.

They both stilled. He expected her to step back and start yelling. When she didn't, he brushed his thumb against her hard nipple, aching to taste what he touched, to see her bare, flushed, wet. He was about to bend down to take her in his mouth, clothes be damned, when she stepped back.

"I can't," she whispered, crossing her arms over her chest. "Nathan, I can't."

She wouldn't. There was a difference.

All the emotions had left her eyes except for one—need. He wanted to tell himself that it didn't matter, that if he made her want him, too, he won. Only he didn't believe the words. She still had enough strength to walk away and, honest to God, he didn't. This round went to her.

"We should get back," he said, and turned toward the door.

She touched his arm. "I don't want it to be like this. You're angry."

"I'm not anything."

"I'm not playing. This isn't a game."

He looked at her with as much disinterest as he could muster. "Your point is?"

She sighed. "We were having a moment. I liked having a moment."

"Meaning I ruined it by kissing you?"

"No. I like kissing you, too. Stopping isn't about

not liking it." One corner of her mouth turned up. "It's been a long time. Too long. I turn to jelly even before you kiss me. I know you think I'm crazy believing I have some control over what happens to Cody, but it's real to me. I get so scared, Nathan. I get so scared that he's going to die. He's all I have. He's my reason for living."

"He's only nine. You can't put all that on him."

"I know. I try to make it different, but I can't."

"You don't have to try to make me feel better."

"I can't help it. You matter."

Simple words. Easy words. He would bet a lot of money she meant them. He mattered.

He told himself it was because of the fifteen million or the wheelchair or anything else he might have bought her or given her. That it was about the things, not him personally. Anyone who could do what he'd done would matter.

But a part of him didn't believe that. A part of him thought maybe, just maybe, her words were specifically about him. About what happened between them—in the moments they'd shared.

He was torn—wanting it to be true but knowing there was power in distance, power in the silence, power in being the one who walked away.

"Don't trust me, Kerri. You're in over your head with me."

She smiled. "I know that, but here's the funny

part. If I start to drown, I believe with all my heart you'll come rescue me."

"You're wrong."

"I don't think so."

She walked past him and out of the office. He followed her back to the meeting, cursing the day he'd walked into The Grill for lunch and had instead been accosted by a mouthy fake waitress with a DVD player.

They returned to the conference room. Kerri took a seat, then leaned forward.

"I have an announcement," she said. "You're going to love this. Songwood is having Nathan King Appreciation Day."

If he'd been drinking he would have spit or choked.

"Excuse me?"

"I know. Isn't it cool? I went to the town meeting and suggested it. That's when I found out about all the other stuff you've been doing." She turned to Jason. "Remember that list I gave you about the stuff in town?" She glanced at the other attorneys. "For that, um, thing we agreed to."

Jason looked as if he was trying not to smile. "I remember."

"He did it all. The baseball uniforms, the fence, everything. That should be in the press, don't you think? He's made a huge difference in Songwood. The money for the lab means the town will survive. Everyone is very excited about the increase in work and house values. It's practically a miracle. So when

I suggested Nathan King Appreciation Day, they thought it was a great idea. There's going to be a parade." She turned back to him. "You're the grand marshal."

"Shoot me now," he told Jason.

"It's not a bad idea," his attorney said.

"It's terrible. I'll look like I'm sucking up."

"It's brilliant," Kerri snapped. "You should be thanking me. Plus, hello, a parade in your honor. How often does that happen?"

Never would be plenty of times, he thought grimly. "It's not a good idea."

"I busted my butt for this," Kerri said.

"You told us everyone in Songwood was excited."

She rolled her eyes. "It was an easy sell, but there's a lot of work. I've been making calls and I have to help with a couple of the floats. Plus finding a car for you to ride in. Oh, Cody wants to be in the car with you. He asked me himself. Is that okay?"

"It would be great press," one of the associates said. The others agreed. Jason didn't say anything.

Nathan would have preferred a couple of hours of serious torture to a parade, let alone Nathan King Appreciation Day. It would be press, all right, but not the kind he liked. Every part of him wanted to say no, but how could he throw Kerri's gift back in her face?

"It could work," Jason said. "It won't hurt."

"You don't know that."

"Small town embraces benefactor?"

"Rich bastard buys good press."

"We'll make sure it doesn't play that way," Jason said.

"*I* think it's brilliant," Kerri grumbled.

"It was very thoughtful," Jason told her.

She glared at Nathan. "I did it for *you*."

She had, he thought in surprise. To help. Maybe because she was worried about him. When was the last time someone had worried about him?

"Thank you," he told her.

"About time."

"Really. I appreciate it."

She didn't look convinced.

"I mean it," he said.

"All right. You're welcome."

Jason looked amused again. "We need to talk about interviews," he said.

Nathan groaned. "Only a few."

"Not for you."

It took him a second to process that. "You're not feeding Kerri to the press."

"She can handle it."

"I can handle it," she said at the same time.

He ignored Jason. "You have no idea what you're getting into."

"So teach me. Don't you have professionals who give training for interviews? I'm a fast learner. Plus I can talk about Gilliar's Disease, maybe get people aware and interested. If more people knew about it, there might be more research."

Because she was an optimist, she always looked for the bright, shiny, silver lining.

She leaned toward him. "I'll do great. I'll probably throw up, but that will be off camera." Kerri winked at the associates.

He turned back to Jason. "Two interviews at most. One print, one TV. I want a media expert with her at all times and we stop the interview if it gets out of hand."

Kerri was torn between being happy that she was going to get to defend Nathan and a sudden knot in her stomach at the thought of dealing with any kind of interview. But she knew this was important—Nathan's future was on the line and she owed him.

They worked out a schedule for her training—apparently it was only supposed to take a couple of hours. She could only hope. Next up was the details for the parade. An hour later, the meeting wrapped up.

Nathan walked her down to the parking garage where she'd left her car.

"Next time I'll send Tim," he said as they stood next to her beat-up import. It looked kind of sad in a garage filled with BMWs and Mercedes.

"I don't mind driving."

"You don't need to. What are the odds of you letting me reimburse you for gas?"

She wrinkled her nose. "Not necessary."

If she could harness the sexual hum she felt inside, she might never have to fill her car again.

It was safe to want, she told herself. As long as she didn't act. Oh, but he tempted her. While he wasn't anyone she would have thought she wanted, he got her on a primal level.

"We should go to a Mariners game," he said.

She took a second to catch up with the change of subject. "Okay."

"With Cody. You said he likes baseball."

"Like isn't strong enough. He would love to go to a game."

"I have a suite."

She smiled. "Of course you do. Name the date. We'll be there."

He stared at her, his expression unreadable. She wanted to touch his face, smooth away his worries, which was just plain dumb. Who was she to ease anything for a man like Nathan?

"I'm sorry Cody's in a wheelchair," he said quietly.

She eyed him. "Thanks. Me, too."

"I know that hit you hard. You weren't expecting it."

"I was hoping it wouldn't happen," she admitted. "But it did. We're dealing."

"He's strong. He's fighting the disease." He looked past her. "It was faster for Daniel."

Her chest tightened. "I'm sorry."

He shrugged. "I guess it's different for every kid. It was bad for him. I wasn't ready for it to happen."

"Why would you be?"

"Paige, his mother, fell apart when he went into the hospital. She was hysterical. They kept her sedated most of the time. So it was up to me to take care of things. Of him."

Kerri touched his arm. "That can't have been easy."

"It wasn't. I worked long hours. I didn't spend as much time with him as I wanted. As I should have." He took a step back and shoved both his hands into his slacks. "He was in so much pain. That's what I remember. At the end, there weren't enough drugs to help. He was in so much pain."

His voice vibrated with anguish. She was torn between offering comfort and running away. She didn't want to hear this. Didn't want to know what Cody was up against. But she couldn't leave. Nathan obviously needed to talk and she needed to listen.

"I told him it was okay to let go," he said.

She stared. "I don't understand."

"I told him it was all right to die. I stood by his bed and told him to let go. So he did. And I've always wondered—did I do the right thing? Was it up to me? Did I let him go too soon? Should he have tried? But the pain was too hard to watch."

Her heart twisted in her chest. "Oh, Nathan," she breathed. "You did the right thing."

"How do you know? You weren't there. What if

he thought I wanted him gone? What if he thought he was too much trouble?"

"No. He wouldn't. You were his father."

"I wasn't anyone he really knew. I practically lived at work. His mother was drugged out and didn't come to see him the last week. I told him to go. He was everything and I told him to die."

"What else were you supposed to say?"

"Are you going to tell Cody to go?" he asked bluntly.

She pressed her lips together, unable to answer. They both knew the truth—she would never willingly let her son go.

"The circumstances are different," she told him.

"No, they're not. I took the easy way out. Daniel was everything to me and I don't think he knew that. He sure didn't know it at the end."

He was hurting and she couldn't figure out what to say. Everything about the situation was impossible. But as she reached for him, he backed up.

"I thought you should know," he said. "What happened. How it was. Why no one gets in."

Then he was gone, leaving her standing alone in the dim parking lot.

CHAPTER THIRTEEN

THE TRIP TO SEATTLE had never seemed so long, Kerri thought. Some of it was Cody's never-ending "Are we there yet?" There was nothing like the thought of a baseball game to get a sports-loving nine-year-old boy quivering.

"We'll be nearly there when we cross over the lake," Kerri reminded him.

"You can see the field from the freeway," Tim said from his place behind the wheel.

"And Nathan really has his own suite? Just like the owners?"

"That's what he told me." Knowing Nathan, it might be nicer than the owner's suite.

She was happy to answer Cody's questions. They kept her attention on him and away from her own issues with anticipation. Even though she knew she couldn't get involved, she wanted to see Nathan again.

Being attracted to him was dangerous in more ways than one. Not only did she have her deal with God, but there was the man himself. Yes, he'd proved to be one of the good guys, but that didn't mean they were even remotely on the same planet. He was a billionaire developer. She did hair. They had as much in common as a fish and an armadillo.

Still, as they neared the stadium, she felt her stomach tighten, while other parts of her got very…relaxed. For a successful businessman, he knew how to kiss—something she could appreciate. Along with all the other women in his life, she reminded herself. For all she knew, Nathan was involved.

Then she remembered what he'd said the last time they'd been together. About Daniel's death. She remembered the pain in his voice when he'd talked about giving his son permission to die. Could he still hurt as much as he did and open his heart to anyone else? She had her doubts. Of course, he didn't need to be in love to be dating. Or having sex.

She didn't want to think about Nathan in bed with someone else, so she pointed out various landmarks in the skyline and counted down the miles to Safeco Field.

As they pulled up to the stadium, Kerri had to hold in a laugh. Tim didn't bother with the parking structure across the street. He just pulled up to let them out.

Kerri grabbed her purse, prepared to slide across the seat.

"I don't want to use my wheelchair," her son told her. "I'll use crutches."

Kerri glanced up at the massive structure. "It's a long way to go."

"I don't care." Cody's expression turned stubborn. "I won't use the chair."

The passenger door opened. "Ready for a great game?" Nathan asked.

Cody shook his head. "I won't use my chair."

Kerri knew there were a dozen ways to handle the situation, but which one was best? She didn't want to start the day with a big fight, but she wasn't happy about just giving in. There was the reality of Cody's lack of strength. What if he couldn't make the long trip?

Nathan helped her out of the car. "Did you bring crutches?" he asked the boy.

"Uh-huh. I'm fine."

"I know that. I've seen you. But it's a long way to the suite. Why don't you use your chair until we're close, then change to your crutches to get into the suite? It'll be easier to maneuver that way."

"That would be okay," Cody said slowly. "I don't want to be a total cripple, you know?"

"I know."

Kerri fought against the sudden rush of emotion, feeling grateful for the compromise and aching for her son and his pain. There were so many difficult decisions and hard conversations. How could she be sure she got them all right?

Tim was already waiting with the wheelchair. Kerri grabbed the crutches they'd brought to help Cody get around in the suite. Nathan bent down and scooped Cody into his arms. He straightened, then staggered.

"You should have warned me he was so big," he told Kerri. He staggered again. "I think I just broke my back."

Cody giggled. "I'm bigger than I look."

"Yes, you are. Much bigger. Practically a line-backer. Tim, do we have the number of that chiro-practor?" He staggered a little more, heading toward the wheelchair. Cody was still laughing when he was placed on the seat.

Kerri watched them both. She appreciated that Nathan was making the effort with her son, but how much better would things be if that weren't neces-sary? If Cody could be well and live like other kids?

A miracle, God, she prayed silently. *I'm asking for a miracle.*

Cody moved the chair forward, leading the way to the elevator. Kerri hung back a little.

"Thank you," she murmured. "I know this is hard for you. Being around Cody."

"Sometimes," he admitted. "Sometimes it's good. Like today." He smiled at her. "Thank you for com-ing."

"How could we refuse?"

Their gazes locked. The rest of the world seemed to blur and fade until there was only this man who had carried her son so easily and confidently. What would it be like to have someone to lean on? she wondered. To not do it all herself?

Dangerous thoughts.

They went up to the suite. Cody struggled to his feet, then reached for the crutches. Nathan held open the door. Kerri waited until her son had gone in before she moved into the suite. Only to find it filled with people.

She hadn't been sure what to expect. The plush seats, buffet and bar seemed par for the course, but the crowd was a surprise. Cody yelled out a greeting to Brandon. Kerri saw Michelle talking with another woman. There were about a dozen other children, several adults and a clown making balloon animals.

Kerri turned to Nathan. "It's a party," she said, hoping she didn't sound disappointed. Until that moment she hadn't realized she'd expected to spend time alone with him.

"I thought Cody would have more fun with one of his friends here, so I contacted Michelle and asked her if she wanted to bring Brandon. Then I realized a few more kids wouldn't hurt. The ones here are living in a shelter. There are a few parents along with some people from the press. I'll be doing the interviews, not you. Don't worry."

"I won't."

She reminded herself that Nathan was a man on a mission. Nothing about their relationship was supposed to be personal.

She walked over to Michelle. Brandon's mother grinned.

"If Don and I ever break up, I want to date Nathan King."

Kerri laughed. "We're not dating, remember. This is about his donation."

"Uh-huh. He's still really good-looking. And rich. Rich buys a lot."

"You know what they say. People who marry for money earn every penny. You couldn't stand that."

"I know, but it's fun to daydream about." Michelle watched the boys. "Cody's looking better."

"I know. I think maybe using the chair is allowing him to conserve his strength. He doesn't seem so exhausted at the end of the day."

"Which is what you want." Michelle pointed out the large windows overlooking the field. "I think this is a better view than on TV. You have to admit, the man knows how to live."

Kerri nodded, but she was remembering what Nathan had said about not caring anymore. How no one got in…ever. That didn't sound like the words of a man content with his place in the world.

One of the women from the shelter came up and introduced herself and the three of them started talking. A few minutes later, a man walked over to Kerri.

"Hi," he said. "I'm Grant Pryor. Can I talk to you for a second?"

"Sure," Kerri said, knowing the name was familiar but unable to place it. "You're a friend of Nathan's?"

"I've known him for years. You're Cody's mom, aren't you?"

"Yes."

"I've done a little research on Gilliar's Disease. It's devastating."

He had no idea, she thought. No one could. Not without living through it—knowing your child was going to die horribly and that there was nothing you could do about it.

"It's not something I'd wish on anyone," she said.

"It's nearly an orphan disease, isn't it?"

"Close, but we have more children sick than that. A disease is considered an orphan disease when there are less than ten thousand afflicted."

Grant smiled. "You know your stuff."

"I've done a lot of research."

"Is the best work being done here?"

"Up in Songwood. Dr. Abram Wallace is leading a team there."

"Hasn't he been doing that for years? Shouldn't there be a cure by now?"

"It's not that easy. There were complications," Kerri said, not comfortable with all the questions.

"But now you have funding. At least that's what I've read. What did Nathan King donate? Fifteen million?"

Kerri nodded.

"Kind of cheap, if you ask me," Grant said. "His son died of the disease. Shouldn't he be giving more? He's worth much more. It's like you or I giving five bucks."

This conversation was starting to sound off. "Who are you?" Kerri asked.

"Someone interested in a lot of things. You're remarkably forgiving. I don't think I would be. After all, you had to blackmail him into donating that much."

Her memory kicked in and she took a step back. "You're that reporter."

"I am."

Kerri felt both used and set up. "I have nothing more to say to you."

"Then I'll talk. Don't you think it's interesting that his own sister hates him? Nathan isn't a good man, Ms. Sullivan. He's a bastard who uses people and right now he's using you."

"So you two have that in common," she said bitterly, wanting to escape but not comfortable leaving the suite.

"Maybe, but I'm just doing my job. He's profiting from your pain."

She turned to leave, but Grant grabbed her arm. "Are you sleeping with him? Was that part of the deal? You're whoring yourself for your son's cause? How much more are you willing to do to find a cure? What if I had the answers? Would you sleep with me?"

Kerri didn't know if she should slap him or throw her drink in his face. Then Tim was there, casually grabbing Grant's arm and twisting it behind his back.

"It's time for you to leave," the driver said.

"Easy," Grant told him. "You don't want a lawsuit on your hands."

Tim ignored that and pushed the man to the door. Kerri turned away, staring at the field but not seeing the activity below.

"I'm sorry about that." Nathan came up behind her. "I keep forgetting that other people consider Grant Pryor legitimate press. He shouldn't have been here. Are you all right?"

She put down her drink because she was shaking too much to hold it without spilling. "I'll recover."

"What did he say to you?"

"Nothing earth-shattering. I just wasn't expecting the attack. He has it out for you," she said.

"I know. You want something to eat? Or we could go walk around for a few minutes to give you a chance to catch your breath."

She shook her head. Grant was nothing but an opportunist, she told herself. A weasel. But there had been some truth buried in the ugliness

"Why didn't you do something?" she asked Nathan. "Other people lose children to tragedy and they use that as an opportunity to change the world. Mothers Against Drunk Drivers. AMBER Alerts. America's Most Wanted. You have more resources than most, but you didn't do anything. You could have fixed this already. If you'd wanted to, Gilliar's Disease would be a thing of the past."

"It's not that simple."

"That's what I told Grant. But why isn't it that simple? You weren't even trying. I had to trick you into helping. I think it's because you were telling the truth, the first time we met at the restaurant. That your kid was already dead so why should you care about mine. Cody could have been okay. We could be done with this. You had a responsibility to help."

"Why?" His voice was bitter. "Why should I have to help anyone else? Daniel is dead."

"Because that's what we're supposed to do. Be more than our circumstances. Think about other people."

"Maybe I don't give a damn about other people."

"Not any of us?" she asked, when the real question was, *Not me?*

Before he could answer, she heard a sharp cry. Cody lay on the floor of the suite, his leg twisted at an unnatural-looking angle, his mouth tight with pain.

AFTER DANIEL HAD DIED Nathan had vowed that nothing would ever get him into a hospital again. Yet here he was, making his second trip in less than two weeks.

An ambulance had rushed Cody, Kerri and himself to Children's. Cody had been taken for X-rays, although it was obvious what had happened.

"I hate this," Kerri muttered as she paced in the waiting area. The doctor had asked her to wait while they took Cody to radiology and her son had agreed, claiming he was fine.

Now Kerri clutched her hands together so tightly Nathan thought she might break a bone, too.

"I'm sorry," he said, feeling out of place and useless.

She turned on him. "About what? That he broke his leg? That he's still alive?"

He didn't react to her attack. "That both of you have to go through this."

Her blue eyes were bright with anger. "My son isn't going to die. Just so we're clear. I'm not giving up on him."

It was like she'd shot him. He turned and walked away, knowing it wasn't a fight he could win.

Had he given up on Daniel? He'd always agonized about doing the right thing. Had he given up too easily? Had he pushed his child closer to death to spare himself more suffering?

He turned a corner, then sank onto a bench. Present and past blurred and he was caught up in the memory of another hospital and another boy in pain. He remembered how tightly Daniel had clung to his hand, how the boy had begged him not to leave.

"I don't want to be alone."

So he'd stayed, because Paige couldn't and there wasn't anyone else. And in those last days, he'd gotten to know the boy and mourn the man he would never be.

That was the worst of it, he admitted to himself. That it was only as his son lay dying that they had finally gotten to know each other. It had been too little, too late.

A soft giggle drew him back to the present. He looked up and saw a pretty little girl walking down

the corridor, dragging an IV with her. She had a
teddy bear nearly as big as herself in her arms. A glit-
tering sticker of a fairy twinkled from one cheek and
a bright pink scarf covered her head.

"Hi," she said when she saw him.

Her smile was bright and friendly, as if she didn't
know about the disease obviously ravaging her body.
Cancer, he would guess.

"Hi."

"This is Fred." She held out her bear. "I got him
for my birthday. I'm seven."

"Fred is a very handsome bear. He's kind of big."

"I know. I'll grow into him."

Her confidence made him ache. Would she grow
into her bear?

She waved and kept walking. Nathan watched her
and knew that Kerri was right. He should have made
a difference after Daniel had died. He should have
used his son's death to create something more significant than grief and emptiness.

He walked outside and pulled out his cell phone.
Less than a minute later he had Dr. Wallace on the
phone.

"Do you need anything else?" Nathan asked.
"Money? Equipment?"

"Mr. King, you've already been more than generous."

"I don't care about that. Is it enough?"

Wallace cleared his throat. "Well, another five

hundred thousand would be most helpful. We could add another researcher and purchase more—"

"It's done," Nathan told him. "The money will be transferred today. Anything else?"

"Not right now." Wallace sounded stunned.

"If that changes, let me know. You have my direct number, don't you?"

"Yes. Ah, thank you. This will make a difference."

"If there's anything else, let me know."

"I will."

Nathan hung up.

It was so little—practically meaningless. But it was all he had to offer—money. What did that say about him?

He went back inside and found Kerri talking to the doctor.

"It's a clean break," the man was saying. "Cody slipped and the bone snapped. It should heal. Not that it will be any stronger when it does. Ms. Sullivan, you have to prepare yourself for more episodes like this. Gilliar's Disease is progressive."

The doctor wasn't a large man, but Kerri looked small next to him. It was as if she were shrinking, unable to bear the news about Cody.

Nathan crossed to her and put his arm around her. He expected her to pull away, but she didn't.

"We don't have to set the break," the doctor continued. "We'll put on a cast and he'll be ready to go. You'll have his regular doctor follow up?"

She nodded.

The doctor left. Kerri sucked in a breath. "I'm okay. I just need a minute." But as she spoke, tears filled her eyes.

"It's happening," she whispered. "It's happening and I can't make it stop. He's going to get worse. I would do anything to make it go away. I would be sick instead of him, but I can't. There's nothing I can do."

Tears flowed faster and faster. Nathan pulled her close and held her, wishing he could take some of her pain.

Tears turned into sobs. Her body shook.

"I can't do this," she said, her voice muffled against his shirt. "I can't be strong. It hurts too much. I don't have it in me."

"Sure you do."

"I'm faking it."

"Does it matter if you're the only one who knows you're faking it?"

"You know."

"I won't tell anyone."

She looked up at him, her face blotchy, her eyes red. "Why are you so nice to me?"

"Not a clue."

"You feel sorry for me."

"Not in the way you mean."

She was beautiful and he wanted to hold on a lot longer. But this was Kerri—all mouth and bravado.

The weakness would pass and then she would be back in his face, holding the world at bay by sheer force of will.

She swallowed. "He's dying. I know he's dying."

Her words were like a sucker punch to the gut. "Kerri…"

"I'm dying, too. Watching him. Knowing what's ahead." She held out her hands, turning them over, as if examining them. "I can't do anything. Do you know how useless that makes me feel? How ridiculous and stupid? I'm his mother. He's a part of me, of my blood and bone and I can't make him better."

"I know."

She curled her hands into fists and hit him on the chest. "Fix it, dammit. Fix it right now. Make me strong."

She hit him again and again. He let her, then caught her as she collapsed against him.

"I can't," she whispered through the tears. "I just can't."

He held her close and rocked her, feeling her pain, remembering his own. Knowing the futility of anger.

He kept her close, willing his strength into her, knowing it wouldn't help. That in the end, she had to find what she needed inside herself.

At last the tears slowed. She drew in a breath and stepped back.

"I said some awful things to you," she murmured.

"Maybe I needed to hear them."

She sniffed. "You really confuse me." She used her sleeve to blot her face. "I look terrible, don't I?"

"You're a little puffy."

"I have to go wash my face and attempt to hide the breakdown. I don't like Cody to see me upset."

"Wonder Mom doesn't cry?"

"Something like that." She squared her shoulders. "I'll be a couple of minutes. Can you go sit with him?"

"Sure."

She sniffed again. "Thank you for not freaking out. I didn't mean to lose it."

He wanted to tell her that she couldn't be strong all the time—no one could. That she was dying as much as Cody, just in a different way. But she already knew all that.

"I've seen worse," he told her.

She laughed. "Don't challenge me. I won't believe you." She raised herself up on tiptoe and pressed her mouth to his. "Thank you."

He watched her walk away, then headed for the E.R., where he found Cody in a bed, flipping channels.

"Still waiting for your cast?" he asked.

Cody nodded. "The break's really clean. It doesn't hurt that much. Is my mom okay?"

There was worry in the boy's voice.

"She's great," Nathan told him. "Being Wonder Mom gives her superpowers."

Cody rolled his eyes. "She's not really Wonder

Mom. She has the costume and she wears it sometimes. But it doesn't mean anything."

"I'm not so sure about that. She believes and faith is a tricky thing. Sometimes it makes all the difference in the world."

"Really?"

"Uh-huh. Don't underestimate the power of believing. Your mom believes in you."

"She tells me all the time that I'm going to get better. Sometimes I sort of believe her."

"I believe her."

Cody looked at him. "For real?"

"Your mother can do anything and you're the most important person in her life. You have some powerful mojo surrounding you."

Cody laughed. "What's mojo?"

"Magic. More than magic. It's strength and will combined with magic."

"In one of the Harry Potter books, Harry finds out he lived because his mother loved him so much, he couldn't be killed by a bad spell. Is it like that?"

"Yes, but bigger."

"Sweet." Cody shifted on the bed, wincing slightly as he moved his leg. "The game's still on. Want to watch?"

It took Nathan a second to realize the boy had made room for him.

Slowly, carefully, so as not to jar the mattress or

the child on it, he settled next to Cody. The kid leaned against him.

He was small and defenseless, Nathan thought, his throat unexpectedly tight. He faced a long, torturous battle with courage and grace. The odds were against him, but he had his mother on his side. Maybe, just maybe, everything would work out.

Nathan put his arm around Cody. "The game would be great."

CHAPTER FOURTEEN

"I FEEL LIKE AN IDIOT," Nathan grumbled. "I don't have time for this."

"I think we all should take time out of our day to be adored," Kerri told him, trying not to laugh at his obvious discomfort. "I would have thought you, more than most, would appreciate the thrill of being worshipped."

"I never wanted a parade."

"All hail Nathan King," she teased. "I wonder if the crowd will throw flowers. You might be offered young virgins. It's hard to say what a grateful people will do."

His gaze narrowed. "Just so we're clear, I'm not interested in young virgins."

"How about old ones?"

"You're not taking this seriously."

"I'm not." She grinned. "It's just a small-town parade in your honor. How horrible could it be?"

"This would be a whole lot easier if you didn't enjoy mocking me so much."

"Where's the fun in that?" She smoothed the front

of his well-tailored suit. "For what it's worth, you look very worship-worthy."

"You're still mocking me."

She didn't have much choice. Teasing him kept them at an emotional distance that was a whole lot safer for her peace of mind. She and Nathan had been through too much in too short a time. The emotional ups and downs left her feeling exposed and vulnerable. She didn't know if she wanted to throw herself in his arms and beg him to keep her safe, or just rip off his clothes and have her way with him. Neither option was especially smart.

Cody rolled into the room. "Hey, Nathan. You ready for the parade?"

"Do I have a choice?"

Her son grinned. "They'll be cheering. That's sweet."

"Then you go without me."

Cody grinned. "Mom won't let me."

"You already have plenty of ego," she told him. "You don't need to be the center of attention any more than you are."

She walked over and smoothed his hair. "Are you ready?"

Cody looked at Nathan. "Women," he said.

"Tell me about it," Nathan said.

Kerri looked between the two of them. "I'm a whole lot more than just *women*," she said, wondering when they'd connected.

Cody sighed heavily. "See what I have to deal with?"

Kerri glared at him. "Let's be clear. I don't care how big you get—I can still take you."

"Not with this," Cody said, motioning to his cast.

"Want to bet?"

"Oh, Mo-om. You know I love you."

"I've heard rumors." She turned to Nathan. "We should probably go. We don't want to be late."

If only they could skip the event altogether, Nathan thought grimly.

Cody led the way to the limo waiting in front of the house. "Mom, was Dad ever in any parades? You know, for Veterans Day?"

"Once, I think," Kerri said. "It wasn't his thing. The dress uniform was really hot. He didn't like to do showy things."

"Because he was a real soldier?"

Kerri smiled at him. "He was. Serving his country was important to him. He wanted to keep us safe."

Nathan had never thought much about the man who had been Kerri's late husband and Cody's father. The man who had died too young, never knowing he was going to have a son.

What would have been different if Brian Sullivan had lived? Kerri wouldn't have had to deal with Cody's illness on her own. He was sure she would have appreciated the support. She wouldn't have come looking for him, or his help. Or would she?

Would she still have blackmailed him and would he have let her?

He didn't have any answers, so he told himself it didn't matter. He wasn't in competition with a dead man and even if Brian were still alive, he, Nathan would win. He always won.

THE STAGING AREA for the parade was a small park at the edge of town. There were less than a dozen floats, each cheesier than the one in front of it. They had obviously been pulled out of storage and hastily decorated, the fresh flowers and draped fabric not totally covering the St. Patrick's Day decorations. There were three open cars and the high school marching band, led by color guard, cheerleaders and some girl with a baton.

"This is not happening," Nathan muttered.

"It's not the Rose Parade, but it will be fun," Kerri told him.

"It's humiliating."

"They spelled your name right on the big banner. That's something."

"You need higher standards."

"You need to loosen up and have fun. When was the last time someone held a party in your honor?"

"I could go my whole life and not miss it."

"Now you don't have to."

She led the way over to the convertibles. Each of them had a banner proclaiming Nathan King Day In

Songwood, which was a lot of text for a small area. It meant the font was small and probably unreadable from more than ten feet away.

Just then, some kid with a camera came up and snapped his picture.

"For the local paper," Kerri said. "We want the moment immortalized."

"I'm having my doubts about that. Lately the press isn't my friend."

"We're going to change all that. Today you are the star. All of Songwood wants you to bask in the glow of our gratitude."

"Spare me."

He opened the back door of the car, while Cody locked his wheelchair into place. The boy stood. Nathan bent down and grabbed him, then carefully set him in the car.

"How's the leg?" he asked, lightly touching the cast.

"It doesn't hurt," Cody told him.

Nathan wondered if that was true or if the kid was just being brave.

Cody had gotten to him. Kerri had been right—he'd done his best to ignore the boy, but he hadn't done a good enough job. Which meant when Cody died, Nathan was going to be reliving Daniel's death. Something he would have walked through fire to avoid.

When the kid was in place, Nathan held out his hand to help Kerri into the car. Her skin was warm to the touch, her body a temptation he didn't want to resist.

Too many complications, he told himself. He should be smart enough to know that. But the truth was, if she offered, he wouldn't say no.

"COME ON," Linda said, taking Abram by the hand and tugging him out of the lab. "The parade will be here any minute."

"I don't have time for parades," he grumbled, even as he went with her. "I have important work."

"I know, but you also need to get out and see the world you're saving. Ten minutes won't make a difference."

They emerged into the warm, sunny day. Most of the staff was lined up on the main street in front of the lab. He could hear music from the marching band and see several teenagers holding a large banner reading Nathan King Appreciation Day.

"He called me a few days ago," Abram said absently. "Offering more money."

"I hope you took it."

"I did."

"More equipment will help, as will more researchers."

If only it were a matter of money, he thought. Then the problem would already be solved. They would…

He glanced down and saw that Linda still held his

hand. She was watching the approaching parade and he wondered if she noticed.

He told himself it meant nothing even as he enjoyed the feel of her skin against his.

"Thank you for agreeing to come back," he told her.

She looked at him then, her eyes bright with humor and caring and something that made him think about her as much more than just his assistant.

"This is where I've always wanted to be," she told him. "I thought you knew."

He hadn't, but he did now.

KERRI ADJUSTED the tiny microphone clipped to her collar. "This is weird," she whispered. "Do I have to have the microphone? It's making me really self-conscious."

Tina, a pretty redhead in a designer suit and power high heels, smiled. "We want to make the experience as real as possible. That's what media training is about. You need to be able to deal with the nerves, the lights, the camera and the unexpected questions. Remember to relax. You know the material. You don't have to answer the question if you don't want to. There's no law. You have a message—that's what's most important."

Kerri wished she had note cards, because currently she couldn't remember anything about the message. Helping? Healing? She felt her palms getting damp.

"I'm not going to panic," she murmured quietly. "This is me—panic free. I'm calm and serene."

Tina looked at her. "You're also miked. Keep the chanting to yourself at a minimum unless you want the whole country to know about it."

"Right." She knew that. "Ah, this is local, right? We're not really talking about the whole country."

"Your interview is with the local affiliate, but if it's interesting enough, it could be picked up nationally."

Kerri's chest tightened. Nausea rose in her throat, nearly gagging her.

"I might have to pass out," she said, hoping she either passed out *or* vomited. She'd seen enough medical shows to know doing both at the same time was risky, not to mention disgusting.

Tina settled across from her. "We're going to start now. Remember, the interviewer isn't your friend. It's his or her job to make you think you're friends so you say things you didn't plan on saying, but the reality is you want different things. You want to get out your message and the interviewer wants a great story. Are you ready?"

Kerri nodded. She did her best to ignore the camera, the flipping of her stomach, the bright lights and the burning need to hyperventilate.

Tina smiled. "Kerri, thanks so much for agreeing to this interview. You find yourself in what I'm guessing is a very uncomfortable situation."

Kerri opened her mouth, then closed it. Don't answer the question before it's asked, she reminded herself. She smiled.

Tina raised her eyebrows, then nodded. "So, you blackmailed Nathan King into giving you fifteen million dollars for your dying son. How did that happen?"

Kerri drew in a breath. "Nathan donated money to a medical research facility working on finding a way to cure and prevent Gilliar's Disease. It's a horrible, painful sickness that's devastating for both the children and their families. As a parent, there's nothing I can do to stop my son's disease from progressing. It's beyond helplessness. I would take the disease myself if I could. I hate what's happening and I can't stop it."

Tina stared at her. "Excellent. You've made me the bad guy and all of America wants to send you flowers."

"I'd rather they donated the money to find a cure."

"Good point. Okay, let's try another question. Nathan King seems to be using you and your son to shore up his questionable reputation so he can build a high-rise condo complex the average American could never afford to live in. Do you mind being used to line his pockets and rape the environment?"

Kerri laughed. "Shouldn't that be rape and pillage the environment? No one is going to ask that."

"They may. How will you answer?"

Kerri didn't have a clue. Then she remembered

that she was supposed to stay on message. "I don't know anything about Mr. King's business interests. I'm a single mom who makes her living as a hairdresser in a small town. My goal is to be a good mother, raise my son right and keep him from dying. There's not much time for anything else in my day."

"Are you sleeping with Nathan King?"

"Could you ask a more tacky question?"

Tina hesitated. "Okay—that's not what we talked about, but I like it. Make sure you're feeling outraged. It gives your answer more emotion."

"I am outraged. It's no one's business and not the point."

"People are interested."

"Let them get their own guy."

Tina grinned. "You're going to do just fine."

"I hope so."

She owed Nathan and she wanted to pay him back. The irony was she also wanted to sleep with him. Which meant if the question was whether she wanted to go bed with Nathan, outrage was going to be a little difficult to come by.

FRANKIE SIPPED her latte and counted silently. One, two, three, four. The numbers soothed her as they always did. They allowed her to breathe slowly, evenly, bringing her heart rate down.

There was comfort in the familiar. Comfort in the ritual.

When she was done, she glanced at her watch, knowing that Grant wasn't late, that she had been early. She couldn't help herself. Being early mattered, even though it meant waiting.

She arranged the three napkins she'd taken and sipped her drink. Anger burned at the edges of her consciousness, like a sense of dread she couldn't escape.

It hadn't worked. The story hadn't hurt Nathan nearly enough. Sure, people had wanted to talk about what a rich bastard he was and how he should be stopped, but no one had done anything. No one had stepped forward to make it happen. Worse, he was back in the papers, but in a good way. Just that morning there had been pictures of him at some stupid parade in Songwood. He'd been smiling. Happy. He didn't deserve to be happy.

She frowned as she remembered the article itself. How he'd been so charming and self-deprecating about Nathan King Appreciation Day. Like he was embarrassed. Like he didn't love every minute of the attention. She hated him. Hated him. Hated him.

Her chest tightened and she started counting again. She'd just finished the first set of numbers when Grant walked into the Starbucks and crossed to where she was seated.

"You should buy something," she told him. "It's what you're supposed to do."

"I don't like their coffee," he said as he sat down

across from her and smiled. "It's good to see you, Frankie. You look nice."

She blinked at him. What did he mean by that? What did he want? She didn't look nice—she looked the same. Nothing was different.

"It's not working," she said. "People aren't mad enough at Nathan. It was a good story, but no one cares. We have to make them care. I have information on the sound, on what's happening there. Statistics. Do you know how many species of plants and marine life are dying out every year? The Black Oystercatcher is living on borrowed time. There are maybe ten Island Marble butterflies left. All this matters," she told him.

Grant leaned back in his chair. "You're not interested in me, are you?"

"What?"

"In me. This is all just about your brother."

"What else is there?"

"I thought you might be into me. You know, as a guy."

"Why?"

His smile turned rueful. "You're an attractive woman, Frankie. A little strange, but I like that. You're passionate, you're smart."

Was he making fun of her? She felt her face get hot. "I'm already helping you get Nathan. You don't have to say that other stuff."

"I'm not saying it for a reason other than I want

to. I find you interesting. Maybe we could go out sometime. To dinner maybe. Or lunch. Lunch is pretty safe."

Was he talking about a date? She didn't date. She couldn't remember the last time a guy had asked. Dating.

She tried to get her mind around the concept, but it was difficult. It was like that part of her was dead. She could remember high school and liking boys and going out, but not for a long time. Not since what had happened.

"I can't," she whispered. "It's too hard."

"Okay. I won't push you."

His voice was gentle, as if he liked her. She tried to remember the last time someone had liked her.

For a moment, it was like the sun coming out on a cloudy day. There was a burst of light and a sense of warmth, of belonging. She could see possibilities. Normal, she thought. She could be normal. It was always there, just out of reach. If she was willing to get help...

No. No. This was better. Focus. She could focus on Nathan. On what he was. On how he'd hurt her. He'd lied. He hadn't come back. He'd left her alone with the blood.

"Part of the problem is Kerri Sullivan," Grant said. "She's a natural. She comes across as honest and engaging. It's a powerful combination. Plus she has that sick kid. She's the underdog. You can't fight that."

"She's lying."

"I don't know that she is and I'm not sure it matters. Plus it's obvious that the kid likes your brother. Kids and dogs. If they like a person, then he must be okay."

She didn't want to think about the boy. That reminded her of Daniel. Daniel, whom she missed. Nathan had loved that little boy.

"The planning commission will be meeting soon," she said. "We have to come up with something before the meeting."

Grant leaned toward her. "Frankie, I like you a lot. I respect your lack of interest in me, so I'm going to tell you the truth. You can't do anything to hurt Nathan. It's too late. He's either going to get the permits or he's not. I'm out of it. I've been chasing him for too many years and I've always come up empty. I'm going to move on."

"I don't understand. You can't give up." She needed him. He hated Nathan. They had that in common.

"I'm going to L.A. I'm tired of the rain and the disappointments. I'd rather chase celebrities and take pictures than keep beating my head against the wall. You should think about letting it go, too. You're still young. Live your life. Find somebody. Be happy."

He rose. "Good luck, Frankie."

And then he was gone.

She stared after him, unable to believe he'd given up and walked out. How could he? She clutched her coffee in her hands and counted quickly, repeating the numbers in her head until she could think clearly.

She could still do this, she told herself. She didn't need Grant. She would keep on fighting…she would destroy her brother. Even if it killed her. Even if. Because there was a voice inside of her. One that warned that if Nathan went down, she just might go down with him.

"YOU'RE A CELEBRITY," Linda said when Kerri walked into her office.

"Hardly."

"I saw your interview. You did great."

"I had a media coach who asked a lot harder questions than the woman from that afternoon talk show. It was pretty easy." Kerri waited while her friend collected her purse so they could go to lunch. "Not that I want to repeat the experience. It was freakish to be in a studio, answering questions. Not my thing."

"You were great and you looked good, which is just as important."

Kerri laughed. "It is, which is weird of us, but there we are."

Linda grabbed a file from her desk. "I have to drop this off in the lab. It will just take a second."

"Not a problem."

Kerri walked with her down the long corridor. She hadn't been in the research center since she'd shown up several weeks ago to yell at Dr. Wallace.

Back then the building had been quiet and dimly lit. Now it was bright and bustling. There were dozens of people in white lab coats going from room to room. The air was warm and filled with…something. Promise, maybe, although that could be wishful thinking on her part.

They stopped in front of a large lab. Kerri could see through the glass into a big room with workstations and complicated equipment and people wearing masks and goggles.

"That's a little scary," she said. "What are they doing?"

"You want the scientific details?"

"I wouldn't understand them."

"Then they're working on a cure. Let me give them this paperwork and we can head out. How about Chinese?"

"Sounds good."

Linda disappeared through a door next to the lab. Kerri watched the scientists at work but had no idea what they were doing.

"Mrs. Sullivan."

She turned and saw Dr. Wallace walking toward her.

"Hi. I'm waiting for Linda. She's dropping something off and then we're going to lunch."

"I see. Well, good." He paused and looked at her, as if expecting more.

She cleared her throat. "So, is it going well here?"

"We have several plans of attack. This group here is looking at how enzymes interact with the immune system. Popular wisdom points us in other directions, but I keep a small team working here. I still think there's something we're missing. I may be wrong. But with the additional money Mr. King provided, I've added more equipment to help us find out."

Kerri crossed her arms over her chest. "Nathan gave you more money?"

"Five hundred thousand. I thought you knew."

"He never said anything."

"He phoned a couple of weeks ago. He said I could have whatever I needed. Of course what we really need is focus and time. Time is the most important thing. There isn't enough."

He stopped talking and looked uncomfortable, as if he realized time was her enemy, as well.

She sucked in a breath. "I need to ask you something. I've been wondering…"

Did she want to know? But she had to hear the truth, even if it was ugly.

"Is it my fault Cody's sick? Could I have done something while I was pregnant? Is it genetic?"

"No," Dr. Wallace said without hesitation. "It's nothing you did. It's not chemically induced or transmitted through food. A gene goes wrong. Who is to say why? A random chance event? Bad luck? As for genetics, I can't say. There is no indication it passes from parent to child. Siblings are no more at risk than the general population. We know it attacks children, mostly boys. Hormones are a possibility. Hormones and the enzymes. I know there's something there."

He continued talking, but she wasn't listening. She was trying to figure out if it was okay for it not to be her fault.

"So it could still be me," she said.

"Do you need it to be you?" he asked. "Do you need someone to blame? Someone other than fate or God or circumstance?"

"I don't know."

"Blame me," he told her. "Blame me for stopping. For not moving forward. For not believing in myself enough."

"I can't."

"Then why can you blame yourself?"

Good point. "I'm not sure this is the right time for logic."

One corner of his mouth lifted. "Life is hard enough, child. Don't make it more than it is."

"Thank you."

"I have done nothing."

"But you will. I have faith."

"The expectation of miracles is a heavy burden."

"I know," she told him. "I'm sorry to put that on you."

"It doesn't weigh as much as blame." He nodded at her and walked into the lab. A few seconds later, Linda came out.

"Ready?" her friend asked.

Kerri nodded. She glanced back at the lab one last time. Would the miracle happen in time? She didn't know and found herself grateful that she couldn't see into the future. Without knowing the outcome, it was a whole lot easier to have hope.

CHAPTER FIFTEEN

REX WAS POSSIBLY the most handsome man Kerri had ever seen in person. He was tall, blond and muscular to the point of being intimidating. If his hands and feet were any indication, he could probably make a living starring in porn films. When he put his hands on her waist and thigh, she practically had to cover her mouth to keep from giggling.

"We will strap you in here and here," he said, his voice faintly accented. Rex had been born in Germany. "It is not comfortable, but it is secure. You are not a professional. Secure is better, yes?"

"Oh, yes. I'm big on secure. Use whatever you want."

"We will have to cut part of your costume for the straps. The skirt will help hide the lines."

"I'll just sew it up later. Not a problem."

"Good."

He reached for a harness and had her step into it. His big hands worked the buckles and Velcro, touching her inner thighs and crotch in the process. Kerri braced herself for the explosion of sensation—after all it had been nearly a decade since a man had touched her *there*. But she felt nothing. Not a quiver or a hint of yearning. Just the need to giggle.

Not good news, she told herself. She was always hot and frothy when she was around Nathan. She wanted to be able to reassure herself that her reaction was about need and not the man, because if she was wrong, she was in big trouble.

After he finished strapping her in, Rex stood. "You will lean into your jump. Like this."

He demonstrated by holding his arms out at his sides and leaning forward, like a runner straining for the finish line.

"You aren't making the jump on your own. You'll be pulled forward, and gravity will help. The lines are made from a special material that is practically clear. From a distance, they almost disappear. We'll use smoke to blur the scene, as well."

"Won't people wonder why there's smoke?"

Rex shrugged, several large, impressive muscles bunching and releasing. "It is the only way. Making someone appear to fly in the real world is a challenge, Kerri. We are doing the best we can."

He sounded almost hurt. She smiled up at him. "You're being wonderful and I really appreciate it. I know this is a lot of work and not how you usually spend your day."

"Working on movies is not always interesting,

but they pay very well and my job makes it easy to get women into bed."

"Always an important consideration."

"I like women," he said, then grinned. "Actually I like sex."

"Why am I not surprised?"

"Are you busy later? We could go to dinner."

"Me?" She doubted she was his usual groupie type. Rex was gorgeous and seeing him naked would provide a memory that would stay with her forever. She supposed she should be flattered. She was pushing thirty and not the least bit glamorous.

Her gaze slid a little left to where a familiar man in a well-tailored suit stood while talking on his cell phone. His mouth thinned with what she guessed was impatience and she had a flash of sympathy for whoever had just screwed up. Nathan didn't suffer fools.

He was difficult, imperious, arrogant, and no one she should get involved with. But there was something about him that called to her and made it impossible to even consider Rex's slightly scandalous invitation.

"I don't think dinner would be a good idea," she told him. "Not that I'm not tempted."

"Are you sure? I'm very good. I have a lot of experience."

"I'm guessing you're beyond good, Rex. But I don't do one-night stands. I get involved, and then what would happen? You'd go back to Hollywood and

I'd have a crush on you. I'd start calling on a daily basis, you wouldn't like that. You'd want to let me down gently, but eventually you'd be forced to change your cell phone number and get a restraining order."

Rex looked confused. "Because of one night of sex?"

She nodded. "I'm trying to save you from a hellish time."

Nathan walked over. "How's it going?"

Kerri smiled at him. "I'm explaining to Rex that I'm not a good person to get involved with. You know how easily I give away my heart. I'll start stalking him and it will get really ugly. I'm not sure I'm getting through."

Nathan frowned. "Are you saying he—"

Kerri moved close. "Tell him how long it took me to get over you, Nathan. How I nearly destroyed your life."

Nathan's expression warned her she would have some explaining to do later, then he turned to Rex. "Trust me. You don't want to go there with her. No matter how much she tempts you."

Rex took a step back. "Okay. Good to know. Thank you for being so honest. I'll get the practice jumps ready so you can try them with the lines."

He scooted away as fast as his massive thighs would take him. Nathan waited until they were alone, then asked, "What was that about?"

"He asked me to dinner, which was really a polite way of asking if I wanted to have sex."

Nathan's gaze narrowed. "He's fired."

"Don't be silly. He can't help himself. Look at his face, his body. He's beyond perfect—he's another species. I can't help but wonder what he looks like naked."

"Apparently he would like you to find out."

She grinned. "No thanks. And don't get all pinchy. I'm curious, not intrigued. He's no one I'm interested in."

"You said you wanted to see him naked and I'm not pinchy."

"You can't see your face."

She had the thought that he was jealous but dismissed it. Nathan couldn't be—that would imply he cared. Theirs was a business relationship with some interesting side trips. Still, it was a pretty cool fantasy. Or as her nine-year-old would say—sweet.

"We have to talk," Nathan said.

"About Rex?"

"About a charity function." He named the date. "Are you available?"

"Sure."

"It's formal."

"Like a ball? I've always wanted to wear a tiara."

"If it's important to you."

"Kerri, we are ready for you," Rex said.

"You can only stay if you promise not to laugh," Kerri told Nathan. "I'm about to make a big fool out of myself. No critical remarks are allowed."

"You don't have to do this at all."

"Yeah, I do. It's time for Wonder Mom to make an appearance."

She followed Rex over to the platform that had been built to simulate the top of a building just beyond the fence at Cody's school. The plan was that she would jump from one building to another, then catch a falling beam. In truth, she would be harnessed and jump with the aid of a line that would both pull her in the right direction and keep her from falling. There would be a net in case she messed up and the beam in question was a Hollywood prop, made of foam rubber and weighing about five pounds. It, too, would be on a line.

Even though she knew nothing was going to go wrong, she was nervous as she stood on the first platform. Rex stood beside her, his huge hand on her shoulder.

"Run straight forward. Not too fast. You need momentum, not speed. Your jump starts at the mark. Lean forward. Gravity and the momentum will carry you forward. Bend your knees for the landing. On the other side, regain your balance and run toward the middle of the building. The beam will fall, you will catch it and the world will be saved."

She laughed. "If only that were true."

She followed him to the starting point—a square on the platform marked with blue tape. Everything was in place. For a second she wondered how much this was costing Nathan—she'd demanded to fly for her son and he'd made it happen.

"Ready?" Rex called.

She nodded and waited for him to call "Go!"

On his cue, she ran toward the edge of the platform. She overshot her jumping point, but launched herself anyway and had to suck back a scream as she began to fall.

Lean, she told herself through the terror. Lean and push and—

Her feet hit the second, lower platform. She staggered a little, having forgotten to bend her knees. When she'd regained her balance, she jogged toward the center of the platform, looked up and shrieked as a massive beam dropped toward her. Rather than catch it, she put up her arms to protect her head. The beam bounced off her and landed on the platform. She straightened and winced.

"We probably need to practice that last bit," she said.

Rex shrugged again, moving those impossible muscles up and down. "Not bad for a first try. We will go again."

So they did. On her second attempt, she managed the jump, but still covered her head and crouched as the beam tumbled toward her. By the fourth practice run, she managed to complete the sequence without messing up.

"Two more runs," Rex told her. "Then we move to the school."

She looked up at the godlike man. "You must think I'm crazy for doing this."

"Nathan said your little boy is sick. That you do this to make him feel better. You're a good mother. I'm happy to help."

A god with a heart, she thought and smiled. "Thank you, Rex. That's so sweet."

"I think we would be good together," he said. "In bed. I can do things women like."

"I'm sure you can, but this isn't the best time for me."

"You're with Nathan, aren't you? That's why you told me you would stalk me."

Her attention slid to the man in question. "We're not together."

"You will be," Rex said glumly. "I can tell. But when you get tired of him, you can call me. I'll give you my card."

She didn't know which to address first—his confidence that she and Nathan would hook up or his unexpected interest in her.

"Are you intrigued because I said no?" she asked. "Does that make me a challenge?"

"Partly," Rex admitted. "But mostly it's because of your son. You really care about him. I like that. You lead with your heart. I don't meet a lot of women like that."

"Then stop dating women in the business."

"But they're so beautiful."

She gave up. Rex didn't want to change and she had no idea why he thought he wanted her. She would take the compliment and let it go.

Two hours later, she was pulling on her Wonder Mom boots in an empty classroom at Cody's school. Second thoughts had been replaced by third and fourth thoughts.

"I'm crazy," she muttered to herself as she straightened and stomped her foot into place in the cheap white boots. "I can't pull this off. Even if I don't kill or maim myself, no one is going to believe the stunt. Talk about dumb."

"Are you trying to commune with a distant planet?" Nathan asked as he entered the room.

"What? Oh." Kerri reached up and fingered the hot rollers. "I decided that I should look good as I plummet to my death. That way everyone talking about what an idiot I was will also add that I looked good doing it."

"You're not an idiot."

"I feel stupid."

"Why? You want to give Cody something to believe in."

"A mom with special powers? He's too old for that."

"No one is too old for a miracle."

She wrinkled her nose. "Hey, you're supposed to be the cynical one, not me."

"I thought I'd check out the view from the other side." He moved close. "You'll do fine."

"I hope so." She stared into his dark eyes. "Thank you for doing this. I know it's been a big pain and a bigger expense."

"I'm happy to make you fly."

She put her hands on Nathan's chest. "Rex told me he can do things women like."

"He's never going to work in this town again."

She smiled. "Don't be mad. It's funny. He's funny. I'm not interested."

Nathan didn't say anything. She supposed there wasn't a good, winning response. He wasn't going to admit *he* was interested, but he didn't want her seeing anyone else. Which she kind of liked.

"Rex isn't my type."

"You said you don't have a type."

"I don't. But if I did, it wouldn't be him."

He stared at her for a long time, then his gaze dropped to her mouth. Was he thinking about kissing her? She found herself wanting that kiss, and his touch and whatever else he was offering.

Someone tapped on the open door. "It's time."

Kerri stepped back and began removing the curlers.

"I'll see you on the other side," Nathan told her. "Good luck."

"Thanks."

Kerri fluffed her hair, sprayed it into submission, then slipped on her cape and took the stairs to the roof.

The school looked a lot different than the mock-up she'd practiced on. There was also the unfortunate issue of the building being much higher than the platform. There were several people hovering just out of sight, behind large pieces of complicated equipment. Rex waved her over.

"There is smoke," he said as he secured her harness and the lines, then tugged on them. "It will not hurt you. You will be afraid, but you are safe. The worst that will happen is you will fall into the net. The lines will slow your fall and you will be fine."

Kerri had a vision of herself tumbling to a broken arm or leg. Neither fell under her definition of fine.

"You will go to your mark, then begin to run. Lean forward as you jump."

"Bend my knees when I land, keep my balance, catch the beam," she finished. "What was I thinking?"

"That you will make your son proud of you and that will give him hope."

She smiled at Rex. "Good answer."

Without warning, he grabbed her shoulders, pulled her close and kissed her.

His mouth was as hard as the rest of him, but yielding. He kissed as if he meant it, with interest and just enough urgency to be flattering. He didn't push, pressing his lips to hers but not taking things further. So much for not kissing any man in ten years, she thought humorously. Apparently she was making up for lost time.

She put her hands on his and gently pulled him away. If she could find the mental time and energy to amuse herself while she was being kissed, then something was really wrong.

Rex stared at her, then sighed. "I tried."

"You did good."

"Not good enough. Come on, Wonder Mom. It's time to save the world."

Kerri walked alone to the mark on the roof. While she'd practiced and in theory should be fine, she found herself shaking as she stared across what seemed like an impossible distance to the building in front of her. Smoke swirled around her, creating a sense of otherworldliness, as if she'd stepped into an alternate universe. She could see much of the town, the blue sky, feel the light breeze on her face.

"I can do this," she told herself. "I have powers. The power of love for Cody. The power of belief. I can do this because he needs to see me do this. I'm fine. It's easy. I can fly."

She drew in a breath and squared her shoulders. Then she began to run.

The edge of the roof seemed to race toward her. She timed her mark okay and started to jump. From the practice sessions, she was prepared for the sense of falling and refused to look down. She leaned forward and, at the last second, remembered to bend her knees.

When she landed on the other roof, she was so stunned, she nearly fell. Then she regained her balance, hurried forward a few steps, looked up and caught the beam. She raised the Hollywood-constructed piece above her head in victory, then set it on the roof and spun in a circle.

"I am Wonder Mom," she yelled. "I can fly!"

Five minutes later, minus the harness and the lines, she walked into Cody's classroom. The kids there clustered around her.

"Mrs. Sullivan, that was so cool. How did you do it?"

"Did you really jump between the buildings? Can you teach me to do that?"

She crossed to her son, in his chair in front of his desk. "So what did you think?"

He ducked his head. "Mo-om, you didn't have to do that."

"I kind of did. If that beam had fallen, it would have crashed through the roof and possibly hurt students in their classrooms."

He looked at her and rolled his eyes. "It didn't look that heavy."

"Trust me, it was."

"Uh-huh."

But he was smiling as he spoke and there was a light in his eyes she hadn't seen in a long time.

"Cody, you're so lucky," one of the kids said. "I wish my mom was Wonder Mom."

"Me, too. Mrs. Sullivan, can you do that again?"

She doubted she was up to an encore. "Everyone is safe now. I think I'll head home."

She turned to leave. Cody grabbed her hand. "Thanks, Mom."

"You're welcome. I'll pick you up at eight at Brandon's. Have fun."

"I will."

"Maybe when you get home tonight, we can pick out a theme song. Or I could just borrow the one from Wonder Woman. What do you think?"

"That I'm lucky to have you."

Kerri had been worried about falling or failing or making a fool out of herself. She hadn't thought about crying.

Still, she managed to hold back the tears. "Me, too," she said, then waved at Cody's teacher and left.

Hope, she told herself as she leaned against the school hallway wall. She'd given him hope. Sometimes that was enough for a miracle. Pray God it was this time.

ABRAM WALKED into Bill's Food and Feed late in the afternoon. "I'm here for my order."

"Sure thing, Professor. I had it ready last night."

Had he ordered it for last night? It was possible. He was attempting to take care of more of the details in his life himself, rather than depend on Linda. It wasn't that he didn't want her help—it was more that he needed to prove something to her. And possibly himself.

"You can check that I have everything," Bill told him.

"Not necessary. I wouldn't know if something was missing or added."

Bill grinned. "You really are the absentminded professor, aren't you?"

Doctor, Abram thought, less annoyed by the title than usual.

"Hello, Dr. Wallace," a woman said as she came into the store. "Aren't we having a nice summer?"

"Ah, yes," Abram answered, not sure he'd ever seen her before. For all he knew, she was employed at the lab. Except for the researchers he worked with, he didn't pay much attention to staff.

Two more people spoke to him before he could pay for his order and escape. Because the lab was back in business, he thought as he picked up the box. They appreciated the work he brought to the town. Did that mean they'd forgiven him for what had happened before? Was it possible?

He turned to leave, then spotted a display of floral bouquets all wrapped up in plastic and sitting in a bucket.

"I'll, ah, take one of those, too," he said.

"Sure thing, Professor," Bill told him. "I'll put it on your tab."

He shook off the flowers before adding them to

the box, then walked out to his car. When he'd put everything in the backseat, he turned and looked at the storefront.

He'd redeemed himself in their eyes. A foolish sentiment. All he'd done was unwillingly accept a grant and make use of Nathan King's money. He had yet to find a cure for Gilliar's Disease.

But he would, he told himself firmly. He would.

KERRI POURED from the bottle of wine Nathan had brought over and wondered how much it had cost. Fifty dollars? A hundred? If it was the latter, it was her food budget for the week. Ah, to have spare cash.

"To a successful flight," he said, taking the glass she offered.

She picked up her own. "Because of you. Is there any way I can get you to tell me what my stunt cost?"

"No."

"I had no idea how complicated it would be or what was involved. You should have told me. I would have found a different way."

"Why? This one worked. Like you said, Kerri, I got one of my assistants to take care of the details. Don't give me too much credit."

"What happened to the heartless bastard who got me fired from my waitress job several months ago?" she asked.

"He's still alive and well and pissing off the world."

She wasn't so sure. Nathan had been more than

kind to her, more than generous. He'd been patient, been a friend.

"I've never had anyone to lean on before," she told him. "I'm afraid to get used to it."

"Don't be. You don't always have to fight the battle alone."

Didn't she? Wasn't that what made it work? Her sacrifice?

But sometimes it was hard to be the only one. To never be able to depend on someone else. Sometimes she wanted to have a strong shoulder to lean against.

She put down her glass of wine and leaned toward him. His eyes were dark and mostly unreadable, except for the fire flaring there.

She felt an answering heat inside—one that made her tremble and want and wonder.

There was danger in desire, she told herself. But he was so much more than she'd imagined a man could be. She didn't just like him, she admired him.

She put one hand on his shoulder and shifted so she could press her mouth to his.

For a second he didn't react, then his mouth moved against hers, claiming her. There was heat and a familiar living need that consumed her. Rex's kiss had left her unmoved, but Nathan's kiss made her want to melt into a puddle. Except a puddle couldn't really appreciate the nuances of a man's mouth.

He set down his wine and grabbed her upper arms.

After hauling her against him, he tilted his head and licked her bottom lip.

Jolts of desire shot through her, making her belly clench and her toes curl. She opened for him, then had to hold in a gasp as he claimed her with passionate, heady strokes of his tongue.

He explored her, teasing her, arousing her. She kissed him back, closing her lips around his tongue and sucking. He stiffened, then groaned.

"Dammit, Kerri," he muttered, his voice low and thick.

His hands were everywhere—on her back, her arms, down her sides. She wore a shirt and jeans, and hated when his palm slid from bare skin to fabric. She wanted to feel him touching her everywhere.

But instead of reading her mind like he was supposed to, he pulled back.

"Why are you doing this?" he asked.

"What?"

"Is this about the money? Are you paying me back?"

She supposed she should have been insulted, but a voice in her head told her that Nathan was asking because he was afraid of getting hurt.

Not possible, she told herself. Her hurt Nathan? No one got close—he made sure of that. Or did he?

"It's not about the money," she said firmly.

"How do I know that?"

Good question. She tried to think of some way to convince him, but there weren't any words.

Finally she simply smiled and said, "You're going to have to trust me."

"Not my style."

"New things can be exciting." She eased forward until their bodies were touching. "Believe me."

"Because you want me?"

No one had ever asked her that before. Brian had been her first, her only, and they had eased into love-making slowly. They'd dated and fallen in love. Their times together had been tender and sweet and all about discovery. They'd never talked about wanting or needing.

But Nathan was an experienced man who probably expected the same from his partners. Which was a really good reason to panic, she thought.

"Kerri?"

"Yes," she said, and covered her face with her hands. "Don't make me say it again."

"You're not convincing me."

"I'm embarrassed."

"Why?"

She dropped her hands. "I'm not like them. Those other women who are so practiced. I haven't been with anyone since Brian and I sort of wasn't with anyone before."

He stared at her so long she felt herself blushing. The need to squirm was powerful, but she resisted. She could at least pretend to be mature.

"I really do want this," she told him.

"I believe you."

"Good. There's just one other thing."

He raised his eyebrows.

She drew in a breath. "It's different when your partner has superpowers."

"I'll just bet."

He pulled her close and kissed her. Even as his tongue teased her into playing an erotic game of chase, he slipped his hands below the hem of her T-shirt and ran his fingers down her spine.

She felt shivers and heat and an aching in her breasts. Her thighs trembled, as did her knees.

When he moved his hands to her waist, her breath caught. When he slid them up and cupped her breasts through her bra, she exhaled. When his thumbs brushed her hard, sensitive nipples, she forgot to breathe.

While his fingers worked their magic, he broke their kiss, then nibbled his way along her jaw. He licked the sensitive skin below her ear, then blew on the dampness. She did her best not to groan, but it was too hard to hold in the passion.

Heat sank down to the apex of her thighs, where she melted for him. She put her hands on his shoulders to keep her balance, then had to lift them as he tugged off her T-shirt. Seconds later her bra followed. She was so startled that he could unfasten it more quickly than she could that she nearly forgot to be shy.

But before she could cover herself or worry that

he wouldn't like what he saw, he leaned in and drew her left nipple into his mouth and sucked.

The combination of warmth and wetness and lips and tongue sent her heart racing. It was the most exquisite sensation, outside of orgasm, she'd ever experienced in her life.

"Don't stop," she breathed before she could stop herself. She clutched his head, determined he do that forever. She needed his touch, his tongue, the sensations shooting through her.

It was as if there was a direct line from her breasts to the center of her body. With each tug on her nipple, she felt an answering tension between her legs.

He shifted to the other breast, sucking and licking and taking her higher and higher. She ached for more, for him to touch her everywhere. She was both hot and cold, trembling with need and yet wanting to make the moment last forever.

When he reached for the button at the waistband of her jeans, she found herself frantically trying to help. Naked, she thought, burning with an unfamiliar need to take and be taken. Naked would be good. She wanted naked. Now!

The good part was after she kicked off her sandals, they managed to push down both her jeans and her panties. The bad news was he stopped touching her breasts to do it.

Then she was naked in her living room, which seemed awkward. But before she could try to figure out what to do next, Nathan urged her to sit on the sofa.

"We're going to do it here?" she asked.

He knelt between her thighs and gave her a smile that spoke of a man who was very comfortable with his skill set. "Why waste time traveling?"

Good question, she thought as he reached between her thighs and parted her skin. Then he bent forward and gave her the most intimate kiss of her life.

His tongue was soft and warm and wet and he used it to explore every inch of her. He found the places that made her squirm and sigh and that one spot that made her want to beg.

He went slowly at first, setting up a rhythm that seemed impossibly leisurely, especially when all she wanted was more. But then she relaxed and forced herself to accept his pace. After a while she even started to like it.

He moved over that one sensitive place at first. Slipping around it, ignoring it, then brushing it again. She tensed in anticipation before relaxing again. Wasn't the journey supposed to be the best part?

She kept her eyes closed, all the better to feel what he was doing, and did her best to ignore the fact that she was naked, with a man between her legs in her living room.

Over and over he touched her, patiently driving her higher and higher. Tension pulled her muscles tight. He circled again, this time brushing that spot more firmly, more regularly. Her breathing quickened as she moaned her pleasure.

Nothing was supposed to feel this good. Nothing ever had. She had forgotten her body was capable of this kind of sensation.

She spread her knees farther apart, wanting more of what he was doing. As she grew closer and closer to a release that would probably cause her to explode from the inside out, she began to pulse her hips. Tremors claimed her. She clutched at the cushions, wanting the crash.

Pleasure heightened, pushing her until she didn't have any control. "Don't stop," she begged, needing what he was doing more than she'd ever needed anything.

Unexpectedly, he began to suck on that swollen center, while flicking it with his tongue. The sensations became so intense, she knew she was about to lose control. Pressure built as release became inevitable. She was hurtling toward that perfect moment and there was nothing anyone could—

Her orgasm crashed through her with the subtlety of a train. It knocked her back, made her shake and shudder and scream. Every cell got involved; every inch of her skin quivered. Her entire body found bliss as her release flowed through her.

On and on, an endless river of rippling ecstasy. It was as if she'd spent the past ten years storing up for this moment and she was going to get every drop she was owed.

After nearly a minute, Kerri became aware that maybe she was carrying this on a little too far. After a few more seconds, she told herself she could stop, but it all felt too good. As long as he touched her, she kept on coming. Could a person actually die from too much sexual pleasure?

Awkwardness battled selfish need and awkwardness won.

"I'm, ah, you can stop now," she said, trying to hide the fact that a delicious contraction continued to rip through her.

Nathan raised his head and smiled at her. "I don't think so."

"What?"

He slipped two fingers inside of her, filling her, stretching her, making her gasp and bear down on him.

He moved them in and out, mimicking the act of love, forcing her over the edge again. With his other hand, he rubbed her swollen center. She probably could have handled that, but then he leaned in and licked her nipples and she had no choice but to come again, clutching at him, pulling her knees back, wanting everything he could give her.

"I can't stop," she breathed.

"Then don't. Dammit, Kerri, do you know how much this is turning me on? I want to be inside of you. I want to feel you coming while I'm there."

"What's stopping you?"

He stared at her for a long second, then shifted back and reached for the belt on his slacks.

It took him about three heartbeats to get his pants and briefs down and pull a condom out of his pocket. Then he was protected and thrusting inside.

His erection felt a whole lot better than his fingers, she thought, as he pushed his way inside. He was large enough to stretch her, to fill her, to hit all the right spots.

He grabbed her hips. She arched into him, taking his thick length and then surrendering to another wave of release. He took her again and again, and she came and cried out and held on for the ride of her life.

At last her exhausted body gave up. The ripples trickled away as she held on to him. Then he pushed one last time and groaned. She felt his body stiffen as he came.

Five minutes later they were facing each other across the sofa. She'd pulled on a robe, he'd pulled up his pants. As they stared at each other, she had the feeling this was going to be a defining moment in their relationship. Which could be really interesting, because Nathan actually looked…sheepish.

"You probably want an explanation," he said.

For what? The sex? Hadn't they both wanted it? "Okay," she said cautiously.

"It was that first kiss. I didn't know what the deal

was. Were you playing a game because of the money or was it real? I couldn't be sure. I just knew how sexy I found you. The more I got to know you, the more I wanted you. I was hopeful more than anything."

Even though he was speaking English, Kerri would have appreciated some subtitles. Or at the very least, a soft-voiced announcer explaining that what Nathan really meant was…and then fill in the blank.

"I have no idea what you're talking about," she said.

"The condom. I had a condom with me because I'm an optimist. I wasn't expecting anything."

Oh. Was that all? "I'm glad you planned ahead."

"You're not mad?"

"Do I look mad? Mad would require more energy than I'll have in the next five years. I'm totally drained. I've never experienced anything like that in my life."

He grinned like a proud male and moved closer. "It was good."

"Are you asking or telling?"

"I know it was good."

She'd just experienced the longest orgasm in modern history. Who was she to be critical? "It was amazing."

He cupped her face and kissed her. "We could do it again."

"I don't think that's possible."

Instead of answering, he bent down and drew her nipple into his mouth. Then he reached between her legs and lightly touched her.

Instantly jolts shot through her. She found herself wanting to pull him close and beg to be taken.

He drew back. "What do you think?"

She looked into his amused eyes. "That maybe I might have a little more time to make up for."

"I figured."

"Did you bring more condoms?"

"Yes."

"Thank God."

CHAPTER SIXTEEN

KERRI HOVERED outside of Cody's room. She rubbed her hands on her jeans, then smiled and walked in.

"How you doing?" she asked. "Is the game going well?"

Cody paused his video game and looked at her. "I'm fine."

"Good. Good. I was thinking of maybe making cookies or something. Would you like that?"

Cody stared at her as if he'd never seen her. "Mom, you're acting weird."

"What? How?"

"You keep coming in here and checking on me. Are you okay?"

"I'm perfect. Really. Just terrific. I'm not checking on you that much."

"You've been in here three times since I came home."

Had she? Guilt was a powerful force in the universe. Too bad she couldn't use it for good.

"I, um, guess I missed you while you were at

Brandon's," she murmured, knowing she hadn't actually thought about Cody once in those few hours. She'd been too busy having hot monkey sex with Nathan.

"Go back to your game," she told him. "I'll leave you alone."

"Okay." While he didn't sound as if he believed her, he did return his attention to the space creatures on the TV screen. She backed out of the room and vowed to quit acting like an idiot.

Once she was in the kitchen, she started emptying the dishwasher. Maybe housework would distract her. There were always a thousand things to do at home. Cleaning, dishes, laundry. She could change her sheets and—

Kerri squeezed her eyes together. Thinking about the sheets reminded her of the bed and the bed reminded her of Nathan.

She straightened and crossed to the window. It wasn't that she *wanted* to regret being with him. She liked him and respected him. He'd been good to her and Cody. He was a friend. He mattered. Not to mention the fact that he'd made her feel things that were beyond anything she'd ever experienced before.

She brushed away a whisper that Brian was supposed to have been the best. In truth they'd been young and inexperienced together. He'd been with one other person and she'd been a virgin. Sex had been fun and, given more time, they would have figured it all out. Nathan had time and practice on his side.

She closed her eyes as she remembered the feel of his hands on her body. The way he'd touched her, she'd had no choice but to surrender. But it wasn't just about the pleasure. In his arms, she'd felt safe for the first time in a long time. She'd felt as if she belonged. As if they belonged.

Which was the problem—she wasn't supposed to have a life. It wasn't part of the deal. So after making love with Nathan, all she could do was wait for whatever bad thing that was going to happen.

She knew that, logically, there wasn't any punishment lurking. Life wasn't that tidy. But she couldn't shake the feeling. She had to give everything to Cody. She'd always accepted that, embraced it even. Giving willingly because there was nothing else she wanted. Only now she wanted more.

She wanted her son to be well and she wanted something for herself. A chance to be happy with a man. And not just any man—she wanted a chance with Nathan King.

As the truth settled into her bones, she sucked in a breath against the pain. Because Nathan wasn't up for grabs. Not only was he rich and powerful and he moved in a different world, he wasn't interested. Hadn't he told her that he didn't allow himself to care? That no one got in? She had a feeling he hadn't been lying.

Even if she was allowed to have more, Nathan was the wrong man to have it with.

ABRAM STOOD in the center of the lab, his fists clenched, his body tense. The evidence of failure sat before him, a few typed numbers from a report. How could so little information mean so much?

"Dr. Wallace, we'll get it right next time," one of the other scientists told him. "We're close. We can all see that we're close. We'll try again. Vary the levels."

The woman kept talking, but Abram couldn't hear her. He could only see the failure and remember how Kerri Sullivan had brought her son to the lab. When the boy died, it would be his fault.

He walked away from the still-talking woman and went into his office, where he closed the door and sank into his chair.

He'd been so sure, so confident. He'd believed in his gut that they were on to the solution. That they were close. And now there was nothing but failure.

Linda knocked on his door, then entered. "I have requisitions for you to sign," she said. "More lab equipment. It's nice to have the money to buy new—" She frowned. "What's wrong?"

"The experiments failed. I was so sure. Now there's nothing. I keep thinking about that boy. Cody. I can't save him."

Linda crossed to him and crouched in front of

him. "You don't know that. You're not going to give up. You're going to review the experiments and look at what you can change, what you can get better."

She was so beautiful, he thought as he stared into her blue eyes and saw the total faith blazing there.

"I have nothing left," he told her.

"Bullshit. You're not allowed to give up. We've been through this before."

He nodded slowly. "I'm not giving up. I'll never give up. I know it takes time, but I feel the weight of that small boy with me everywhere. I have to save him. I promised I would try. But will it be enough? Time is my enemy."

"Cody's, too."

Her hand was on his thigh. He took it in his, looking at her long fingers, the painted nails. Bright pink, he thought. A ridiculous color. Yet so right on her.

"They talk to me now," he said. "The people in town. They talk to me. I know it's because of the lab. The jobs, the opportunity. If I fail, I fail them all."

Linda pulled her hand free and stood. "First, you're not going to fail. I refuse to believe that. Second, they've always talked to you. You just never noticed before. You were too busy feeling sorry for yourself."

He stood and faced her. "Is that what you think of me?"

"Not anymore."

"But before?"

She shrugged. "You were mopey."

"Then why did you stay?"

"Where else was I supposed to go?"

She'd been with him nearly twenty years and until these past couple months, he wasn't sure he'd ever seen her before. Emotion crashed through him—unfamiliar and terrifying. He wanted to pull her close and hold on like he would never let go. He wanted to beg her to stay. He wanted her to tell him again how she believed in him, because her belief had power.

"Don't leave me," he said, his voice low and hoarse, his hands clenched into fists to keep from dragging her to him. "Please, don't leave me."

She smiled. "Abram, I haven't left yet. Why would I leave now?"

His throat tightened. "You are too good to me."

"That's true. You don't appreciate me enough. Always the absentminded scientist. Always thinking of your work."

"Not always," he told her, and lightly touched her cheek. "I haven't been there for you. Not the way I should have. I've taken you for granted. You could have left a thousand times. No one would have blamed you."

"Where else would I go?" she asked again.

He hadn't realized how he'd been living in darkness until there was suddenly light. "My ex-wife complained that I loved the work more than her. That I wouldn't notice when she was gone. She was right.

It's not like that with you. I can't survive without you. I am a selfish man who gets lost in what he does. You have no reason to care about me. I accept that. But I love you, Linda. Perhaps I always have."

He dropped his hand. "Why would I tell you that today? When I've failed? I'm a fool."

"You're not," she told him, then raised herself onto her toes and pressed her mouth to his. "Today is the perfect day. I love you, too, Abram. Moping and all. You're brilliant and I have complete faith in you."

She loved him? Why? What chain of events, what quirk of fate, would allow him to be so fortunate?

Energy swept through him, filling him with ideas. In a nanosecond, there were possibilities where there had only been failure.

"She was right," he said more to himself than Linda. "Varying the levels could change everything. I must get back to the lab."

He turned to leave, then hesitated. "Should I say more to you? Do you want me to stay?"

Linda smiled, brightening the room and causing his old, nerdish heart to flutter. "I want you to find a miracle."

"I'M NOT SURE about this," Kerri muttered as Nathan led her through the downtown Nordstrom. "It feels borderline icky. Cheap even."

He took her hand and pulled her along. "We're looking in the designer section. It won't be cheap."

SUSAN MALLERY   299

"That doesn't help." She pulled her hand free and stopped in the middle of the aisle. "I'm not comfortable."

"Why?"

"Because."

He was far better at power plays than she would ever be, she discovered as he simply stared at her.

"You're buying me clothes," she said, her voice low.

"I asked you to go to a charity event with me. It's formal. Your lifestyle doesn't lend itself to dressing for events like that. The deal is you help me out, not that you incur expenses."

Now he was talking like an accountant, she thought with a sigh. Even though he was telling the truth. There was no way she could have afforded a suitable dress. Nathan's logic made perfect sense, but she didn't have to like it.

Maybe what she really hated was the reminder that there were too many differences between them. When they were alone, it was easy to pretend they might have something in common, but here…not so much. Not in an elegant store surrounded by pricey merchandise. While she'd never actually been in the designer department, she had a feeling the clothes there went for a whole lot more than she paid in rent. Possibly more than she'd paid for her car.

"I know a couple of great thrift stores," she muttered. "Or we could have gone to a consignment store."

He raised his eyebrows.

"Not your style," she said.

"Not my style. Come on. We have an appointment."

She blinked at him. "Excuse me?"

He took her hand again. "We have an appointment with one of the shoppers. She'll help with coordinating shoes and an evening bag. Whatever you need."

Kerri had never made an appointment to shop. The most organized she ever got was being at Target at five in the morning after Thanksgiving to pick up a couple of bargains for Cody for Christmas. She had certainly never used a shopper.

The "she" in question was a tall, slender beauty in her forties named Antonia. She was graceful, well dressed and spoke with a slightly foreign accent. Kerri immediately wanted to be her.

Antonia introduced herself, shook hands, then stepped back and studied Kerri. Kerri pressed her lips together to keep from apologizing for the worn jeans and T-shirt.

Either Antonia was used to badly dressed clients, or she was too polite to notice. She smiled at Kerri and said, "I am familiar with the event in question." She wrinkled her nose. "Very expensive dresses and jewelry, but they are a little short on good taste, yes? You have a beautiful face and wonderful figure. You will be a goddess. They will all whisper, wanting to know who you are. It will make for an excellent evening. What do you think?"

"That if you can make that happen, it will be amazing."

Antonia laughed. "I have so much to work with. Your excellent genetics and Mr. King's credit card. Both make my job very easy. Come. This way. I have picked out a few dresses. We will see how they look on you. That will give me an idea for direction."

As they walked toward the dressing area, Nathan leaned close. "Good trick," he murmured in Kerri's ear. "She put both of us in our places."

"At least you have value because of your business success. I'm nothing but good genetics."

He grinned at her. "I've always admired that about you."

"Don't let my excellent bone structure fool you. I know how to throw a punch. I could have you doubled over in pain and gasping for breath in about three seconds."

"Tough talk."

They stared at each other, both smiling. Kerri found herself getting lost in his eyes, in the humor there, and something else she wanted to call affection. She knew he liked her, so it wasn't a huge stretch. What she didn't know was how much he cared. Was it friendship or something more?

She started to tell herself it didn't matter, when suddenly she realized it did. It mattered a lot. She wanted Nathan to think well of her, to like her. But why? He was a means to an end. At least he had been.

Panic swelled up like a blowfish, making her stomach hurt and her chest tighten.

Don't think about it, she told herself. This wasn't the time. They were shopping. She needed to focus. She would panic later, when she was alone and could think things through. Tonight she would wrestle with the fact that she'd been so busy being sure no one could possibly touch her heart that she hadn't noticed someone had.

"Mr. King, I have the *Wall Street Journal* here for you, along with the remote." Antonia motioned to a comfy-looking leather chair in front of a flat-screen television.

"Would you like me to order you coffee or something to eat?" she asked.

Nathan shook his head. "No, thanks."

"If you change your mind, let me know."

"I will."

Kerri leaned close. "It's not like this at the discount store, although you can certainly go stand in electronics and catch the game."

"I'll keep that in mind." He gave her a push. "Quit stalling and go find a dress."

"Yes, O great leader."

She followed Antonia into the biggest dressing room she'd ever seen. There was a full three-way mirror against one wall, a love seat and five dresses hanging on hooks on the walls.

Each was more beautiful than the one before.

There was a midnight-blue strapless gown with a draping skirt, a pale pink slip dress with exquisite lace and beading at the bodice and tulip hem. A simple black dress seemed out of place until Antonia turned it, exposing the plunging back.

"I don't have a bra that will work with any of these," Kerri said.

"Not to worry. Someone from our lingerie department will be by shortly to fit you with an assortment of bras. Everything is to be perfect."

Kerri wasn't sure she was up to perfection, but she kept that thought to herself.

Twenty minutes later her breasts had been through their most thorough exam ever. She had been fitted for several bras, each designed to go under a different dress. Any lingering hint of shyness had long since disappeared. There was nothing like having a tiny woman in her sixties staring at one's breasts to get over the whole being-naked-in-front-of-strangers thing.

Antonia slipped a long, flowing print dress off the hanger and held it out. "We'll start here. The pattern is bold enough to be noticed, but not so large as to overwhelm your body."

"Lord knows we don't want that," Kerri murmured as she stepped into the dress and pulled it up. Antonia worked the side zipper, then fluffed the skirt and walked around Kerri.

"We can pull it in some," the personal shopper

said, apparently talking to herself. "The straps sit well. I don't like the way the front hangs."

She moved in front of Kerri and began gathering pinches of fabric. Kerri stood still, waiting to see how this all would end. Finally Antonia stepped back.

"What do you think?"

"That I don't love it. I would prefer a solid color."

Kerri half expected to be told she was wrong, but Antonia only nodded.

"Then that's what you will have."

Three dresses later, Kerri held the midnight-blue strapless dress in place while Antonia fastened it in the back. There was a zipper and several small hooks and eyes. The bodice was tight, pushing up Kerri's boobs until she looked positively lush. Of course, some of that was the very expensive, very well-fitted bra she had on.

Antonia set a pair of metallic high-heeled sandals on the carpeted floor. "Try these on. With a long dress, a sense of length and height is important."

Kerri slipped into the shoes, then stared at her reflection. She looked tall and thin and sophisticated. All she needed was some serious jewelry and a small dog on her arm and she could easily pass for a B-list starlet.

"I like it," Kerri said.

"I agree." Antonia fluffed her hair. "Up, I think. In a simple but sophisticated style. Some jewelry and you'll be set. Come. You can show Mr. King."

Kerri wasn't sure if she was being offered a suggestion or given an order. Either way, she walked out of the dressing room to the alcove where Nathan waited.

He glanced up from his paper, then set it aside and stood. "Wow."

"Wow's good."

"You're beautiful. The dress isn't bad, either."

She laughed. "Flattery really works." She turned in a slow circle. "I love the dress. I love it with a fiery passion that borders on unnatural."

"Should I be jealous?"

"Of course. You don't make me look nearly this good."

"Can you dance in it?"

Before she could answer, he slipped one hand around her waist, grabbed her fingers with the other and began moving to an imaginary beat only he could hear.

Kerri laughed as he dipped her, then caught her breath as she straightened.

There it was again—a sort of fluttering inside. One that warned her she was in big, big trouble. Telling herself he was the wrong man didn't seem to be working, so she reminded herself that there was more at stake than her foolish heart. There was the life of her son.

She stepped back. "So you like it?" she asked, not looking at him. "I haven't dared ask what it costs. I don't think I want to know. I'm going to need shoes, too. I'm sure I can find some at a consignment store."

He stared at her for a long time, as if he knew what she was thinking. As if he understood there were choices to be made and that when the outcome was her son's life, there wasn't much of a decision.

"If you like those shoes, we'll get them," he said at last. "Or you can try on more."

"No, these work." She reached out to touch him, then dropped her hand to her side. "The dress is beautiful. Thank you."

"You're welcome."

"I have no idea where I'll wear it again. There aren't exactly formal events in Songwood."

"You'll figure out something."

They were still only feet apart, but she actually felt him moving away. Emotional distance yawned. He knew her well enough to understand what was wrong. She knew him well enough to know he didn't agree or approve. That he thought she was punishing herself and possibly him for something that neither of them could control.

She wanted to explain, but what was the point? Their positions were clear.

"Thank you," she whispered again.

"Something to remember me by."

She bit her lower lip. "I'm sorry."

"You can't change what you believe. Not when you don't want to."

She walked back into the dressing room and waited for Antonia to return and unfasten the dress.

As she stood in front of the triple mirror, she wondered why her reflection was so blurry. Then she saw the tears on her cheeks.

How odd, she thought. It had been years since she'd cried for herself. Until now, all her tears had been spent on Cody. Until now, she'd had nothing else to lose.

NATHAN STOOD outside the apartment building and stared at the main door. There wasn't a doorman, or even a lock. Anyone could go inside. Yet he felt as if there were a thousand miles between him and Frankie's apartment and light-years between him and Frankie.

He told himself there was no point in speaking with her. While he didn't know what she was going to say specifically, he could guess the message. Still, he felt compelled to reach out, to try to…what? Connect? Was that possible? Wasn't he doing her a favor by staying away?

A coward's question, he told himself as he crossed the street and entered the building. He climbed the stairs to the right floor, then knocked on her door.

She answered without asking who was there, then stared at him across the threshold.

"Hello, Frankie," he said quietly. "How are you?"

She looked like crap—wild-eyed and pale. Her clothes were mismatched and oversize, her hair was stringy. She wasn't the pretty younger sister he remembered, but then he doubted he'd lived up to her memories, either.

"Go away," she told him, her fingers clutching the edge of the door so tightly they turned white. "Go away."

"I want to talk to you."

"I'll bet you do. You want me to change my mind. Ha! That's never going to happen. I'm speaking at the hearing. Did you know that? I sent in a letter and they've agreed. I have so much I want to say. I have facts and figures and sad pictures of dying fish and animals. I'm not going to talk about the plants. No one cares about them. Not really. But if it has fur and big eyes, I'll get TV time." She smiled. "You are so screwed."

"Is that what you want?" he asked. "Will that make things better?"

"It won't make them worse. I hate you, Nathan. Hate you. Do you hear me?"

He did, and the words were so profoundly sad that he ached for her—for them both. She was his sister—he was supposed to take care of her. But he'd failed her and she would never forgive him for that. Fair enough—he hadn't forgiven himself.

"I'm sorry," he told her. "I'm sorry for not being there. I was a kid and I just…"

"I was younger," she shrieked. "I was younger, Nathan, and you left me alone. With him. Every day was worse. I begged you to come home, but you wouldn't. You were gone and I was alone."

Tears filled her eyes. She brushed them away. "So now you'll pay. I'm going to destroy you." The smile returned. "I'm your sister. I think people are going to find it real interesting that I'm so against your towers. People don't like you, Nathan. You haven't made a lot of friends. You're too rich, too mean. You're a bastard. People like the underdog. That's me."

She trembled as she spoke and there was an eerie light in her eyes.

"I don't care about the towers," he said. "I care about you. You need help."

"You'd like that, wouldn't you? You want to lock me away. Get rid of your problem by locking it away. That's not going to happen."

"I don't want to lock you away. I want to make things better."

"You can't," she screamed. "They're dead. Dead. Dead." She went pale and her voice dropped. "I'll stop you. That's what matters. Go away."

She slammed the door and locked it. He stood in the hallway and listened to his sister count to four over and over. He ached for her and some for himself. For what he'd callously thrown away, never imagining how much it would matter later.

She'd been right. He'd only wanted to escape. He'd ignored her pleas because he'd been young and selfish and busy. Now they were both paying the price.

"Did I do this to you?" he asked aloud.

The hallway was empty, but that didn't matter. He already knew the answer.

He had.

CHAPTER SEVENTEEN

KERRI HAD NEVER BEEN at a commission hearing before and she hoped to never repeat the experience. The panel sat in front of a dais, behind desks. There were several people down in front, then a packed hearing room filled mostly with protesters and the press.

She was tucked into a corner, her goal to be supportive and yet unnoticeable. She wasn't sure she could do one without triggering the other, but she was going to do her best.

She pressed a hand to her churning stomach and wished away the pain in her belly. From where she was sitting, she could see Nathan. He looked calm, as if this meeting was no big deal, when she happened to know he had nearly a billion dollars on the line.

So far the speakers that were called had been spread fairly evenly. There had been a couple of good points against the towers, with more in favor. But Kerri couldn't relax. Not after reading the *Seattle Times* that morning and learning that Nathan's own sister would be speaking against him.

She told herself that it wouldn't matter. That Frances King was part of a fringe environmental group and no one would be impressed by whatever she had to say. Unfortunately she knew that having a family member speak out against the towers wasn't going to be good, no matter how anyone spun it.

Kerri sucked in a deep breath and willed herself to relax. Whatever happened, happened. She was not part of the outcome. Nathan was used to this sort of thing. He'd prepared. He'd—

A petite brunette stood up and approached the witness chair. She had dark hair and pale skin. There was something strange about the way she moved. Something stiff or jerky or…

Kerri leaned forward as she saw a resemblance between the woman in her early thirties and the man Kerri had come to know really, really well.

"This is it," she murmured to herself.

If she'd had any prayers left, she would have offered one up. But all her faith was reserved for Cody. Still, she crossed her fingers and hoped for the best.

"Please state your name," the clerk said.

"Frances King."

"Ms. King, you've asked to speak with us today on the matter of Mr. King's request to build his towers on the edge of the sound." The commission member frowned. "You have the same last name."

"He's my brother."

"I see. And you're against the towers?"

"Very much." Frankie, as Nathan called her, pulled several papers from her bulky purse. "While I support everyone's right to make a living, there is no need for this monstrosity to exist simply to satisfy the overblown ego of Nathan King. Development should be a celebration of a culture and a people. It should be in service of those who live around it. Take the Seattle Center. There are concerts and open spaces. Restaurants, plays, street performers. You don't have to like fish to enjoy an afternoon at Pike Place Market. But Mr. King's plan is not for the citizens of Seattle. Not unless they have a few million dollars to spare."

She took a sip of water from a bottle she'd brought with her. "My brother doesn't care about ordinary people. Only those with the means to pay for what he proposes. There's no way any of us could afford to live there. I certainly couldn't. I have a one-bedroom apartment. It's next to one of his other projects. I don't get a lot of sun in my windows."

She gave a slight smile. The knot in Kerri's stomach doubled in size.

"But there is more at stake here than a condo with a view for the very wealthy," Frankie continued. "There are hundreds of indigenous species in the sound that are at risk. Hundreds that will go extinct if these towers are built. Not just tiny little single-celled organisms we have trouble seeing, but beautiful birds and animals. These creatures have as much right to live as we do. As much right to be safe. My brother has made a habit out of not caring about anyone but himself. That's wrong. Someone has to stop him. I can't. I hope you will."

Kerri held in a groan as Frankie finished. The other woman stood and suddenly her odd manner and ill-fitting clothes didn't matter. She'd made her point eloquently and with great conviction. Kerri wanted to side with her and she was supposed to be on Nathan's team.

Later, when the presentations were complete and the commission had adjourned to consider the vote, Kerri left the building and stepped into the back of Nathan's limo. Their prearranged plan was that he would join her as soon as he'd finished with the press and they would go out to dinner. She wondered if he would be much in the mood to eat.

It took him nearly forty minutes to make his way to the car. "Sorry," he said as he settled next to her and Tim got behind the wheel. "I didn't mean for you to wait so long."

"It's okay," she told him. "How are you?"

"Screwed." He loosened his tie. "Wrong project at the wrong time."

"You don't think you're going to get the permits you need?"

He looked at her. "Do you?"

"Your sister was very convincing."

"She always did have a way with words. Even before things went to hell."

"Jason mentioned an appeal process," she reminded him. "So if you don't win now, you'll win later."

"I'm not going to appeal."

Kerri didn't know what to think, what to say. She knew how much the towers meant to Nathan, what they represented. The two of them had a deal because of the towers.

"You don't mean that," she told him. "You can win. I'll help. There's more I can do. I'm sure of it. We'll come up with a plan."

He pulled his tie free and shoved it into his jacket pocket. "I appreciate the sentiment, but what for? It's over."

"No way. You don't give up. It's one of the reasons you are so successful. You can't give up. How much have you already invested in this project? Are you seriously going to walk away from all that?"

"Yes."

She wasn't sure she would have been more surprised if Nathan had told her he'd decided to become a woman.

"I don't believe you."

He reached for the decanter of Scotch and grabbed a glass. "Want a drink?" he asked.

"No, thanks."

He poured himself a healthy amount, then swallowed it. "I'm not fighting the decision. I know it doesn't make sense. It's business. I always win in business." He glanced at her. "It's just a feeling in my gut. I don't need my name on a building to prove anything. I'm walking away."

How? He'd been so focused, so sure. They'd made a deal based on how much he wanted the towers. There had to be a good—

"Is it because of Frankie?" she asked. "Does this have something to do with your sister?"

Nathan poured himself a second drink. "Maybe. I don't know."

"What's wrong with her?" Kerri asked softly.

"A lot of things. She has some phobias. Obsessive-compulsive disorder. God knows. She's never been tested or diagnosed." He laughed, but the sound was harsh. "Or maybe she has been. It's not like I kept in touch."

He sipped his drink, staring out the window. Kerri wondered if he saw the streets of Seattle or something else entirely.

"My father worked for the navy in Bremerton. He was a civilian. Blue-collar work, mostly construction. It was a hard way to make a living, which suited him. He was a hard man." Nathan shook the glass. "He loved to drink. He wasn't bad when he was sober, but when he was drunk, he was mean, and that was most of the time. He hit my mom a lot. Beat her up every now and then. That was always his answer to something he didn't like—beat his wife."

Kerri didn't know what to say. She'd researched Nathan and nothing had even hinted at a difficult childhood. She knew he'd grown up without a lot of money, but not this.

"When I was about five or six, he started going after me, too. That lasted until I was fourteen and big enough to hit back." He finished his drink and poured a third. "I remember talking to my mom, begging her to leave. She said she couldn't. That she couldn't support us herself and that she'd married for better or worse. Those vows meant something to her."

He shook his head. "The only good thing was that he wouldn't beat Frankie. He'd slap her from time to time, but compared with what was happening to Mom and me, it wasn't much. Frankie always said it was because he knew I wouldn't let him get away with it. That I would come after him and kill him. Maybe she was right. I don't know. I did protect her from other bullies. In school, in the neighborhood. We used to talk about running away together, about how it would be when we were grown-up. I always thought we'd be close forever."

Nathan set down the glass and rubbed the bridge of his nose. "Then I got a football scholarship to USC. Frankie begged me not to go, but I couldn't wait to get out of there. I packed my bags and took a plane to sunny Los Angeles."

Kerri swallowed against the rising bile in her

throat. She didn't know how the story was going to end, but she sensed it wasn't a happy resolution.

"He never hit her, but he still tortured her," Nathan said, his voice flat as if he wasn't willing to give away any emotion. "Calling her names, telling her she was stupid and useless. She'd never been emotionally strong and I'm sure being the center of his sick attention only made things worse."

He looked at Kerri. "I ignored her. When she called and said she couldn't take it anymore, I told her to go stay with a friend. I'd found where I wanted to be and I wasn't leaving for anyone."

"You were barely eighteen."

"I was plenty old enough to know what he was capable of. I had a responsibility to her. She was my sister and I walked away." He swore, then continued. "Apparently it was too much for my mother. The day Frankie graduated from high school, she walked in to find our parents dead. My mother had killed my father, then shot herself. I've seen the police reports. It wasn't pretty. There was blood everywhere."

Kerri felt sick to her stomach. "I'm sorry."

"Me, too. Frankie had to deal with all of it because I was too damn busy at college. I flew up for the funeral. She blamed me for everything, then screamed at me to leave her alone. I did. I walked away because it was easier than dealing with her pain. She was eighteen, so the state left her alone. Even back then I was a heartless bastard."

"You were young and selfish. There's a difference."

"Not a big one. You don't have to make excuses for me, Kerri. I've been doing it long enough. I deserve whatever blame there is. Frankie is the way she is because of me. Because I couldn't be bothered. When I came back to Seattle a few years later, I looked her up. She'd become…strange. It made me uncomfortable, so I disappeared again, this time sending money. I told myself it was enough. Supporting her financially paid my debt. We both knew better. By the time I knew I had to reach out to her, she was too far gone. You're right to be wary of me. I let her down. I've let down everyone I've ever loved."

She ached for him, for the teenager he had been and for Frankie, who had suffered so much.

She slid close and put her arms around him. "You made mistakes. We all make mistakes."

"Not on such a grand scale. I should have taken care of her. I should have been there for her and for Daniel. I should have made it different."

His pain cut her, too. She held him tight, willing him to forgive himself for the past and focus on making it better in the future.

"I've tried to talk to her," he admitted. "I want her to get help. But she doesn't care about that. She wants me destroyed."

"So you're giving up on the towers out of guilt? If you don't build them maybe she'll get better?"

"Something like that."

"Talk about twisted logic."

"Right now it's all I have going for me."

He shifted so he was holding on to her, pulling her close and resting his chin on her head. "Thanks for listening and not saying anything."

"I won't judge you."

"You should. I deserve it."

Too much pain, she thought sadly. For all of them. Poor Frankie, who had suffered so much.

"You're a good man," she said. "You're trying to make things right."

"Too little, too late."

"Better late than never."

He looked at her. "Clichés?"

"You're the one who started it."

"That's a mature and well-articulated response."

But he was smiling as he spoke. Smiling and looking at her as if she mattered. As if she was important to him.

She felt it, again. That tightening in her chest. A slight shifting in her heart. Emotion. Hope. Expectation. A need for...

And then she knew. It had been so long, so unexpected now, so unlikely. She hadn't been looking or even trying to fall in love. It had just happened. When she wasn't paying attention, she'd gone and fallen for Nathan.

Panic came on the heels of her revelation. Panic,

because loving anyone wasn't allowed. What would her punishment be?

But before she could totally freak, she took a deep breath and told herself life wasn't that tidy. Love was the answer. It was the higher plane people aspired to. Why would she be punished for falling in love?

Almost believing her logic, she leaned against him. "Now what?" she asked.

"Now I get on with my work. You go back home to Songwood and pick up the pieces of your life."

Which meant what? She wasn't going to see him anymore? After all, he'd only hired her to help with the towers. Nothing more. She'd fallen in love, but did he see her as anything other than an employee?

Wouldn't that be ironic, she thought, not sure whether she should laugh or cry. To have come so far and missed out on the love train because she'd gotten on the wrong car. Or was it the wrong train?

Hmm, maybe a better example was needed.

"Do you still want me to go with you to the charity event?" she asked. "You don't have to say yes. We can return the dress."

He put his finger under her chin and raised it. After kissing her, he said, "I'd still like to go with you. Is that all right?"

Relief was sweet. "Yes. I want to go, too." Not that she cared about hanging out with a bunch of rich people. She just wanted to be with Nathan.

"Then it's a date."

Date. Did he mean that?

Talk about a disaster, she thought. Life had been so much easier when he was just a means to an end and not the man of her dreams.

FRANKIE FOUND her old boss, Owen, at home. She rang the bell, impatient to share the happy news.

He opened the front door. "Frankie. What are you doing here?"

"We won." She pushed past him, into his living room. "We won. The commission isn't going to give Nathan the permits for his towers. Do you know what this means? We made a difference. We'll get funding. We can start back up again. There will be press. We'll be known as the group that took on one of the biggest developers in the country and won."

She couldn't stop smiling. Her cheeks hurt, but it was a good pain. A happy one. "I was terrified, but I got through it. I said everything I wanted to and it came out perfectly. He's finished, or at least broken. That's a start. I've been thinking about what we can take on next. There's talk about a bridge and I was wondering about—"

"No," Owen said quietly. "Frankie, no."

She stared at him. "What do you mean, no? We won."

"It's too late. We're not starting back up. Look, you did a good thing. You did more in an afternoon than we did in three years."

"No. It wasn't just me. It was all of us. It was working together."

He didn't get it. He had to get it. "We'll start up again. We were a great team."

"The team is finished," he told her. "Everyone has new jobs. I start with the EPA on Monday. We all knew it was ending, Frankie. I tried to tell you. It's over. I don't want to try anymore."

"You're giving up? But you can't. There's too much work to do."

Owen sighed. "Melody's pregnant. I can't keep asking her to live in a shithole like this." He motioned to the tiny apartment. "We want to buy a house, have a couple more kids. I need health insurance, Frankie, a regular job that pays."

Horror swept through her. "You're selling out for a paycheck and health insurance?"

"We don't all have rich brothers paying for everything," he snapped. "Some of us don't have the luxury of taking on losing causes."

She flinched. "I used Nathan's money to help the cause."

"The cause was bringing down your brother. Does anything about that strike you as odd?" He shook his head. "Look, I appreciate your effort. We all do. But it's over. You need to get on with your life. Maybe go see a doctor or something."

It was as if he'd slapped her. Frankie put a hand to her cheek, then stepped back. "I don't need a doctor."

"I'm sorry. I didn't mean to say anything."

"I'm not crazy," she yelled. "I'm fine. I'm fine."

"I know. I'm sorry."

Frankie turned and ran from the apartment. She took the stairs because elevators were unsafe, then walked out onto the street.

It was raining, but she didn't notice the drops hitting her. She stood in the rain, counting to four over and over, waiting for the calm the numbers always brought her. She counted until she was drenched and shivering, still waiting. But all she felt was alone and hopeless. Empty, with nowhere else to go.

KERRI PUT THE LAST PIN in her hair. She'd ridden down in the limo with her hair in electric curlers. Very chic. But she needed curls to pin it up in the so-called casual style that was fashionable right now.

After putting on enough hairspray to withstand a hurricane, she dropped her robe on the bed and slipped into her dress. She pulled on the zipper, but knew she would have to leave the hooks and eyes to Nathan. Last she stepped into her high-heeled sandals.

"This is about as good as it's ever going to get," she said as she stared at herself in the mirror. She crossed to the guest bedroom door and opened it. "I'm ready, except for the back. I need you to do some fastening."

Nathan walked into the bedroom and looked her over. "Impressive," he told her. "You're beautiful."

He looked good himself, the black tux emphasizing his good looks and muscled body.

"Thanks," she said. "I'm nervous about the party."

"You'll do fine. The worst you'll have to deal with is everyone staring at you because you're so stunning."

If only, she thought humorously. "I think I can handle it."

"We'll see."

He fastened the back of her dress, then pulled a black velvet box out of his jacket pocket.

"Don't get too excited," he said. "These are on loan."

Borrowed jewelry? Just like the stars on award-show night?

She practically bounced with excitement. "Is it sapphires?" she asked. "Something so big and bold it's tacky. Because I'm comfortable with tacky. Tell me it's huge, please? Please? It's just for the night. I can handle it."

He opened the box and she nearly fell off her high heels.

It was sapphires and diamonds. Lots of both. Big, beautiful stones that glinted and glimmered and screamed that they were fancy and expensive.

The drop earrings had a yummy square sapphire at the top and bottom with an impressive line of diamonds in between. The necklace was more subtle—alternating princess-cut diamonds and sapphires getting larger and larger toward the center. The matching bangle bracelet was a double row of the same.

Kerri's excitement was tempered by the heady math of figuring out how many lifetimes it would take her to pay back the price of anything lost.

"How much is it all worth?" she asked, not sure she wanted to know.

"About half a million."

"Dollars?"

He picked up the necklace and slipped it around her neck. "It would be less in euros."

"Right." Breathe, she told herself. She had to remember to breathe. "You, um, have insurance, don't you?" she asked, trying not to faint as she held up one of the earrings and realized the bottom stone had to be at least three carats.

"Don't worry about it. We're covered."

"Even if I lose a stone? Not that I want to, but it could happen."

He bent down and kissed her shoulder. "Relax. Have fun. Nothing bad will happen."

She wanted him to be right about all of it. She wanted to relax and enjoy the night. All of it.

Rather than make Tim drive her back so late, she was staying over. Michelle had Cody and had promised the same as Nathan—that nothing bad would happen. Of course her friend had also made her promise to spill details about the upscale party and the hot sex sure to follow. Kerri planned to at least talk about the charity event.

Thirty minutes later they walked into the hotel

ballroom. The space was crowded with the well-dressed cream of Seattle society. There was a stage at one end where the auction would be held later, and draped tables along the side with pictures of the various items available through the silent auction.

"You can bid on a trip to Aruba," she murmured, catching sight of one banner. "I've never been to Aruba."

"It's nice," Nathan told her. "You'd like it."

"I don't even have a passport."

"Do you want to get one?"

"Not tonight."

He drew her hand into the crook of his arm. "Ready to be introduced and gawked at?"

"Sure. I'm okay with this. Hanging out with rich people. I've been telling myself they're not all that different. Some are really nice and some are mean and they all have problems."

"Good attitude."

She let him lead her into the first small crowd. There were introductions and a blur of names and faces. Kerri smiled and nodded, making mental notes about dresses and jewelry and who was drinking what.

"You'll get the tower on appeal," one man said. "Damned commission. Why do they have to care so much about the environment?"

"Hard to say," Nathan murmured.

"Without jobs, without a thriving economy, we'll

have plenty of time to hang out with the spotted owl. You'll get them, Nathan. You'll win. You always do."

The man and his wife moved on. Kerri watched them go.

"I like owls," she said.

Nathan laughed. "I'm not surprised."

"So you're not going to tell anyone that you're not appealing?"

"There won't be an announcement. I didn't see the point."

She faced him. "You're giving up because you don't deserve to win?"

"I'm walking away because it's not worth the fight."

As he wasn't someone to give up easily, she had to believe him. But was his decision a good thing or a bad thing? And what was going to happen to them? Was there even a "them" to worry about?

She knew that all she had to do was ask and Nathan would tell her the truth. The problem was she wasn't sure she wanted to hear the truth. Not tonight.

He touched her cheek. "I'm glad you're staying the night," he told her.

"Me, too."

"Would you be more comfortable staying in the guest room?"

She leaned close. "I'm not here for the charity, big guy. I'm here for the sex."

He laughed. "Good. Me, too. I'll go get us both a

drink. What do you want? They have very expensive champagne."

"I'll start with that."

He kissed her cheek. "I'll be right back."

Kerri watched him go.

"He never looked at me like that," a woman in a beautiful black gown said with a sigh. "I would have given anything for it to happen, but it didn't." She smiled at Kerri. "Betina Hartly."

"Hi. Kerri Sullivan."

"Congratulations. I didn't think anyone would catch Nathan. After his divorce, he simply wasn't that interested in getting serious."

Kerri forced herself to keep smiling. "We're not serious." At least she didn't think he was. "We're, um, friends."

"If that was friendship I saw, then he and I were distant acquaintances. It's all right. I don't mean to pry. I guess Nathan is the one who got away. I'm curious." She held up her left hand and wiggled her fingers to show off the massive wedding set there. "Not that I've locked myself away or anything. Still. Nathan. I'm impressed." She smiled again. "Have a nice evening."

Nathan returned with the drinks. "Who were you talking to?"

"One of your old girlfriends. Betina."

"Hartly," he added. "She married into a big banking family."

"Big banks or lots of family members."

"Big banks."

"You dated her for a while."

He sipped his champagne. "Are you asking or telling?"

"Asking."

"A few weeks. It wasn't serious."

It had been for Betina, Kerri thought, wondering whether she would suffer the same fate. Remembering Nathan and knowing he never thought about her.

"Are there a lot of Betinas lurking in the shadows?"

"A few, but you don't have to worry."

Before she could ask why, her cell phone rang. She set down her champagne and reached for it, telling herself there was no reason to panic but already feeling the cold sweeping through her.

"Kerri? Thank God." Michelle's voice shook. "It's Cody. Oh, Kerri, I'm so sorry. Please. You have to come right away."

CHAPTER EIGHTEEN

N ATHAN LOOKED out the window as Kerri changed from her evening gown to the jeans and T-shirt she'd worn that afternoon on the drive down. Her quickly packed suitcase lay at their feet in the back of the limo.

"You'll want these," Kerri said, handing him the jewelry.

He dropped the pieces into his jacket pocket. "You all right?" he asked, knowing the answer and realizing it was a stupid-assed question.

"Fine."

Sure. Her kid had collapsed and was being rushed to the hospital. She was great.

She slipped on athletic shoes and tied them, then pulled pins out of her hair and finger-combed it until it hung in loose curls down past her shoulders. When she finally leaned back in the seat, he turned to her.

"I'm sorry," he told her.

"I know."

"This isn't your fault."

She looked at him, her blue eyes wide and dark with pain. "You're going to tell me that it isn't anyone's fault. That this was going to happen regardless. Cody's disease is progressive. I know the drill."

"But you don't believe it."

"No, and you're not going to convince me. You're the one who won't pursue the condo tower because you think it will make up for you ignoring your sister for years. We all do what we have to in order to get by."

He knew she was right. The problem was he didn't know how much she blamed him for specifically.

"I can stay," he told her. "At the hospital. I want to stay."

"You'll need to get back to Seattle."

"No, I won't."

She stared out the window. "There's nothing you can do to help."

She did blame him. He shouldn't be surprised. He should walk away—it was what she wanted.

But what did he want—from her, from them? Was there a "them"? Kerri had lied and blackmailed her way into his life. He should be happy to be rid of her. But he wasn't.

An hour later they pulled up in front of the hospital. Kerri was stepping out before the car had come to a stop. Despite what she'd said, he went in with her. A frantic woman hovered by the door.

"Oh God, Kerri, I'm so sorry," Michelle said, her eyes filled with tears. "I don't know what happened.

One second he was fine and the next he was on the floor. I was so scared."

"It's okay," Kerri told her. "You didn't do anything. This was going to happen. I'm sorry you had to deal with it."

Nathan moved next to them. "Go find Cody," he said. "I'll talk to your friend."

Kerri nodded and jogged down the hall. He turned to the other woman. "I'm Nathan."

"Michelle. Brandon's mom."

"It wasn't you," he told her. "You couldn't have done anything to stop what happened."

Michelle shook her head. "You can't know that."

"I can. I've been through this already. Beating yourself up won't help. Kerri's going to need a friend. Don't let unnecessary guilt come between you."

KERRI BENT OVER Cody's unconscious body, her hand holding his as she willed him to wake up.

"Come on, baby," she whispered. "Open your eyes. Say hi. Tell me a joke. You know I love your jokes. You make me laugh and right now, laughing would be a good thing. Come on, Cody. Just open your eyes."

Nothing happened. His breathing was steady and she told herself that was a positive sign. She hadn't seen the doctor yet but knew he'd been paged.

Fear gripped her. Icy-cold fingers of terror twisted

around her muscles and made it hard to think about anything but the worst.

Cody couldn't die. Not now. Not without them talking to each other again.

He was pale and looked so small, lying there in the hospital bed. He had an IV in his arm and there were several pieces of scary-looking equipment nearby. Fortunately none of them were hooked up.

"You're not that bad," she said desperately. "Come on, you know you're not. You've got a long way to go. Stay with me. Stay with me. You're strong. I know you're strong. You're always—"

His eyelids fluttered. "Mom?"

"Hey, you." She kissed his forehead. "You really scared Michelle. She's got a streak of gray hair that has your name on it."

He shifted slightly, then groaned. "I hurt."

She pushed the call button. "I'll get the nurse in here. They'll give you something."

He closed his eyes then opened them again. "What happened?"

"I don't know. Michelle said you were fine one minute, then you hit the floor. I'm sure it was impressive. I'm sorry I missed it."

Cody managed a faint smile. "Me, too. My head hurts."

"Rumor has it that you're fine. No permanent damage. You're going to be a little flat on that side, though. It will make finding hats difficult."

He chuckled, then moaned. "Don't. My chest hurts."

The nurse came in. "Mrs. Sullivan?"

"Kerri."

"The doctor is on his way. He'll want to talk to you."

"I'm not going anywhere."

The nurse walked up to Cody and checked his pulse. "Handsome, you're awake. I know you'll want to start making demands. That's what all this is about, isn't it?"

"He hurts," Kerri told her. "Do you have something for the pain?"

"I do, right here." She winked at Cody. "It's magic. I'll put it in the IV. You won't feel a thing." She injected a liquid into the IV line. "Take a couple of breaths and the whole world will look better."

"Thank you," Kerri told her.

"No problem. We're on a schedule here." The nurse smiled at her. "We'll keep him comfortable."

That was important, Kerri knew. Gilliar's Disease was cruel in many ways.

She pulled up a chair and settled in next to Cody's bed. The painkiller went right to work and in a matter of minutes he was sleeping. She waited until she was sure he was comfortable, then went in search of coffee. It was going to be a long night.

As she stepped out of the room, she was surprised to see Nathan in the waiting area. He rose when he saw her.

"You didn't have to stay," she told him. "I thought you'd go back to Seattle."

"I wanted to hang out here for a while. See what's going to happen."

He knew what was going to happen, she thought, suddenly angry. Cody was going to get worse. He was going to suffer. It was going to be awful for all of them.

"I'm not giving up," she told him. "I won't let him go. I know you're going to tell me I should, but I don't believe that. So you can just forget it."

"I agree. Hang on as long as you can."

What? "You don't mean that."

"I do. You have a kind of faith I could never find. Hold on, Kerri. Hold on forever."

He wasn't supposed to say that, she thought as her eyes began to burn. He was supposed to fight her. Being mad at him, at the world, made her strong.

"I don't want you here," she said. "You should go away."

"You need me."

"I don't. I don't need anyone. Cody and I are fine by ourselves. We've always been a team. There isn't room for anyone else. You've only made things worse."

She knew she wasn't making any sense, but that didn't seem to matter. She was desperate to find the inner strength to go on, by any means. Right now she didn't care about fair.

"You still blame me?"

"Yes. For everything. It's all you. Go away. Go away, now."

She sounded like a petulant child, she thought, embarrassed. But calling back the words was impossible.

"You only hired me for the tower project and if that's over, then you don't have any need for me. I'm fine. You have business in Seattle. Take care of things there."

"Kerri, this isn't helping."

"Do you think I care about that? About you? Do you think you matter? You don't. You never will. I only love Cody. Only him. He's all I have."

Tears filled her eyes. She blinked them away, but more came and more until they were spilling down her cheeks.

She wanted to collapse onto the floor and sob out her pain. She wanted to take it all back and tell Nathan the truth—that she'd fallen in love with him. But if she loved him, didn't that mean Cody would die?

Without saying anything, Nathan wrapped his arms around her and pulled her close. She started to fight him but didn't have the strength. It was so easy to sink into him, to let him be the strong one.

She cried, her tears burning, her body shaking. She cried because her son was dying and no matter what she did or how she bargained, she couldn't make him better.

"I don't want him to g-go," she sobbed. "Make it stop. Make it stop."

"You don't know how I wish I could. I hate feeling this helpless, Kerri. I would do anything to save Cody."

She believed him, because he knew. He'd lost a child the same way. He'd suffered and been empty and a thousand other horrors she couldn't begin to imagine.

"I can't do it," she whispered. "I can't be strong for him anymore."

"Sure you can. It's what you're best at. You'll be Wonder Mom because that's what Cody needs to hang on."

"I can't let him go."

"No one is asking you to."

ABRAM HOVERED in the hallway until he was sure the boy was alone. Right now he had nothing to offer Kerri Sullivan and he couldn't imagine facing the grieving mother. When he saw her leave and heard one of the nurses telling her to avoid the beef stew in the hospital cafeteria, he knew he had a few minutes until she returned.

He knocked once on the open door, then stepped into Cody's room. The boy looked at him.

"Hi. I've seen you before. Are you one of the specialists?"

"No. I'm a research scientist."

"Yeah. We went to your lab. The one here in town. Are you going to fix me?"

"I'm still trying." He reached into his lab pocket and pulled out several small bottles. "I'll be taking these to your doctor. Some may make you better, some may make you worse. We just don't know."

Cody looked small in the adult-size hospital bed. He wore pajamas instead of a gown and there were toys piled next to him.

"It would probably be good to start with the one that works."

Abram smiled. "An excellent point. We'll do our best. There's a whole team working on a way to manage Gilliar's. We want to slow the degeneration, but so far we haven't made much progress." He paused and frowned. "Are you too young to hear this? Should I stop?"

Cody managed a smile. "You're the grown-up. You get to decide."

"I think it is better to know than to wonder. What do you think?"

"I want to know." The smile faded. "I'm going to die, aren't I? My mom says I'll be okay, but she kinda has to, you know? It's a mom thing."

"Yes, it is." Abram wasn't sure what to say to the child. He was a great believer in the truth, but this wasn't his son. "There are always questions about what will happen," he said instead. "You've had a better run at the disease than many."

"But I'm still going to die."

"We're all going to die."

Cody closed his eyes. "That's cheating. Don't cheat. Then you're just like everyone else."

Abram pulled up a chair and sat next to the boy. "Yes," he said slowly. "You will die."

"Soon?"

"I don't know. There's so much I don't know."

Cody opened his eyes. "What's it like to die?"

Abram considered the question. "I have no first-hand experience myself," he began, only to stop when the child laughed softly.

"I think it would be bad to have a dead doctor," Cody said with a chuckle. "Even a really good one."

Abram smiled. "An excellent point. What I meant is I'm a research scientist, not a physician. My experience with dying is limited. I know you will be sedated at the end. You probably won't know what's happening. It will be like sleeping and then you'll be gone."

If he was lucky, Abram thought. For some, the pain could not be controlled. He found himself wanting to pray that Cody was one of the fortunate ones.

"It'll be real hard for my mom. I'm the only one she has."

"Death is most difficult on those left behind."

"Thank you for trying," Cody said. "I know my mom kind of forced you."

"She reminded me about what was important." As had Linda. "I will do everything I can to save you, Cody. I have a whole team working on a cure. We all think about you and pray for your recovery."

"Sweet." He shifted, then winced. "Maybe they could do something to make it not hurt so much."

"We'll put that on the list."

A nurse walked in. "It's time for more medication. How does that sound?"

"Good. I'm tired."

"I'll bet you are." The nurse looked at him. "And you are?"

"That's Dr. Wallace," Cody said. "He's going to cure me."

"Lucky you."

Abram held out the bottles. "There are instructions on each of them. The order and the timing is very important. You'll find the approval is already in the chart."

He rose. "Goodbye for now, Cody. I hope to see you soon."

"Me, too. And if you don't find a cure, I'll let you know what it's like to die. So if you have to, you can tell another kid it's okay."

Abram didn't know what to say to that. Unexpected emotion flooded him, making it difficult to speak. He nodded at both of them, then walked out. When he was in the hallway, he leaned against the wall and tried to catch his breath.

He needed a miracle, he thought grimly. A last-minute reprieve. But as far as he knew, there weren't any in sight. If only he'd started sooner. If only Cody Sullivan's disease hadn't progressed so far. If only…

In science there were no if onlys. Just the truth and protocol and more attempts to find the answer.

Which left the very real possibility that they were all going to be too late to save the boy.

KERRI DID HER BEST to relax. Linda had shown up at the hospital and insisted she go home to her own bed, at least for a couple of hours. In theory it was a good idea, but Kerri couldn't stop thinking about Cody, which made it impossible to sleep.

Everything hurt. Her whole body ached because her son was dying and she couldn't do anything about it. She could only stand by his side and pretend to be strong. It sucked. The whole damn situation sucked.

She sat, then rose to her feet and walked into the living room. Tim and Lance looked up from their card game.

"Too wound up?" Lance asked.

"Too everything."

"Want a foot massage?"

Despite everything, Kerri smiled. "You are the sweetest man I know."

"Actually I was offering Tim's services. He does an excellent foot massage."

"Something other people don't need to know," the burly driver muttered.

"Fear not. I'll pass, although I'm tempted. I'm going to make some tea. You guys want anything?"

"We're good," Tim told her.

As she crossed the living room, someone knocked

on her front door. Her body clenched as she wondered if Nathan had returned. He'd gone back to Seattle the day before but had promised to return. She'd told him it wasn't necessary, but he'd insisted and she knew he always kept his word.

She pulled the door open, then frowned when she saw an unfamiliar woman standing there. Who was...

"Frankie?" she asked, recognizing Nathan's sister. "What are you doing here?"

She looked pale and oddly intense. There was something about her eyes that caused Kerri to take a step back. Then Frankie raised a gun and pointed it at Kerri's head.

"So you know who I am. It's because he talks about me, right? You both talk about me and you laugh because I'm so pathetic. You think I'm a joke, but I'm not. I'm someone you have to take seriously.

"Bitch!" she screamed. "Bitch! It's your fault. It's all your fault."

Lance shrieked and Tim stood. Frankie kept the gun on Kerri.

"Move and she dies. I'm crazy so I'll do it. Just ask my brother. He's here, right? I knew he'd be here. He cares about you and that kid. He never cared about me. Even though he pretended to. I believed him. Stupid, huh? He was always smarter than me. That's why he went away. That's why he left me. He knew I didn't matter. But I matter now."

Kerri's heart pounded so hard and fast that it hurt. She barely breathed, not wanting to upset Frankie. And yet a part of her recognized the pain in the other woman. A deep, permanent wound, maybe because she carried a similar scar herself.

"I know how bad it feels," she said quietly. "To lose someone you love."

"We are nothing alike," Frankie yelled. "Don't think you can make friends with me. We are not friends."

"I know. We're strangers who have both been hurt. I was left, too. My husband died. It's horrible. It's like a big hole no one else can see. You keep waiting for people to notice and they don't."

Frankie blinked and the gun dipped. From the corner of her eye Kerri saw Tim inch closer. Then Frankie straightened her arm.

"You can't talk me down, so don't even try. I want Nathan destroyed. I have to make him suffer. If I can't destroy his business, maybe I can destroy someone he cares about. Maybe I can destroy you."

The terror was much colder than Kerri had expected. "I don't care about myself," she breathed, willing the other woman to understand. "But my son is dying. Please, he can't be alone now. He can't."

"Daniel died. I loved him. I loved him so much and I hated him because Nathan loved him, too." Frankie began to tremble. "I was happy when he died. I was happy because Nathan hurt, but then I missed him. He loved me. No one else loved me. Nathan went away. Did he tell you? Did he tell you about the blood? It's not like in the movies."

Frankie took a step back, but she kept the gun aimed at Kerri's face. "I have to count. One, two, three…" She kept counting, her breathing uneven, her body shaking more and more.

"Oh God," she cried, reaching out her other arm so she could hold the gun with both hands. "It hurts. It hurts so much."

She dropped without warning, falling to her knees and letting the gun fall away. "Help me. Help me. I can't be sick like this anymore."

Tim grabbed the gun. "Call nine-one-one," he told Lance, and held the weapon on Frankie.

Kerri ignored him and moved toward the other woman. She knelt down and wrapped her arms around her.

"We'll find a way to make the pain fade," Kerri told her, both relieved and heartbroken. "We'll get you help. We all want to help."

"Nathan?"

"Yes. Nathan. Your brother most of all. He didn't forget, Frankie. He was young and stupid, but he didn't forget."

Frankie began to cry. Kerri held her even after she heard sirens in the distance. She held her through the questioning, the explanations and the argument about whether or not to arrest her or take her to the hospital. She held her until Nathan arrived and took his sister into his arms.

CHAPTER NINETEEN

NATHAN WATCHED Jason and the D.A.'s conversation, unable to tell what was happening by the looks on their faces. If only he'd learned to lip-read, he thought grimly. On the one hand, there was the temptation to make an example of a rich man's family member. Holding Frankie could make for good political coverage.

On the other hand, no one was going to press charges. Kerri hadn't even wanted the police to take his sister away, and neither Lance nor Tim was interested in having Frankie in jail. But she had gone after someone with a gun. That was going to be tough to overlook.

He paced the long corridor, wanting to go into the meeting and demand they all listen. Dumb idea, he told himself. He would only make things worse. He had to let Jason do his job. But he'd never been a patient man and the time went slowly.

As he walked back and forth, he wondered about Kerri. How was she holding up? She'd been brave and determined for days now, staying with Cody, trying to push all her strength into her son. She was driven by love and fear, a powerful combination. He wished he could help, but there was little any of them could do but wait for a miracle that might never come.

Jason walked out of the office and motioned him closer. "He'll deal," he said. "As long as you're willing to put Frankie into a residential facility for at least three months, then monitor her care when she leaves. She's going to have to stay in therapy and on any required medication for at least two years."

"Not a problem."

Jason looked at him. "This means being responsible for her, Nathan. You can't pass this off to a secretary."

The latter was his friend speaking, not his attorney. "I understand. I'll take care of her."

"Then as soon as you find a place, she's free to go. They'll hold the case open until she completes her preliminary treatment, then they'll drop the charges. It's a good deal."

"I agree. I've been making calls. I know where I want her to go. It's just outside of Portland. One of the best facilities on the West Coast. They have an excellent success rate."

"Give me the phone number and contact information. They'll have to fax us proof of admission before she'll be released."

While Jason went to take care of that, Nathan

returned to the jail where he waited in a small room to see his sister.

Frankie looked small and frightened when she walked into the room. He rose, thought about hugging her, but then waited for her to make the first move. She looked at everything but him, then dropped her gaze to her feet.

"You have two choices," he told her, wishing things were different. That he could hug her or tease her or make her laugh. He hated all the distance between them even as he acknowledged that he'd been the one to put it there. "You can be charged with felony assault or you can go into treatment."

"No one wants to be locked away," she said quietly, still not looking at him.

"I know. But, Frankie, this place is nice. The rooms are large and airy. They have real chefs preparing the food and you'll get the help you need. It's not scary."

"Easy for you to say. You won't be the one locked up."

"You need help."

She raised her head then and glared at him. "You think I don't know that? You think I can't see what's happening to me? The ways that I've changed? But I needed to be that way to survive."

"You don't anymore."

"You don't know that."

He ignored her comment. "The place is just outside of Portland, which is good because I'll be coming down a lot." He shrugged. "The doctor I spoke to made it very clear I have issues, too. We'll work through them together."

She stared out the small window. Tears filled her eyes and ran down her cheeks. "I can't trust you," she murmured. "Not ever again. I can't. I won't. You'll just leave again."

His throat tightened. "I can't convince you with words, so I'm just going to have to show you I'm not going anywhere. Please, Frankie. Don't turn this down. It has to be better than jail, right?"

She nodded slowly, then shuffled toward the door. "When do I leave?"

"In a couple of hours. They won't let me visit for a while."

"How convenient."

He held in the instant anger. "I can come in two weeks to visit. I'll be there."

"Don't bother."

He didn't know if she really would rather he left her alone, or if she was assuming he would let her down again. Maybe it was a little of both.

"I'll be there," he said. "You can refuse to see me, but I'll be there."

She reached for the door handle, then turned back to him. "Tell her I'm sorry I scared her like that. I wouldn't have hurt her. She wasn't the one."

Because the one his sister wanted to hurt was him. "I'll tell her. For what it's worth, she already knows."

"Everyone likes to hear an apology."

She opened the door and left.

"YOU'RE ASKING us to break the law," the doctor said sternly.

Kerri had a feeling he used the same tone when he was scolding his children for making too much noise at bedtime.

"I'm asking you to keep a nine-year-old boy from dying," she said. "I've signed the necessary paperwork, so this is a gray area at best. What is more important than that?"

The specialists exchanged looks. "Sometimes you have to be willing to let go, Mrs. Sullivan. For the sake of the patient."

She'd known it was going to come to this. Linda had shown up with a list of instructions from Dr. Wallace. There were combinations of medications to be tried, supplements, a radical change in diet, not that Cody was eating anything, and incredibly high doses of morphine for the pain.

"I'm curious how you think giving up helps my son," Kerri said. "I thought your job was to save people."

"What Dr. Wallace is suggesting is beyond radical. It's risky."

"Isn't Cody dying anyway? As for doing no harm, explain chemo to me. Aren't good cells killed, as well? There are many treatments that do harm. The theory is they do more good in the long run so we accept the potential for harm. That's what we're doing here. If this works, thousands of other children will be spared. Either you do what Dr. Wallace says or I'm taking Cody away."

The doctors stared at her. "You can't do that."

"Of course I can. He can get quality private medical care at home. I would rather he not be moved, but don't push me, gentlemen. I will do anything to save him and you can't stop me."

"Private care is prohibitively expensive," one of them told her.

As if she didn't know. "Do you think money matters to me?"

"You'll destroy yourself financially."

"So what?"

"They won't send out private duty nurses if you can't afford them."

"She can."

Those words came from behind her. Kerri turned and saw Nathan walking toward her. Relief left her weak and trembling. When he put his arm around her, she leaned against him and enjoyed the reprieve.

"I'll pay for it," Nathan said. "If you're going to help, then help. If not, get the hell out of the way."

The doctors looked at each other again. "Fine," one of them said. "We'll get started on the regimen. But know that there is no reason to think it's going to work."

They walked away. Kerri watched them go.

"I guess in their own way, they're trying to help," she said. "Thanks for coming to my defense."

"No problem."

"Dr. Wallace wants to try some different protocols. I have no idea if they'll work." She tried to shake off the exhaustion clinging to her like wet clothes. Most nights sleep was impossible. She was always getting up to check on Cody. "How did it go with the D.A.?"

"He'll drop the charges if she gets treatment."

"Oh good," Kerri said, knowing Frankie was very much the victim. "Jail wouldn't help at all. Did you find a place?"

"Yes. She's on her way there right now. I can't go see her for a couple of weeks. I hope it helps. I want my sister back." He shook his head. "Not that she would believe me. Not after how I've ignored her."

"You both have a lot to work through, but this is a first step."

One corner of his mouth twisted. "I have to go into therapy, too. That's the deal with the facility. They gave me a list of therapists that are approved."

Nathan? In therapy? She couldn't begin to imagine it. "I'm sure it will be helpful. I've always believed we're all crazy to greater or lesser degrees."

"You're not helping and stop grinning."

She laughed. "Am I?"

"Yes, and I don't appreciate it."

"This is obviously a sensitive topic. I won't mention your therapy again. But while you're healing spiritually, you might want to think about yoga. I hear it's wonderful. Or knitting. It's such a relaxing hobby."

His gaze narrowed. "You're not funny."

"Yes, I am."

He slid his hand under her hair so his fingers rested against the back of her head, then leaned in and kissed her.

The contact was more comforting than sexual. She kissed him back, wanting to feel close and connected.

"Don't give up," he whispered. "Don't listen to anyone else. You know the right thing to do."

"Sometimes I'm not sure."

"You always know, Kerri. Trust your heart."

NATHAN WALKED into Cody's room and tossed the signed baseball onto the bed. Cody grabbed it and turned it over in his hands.

"Sweet," he breathed. "They all really signed this?"

"Yeah, and those are real signatures. Not from a machine. I thought you'd enjoy having it while you watched the games on TV. Later, when you're better, we'll go back to Safeco Field and see if we can get through all nine innings this time."

"Thanks. That's great." Cody kept hold of the ball even if he didn't comment on the promise of another trip to the baseball park.

Nathan pulled up a chair. "Your mom went home for a shower. She'll be back in a bit. I thought I'd sit with you for a while."

"I'm okay alone."

"I know, but I'd like some company if that's okay with you."

"Sure." Cody looked at him. "Do you have the limo?"

"I drove myself in a regular car."

"If I were you, I'd always take the limo."

"Sometimes it's fun to drive. You get to be in control."

Cody didn't say anything. Nathan wondered if it was because he felt sick or the fact that he was nine and adults ruled the world.

"Your mom said the new treatments have started," Nathan said. "You doing okay with them?"

"I guess. Nothing's different." He dropped the ball onto the bed and picked at the blanket. "You had a kid, too, right? One who died?"

"Daniel," Nathan said, doing his best to keep his voice even. "He was a few years younger than you."

"So you know what it's gonna be like…for my mom."

"I have an idea."

"Can you tell her…" Cody swallowed, then looked at him. "Can you tell her it's okay to let me go? I know it's gonna be hard and she loves me a lot, but I'm tired and it hurts all the time. I'm not scared.

I talked to Dr. Wallace and he said I'll just go to sleep. And then I won't feel bad. I just need her to be okay and I don't know that she will be. I'm sort of all she has."

Nathan had gotten through Daniel's illness and death without shedding a single tear, but now, hearing Cody's words, his eyes burned even as his heart tightened into a hard, unyielding knot.

He swore under his breath. He was the wrong person to be having this conversation with a dying nine-year-old. There should be someone smarter in the room. Someone with more experience. Someone who knew what the hell he was doing.

The only thing he knew for sure was the regret he felt at letting Daniel go so easily.

He leaned forward and touched Cody's arm. "You're forgetting something. Your mom has special powers. She's Wonder Mom. You've already done so much better than most kids who get Gilliar's. Who's to say you won't keep doing better?"

Cody rolled his eyes. "She's not really Wonder Mom. I know it's all tricks. I don't believe in it."

"I do," Nathan told him.

Cody stared at him. "No way."

"Way. She's powerful and determined. She has heart and faith and loves you. The power of a mother's love can never be underestimated. There's magic in loving someone. It's like a part of the universe changes every time we open our heart. She loves you, Cody. You can feel the love, I know you can. That's worth sticking around for. Even just a little longer."

The boy looked at him for a long time. "You really love her, don't you?"

The question shouldn't have been a surprise, yet it was. And nearly as shocking as those words was the response that came from deep inside. "Yes, I love her."

When had that happened? At what point had she slipped past his defenses to wind her way into his heart?

"I'm glad," Cody said, sounding older than his years even as he picked up the baseball and studied it. "Then she won't be alone. You can be there for her. After."

"You're not going to die," Nathan told him.

"Yes, I am. We all know that. It's just a matter of when."

"THREE DIFFERENT KINDS of burritos, crispy tacos, soft tacos and Dr Pepper," Nathan said as he laid out the food on Cody's hospital tray.

Kerri stared at the array of food. "There's no Taco Bell in town. How did you keep it warm?"

"Heated seats."

Cody grinned, then started to laugh. Kerri laughed, too, because hey, the rich could use their heated seats for anything they wanted.

She laughed until she felt her control slipping. "I'll go get more napkins," she said. "Be right back."

Then she escaped to the hallway where she collapsed into one of the hard plastic chairs and gave in to the tears that were painfully close to the surface.

It hurt, she thought as she brushed her cheeks and wished she had a tissue. It hurt to watch Cody fade away, his body almost shrinking as the disease dissolved his bones.

She felt someone sit next to her, then wrap his arms around her.

"I can't do it," she whispered against Nathan's shoulder. "Everyone is telling me to let him go and I can't. I keep begging him to stay with me. Is that wrong?"

"I let Daniel go too easily. You're his mother and you love him more than anyone ever will. Listen to your heart."

"It's breaking. I can't hear anything but that."

"Cody is your life, Kerri. It makes sense you don't want to release him. When he's gone, you won't have anything else."

Not exactly the words of comfort she wanted to hear. She straightened.

"What are you saying? That I'm keeping him around for me? That I'm selfish?"

His dark gaze was steady. "We always keep the dying around for us."

"Which doesn't answer the question. You think I'm selfish."

"I think you're motivated by the fact that you love

him and want him to live a long, healthy life. But you've also made him the center of your universe. When he's gone, you'll have no reason to get up in the morning."

"So I need a hobby or two? You want to compare that to losing a child?"

"You need to live for more than just your son. You get to have a life, too."

"I don't want a life," she snapped. "I want Cody back."

"I know. I know how it feels. But when he's gone, then what? Do you die, too? Is that the legacy he leaves behind? Do you think Brian wanted you to bury yourself in grief and raising his child? Do you think he would have been happy to know you haven't even dated for ten years?"

Kerri wanted to hit him. "You have no right to judge me. None at all."

"I'm not judging. I'm trying to tell you that there has to be more than just suffering. That whatever happens, you'll go on living. I'm trying to tell you that I love you and that I want some of that living to be with me."

He... "What?"

"I love you, Kerri. Hell of a time to tell you, but there we are. I love you. I want the best for you and Cody. I want us to be together. The three of us, if there's a miracle. If not, then you and I."

She couldn't think, couldn't imagine, couldn't...anything. "You what?"

His mouth twisted. "I love you. Is that such a surprise?"

Longing swamped her. It was thick and powerful and she was shocked by the intensity of her need to launch herself at him, to tell him she loved him, too, that he was everything to her.

But she couldn't. There was Cody and that had to be all that mattered. Nathan *knew* that. Why was he doing this to her? Why was he making it harder?

"No," she said loudly. "I don't want this. I don't want you. You already know, so why are you doing this?"

He grabbed her upper arms. "Kerri, you're not going to be punished for having something for yourself."

"I am. How dare you talk about us having a life without him?" She jerked free of his touch. "Go away. I don't want you here. I won't forgive you for this, Nathan. Not ever. Go." She sucked in a breath and screamed. "Just *go!*"

He looked at her for a long time. In a way the moment was what she imagined an out-of-body experience to be. She felt strange and light, as if she were floating. As if she were watching from a distance.

She could clearly see herself and Nathan. She saw the pain in his eyes and the way he held himself tensely, as if trying to make sure she didn't know she'd hit him hard. She saw herself looking angry and crazy—a mother desperate enough to fight anyone to save her son.

She also saw the pain—it was the silent third party in the room. There was longing, too, and need. They could have been so good together, she thought sadly, feeling compassion as if this were a situation that didn't involve her directly. Now they would have nothing.

Nathan turned and left without saying a word. The out-of-body Kerri watched him go, watched her hand raise slightly, as if she was going to call him back. Then, when she was alone, a huge sob ripped through her body and she collapsed onto the floor. She felt herself fly back into her body, hitting a wall of pain so thick and strong, it would never go away. She cried out desperately and there was no one to hear. No one to comfort her. She'd lost Brian. Cody would be gone in a few days and she'd sent Nathan away. Everyone she'd ever loved would leave her and then she would cease to exist. She would be nothing but a shell with a heart that slowly came to a stop.

CHAPTER TWENTY

ABRAM STARED at the computer screen and willed the numbers to change. He stared so hard his eyes blurred, but the numbers stayed as they were—written proof that he had failed.

The door to his lab opened, but he didn't turn around. There was only one person who would come and check on him in the middle of the night and he was afraid to face her. Afraid to tell her that he had nothing left to give.

Behind him, Linda sighed. "I don't have to ask. I can see the truth on your face."

"The boy is dying and I can do nothing to save him."

"I thought you were giving him new medications and injections."

"They prolong the inevitable for a few hours. Nothing more. We need to do more than stall the destruction. We need to heal, to make progress." The room seemed to slip a little. He grabbed the side of his desk. "I can't save him."

Linda put her arm around his waist. "You must sleep. You're exhausted."

"I have to work."

"You won't be any good to anyone like this, Abram. Come on. A few hours of sleep will help."

He shook his head. "I have to try. Every time I close my eyes, I see his face. It rips at me." He turned to her. "I have made it personal. Science should never be that."

"A child's life is on the line. Of course it's personal. It only matters if we touch the lives we heal." She smiled. "I am glad it's personal to you. Come. Rest. You can be brilliant in the morning."

He reached out and touched her cheek. "You have always been here for me."

"Yes, I know. Twenty years of loyalty. I think you owe me a watch or at least a pin." She smiled as she spoke.

"More than that, I think. You deserve so much more. I want to marry you." He sighed. "Not that I am so great a prize, but maybe you can make do."

Her blue eyes brightened with humor and affection. "So romantic, Abram. You don't want to talk about the stars or loving me forever? Instead you announce you want to marry me then tell me I'm not getting much of a deal?"

He shifted awkwardly. "I should have planned something romantic. Bought flowers."

"You're exhausted. What you need is to sleep. We'll talk about this in the morning and make our plans."

"Plans?"

"For our wedding."

He stared at her. "You're saying yes?"

"I've been waiting a long time for you. What else would I say?"

Delighted, he allowed her to lead him to the cot in the back of his office. He sat on the edge, then pulled her close and kissed her.

"I love you," he told her. "You are so much more than I deserve."

"I'm sure that's true."

"I want to make you happy."

"You already do."

"I'm serious, Linda. Make a list of demands. I'll fulfill them all."

She hesitated, then nodded. He knew what she was thinking. She was putting "find a cure" at the top of her list.

If only that were possible, he thought grimly.

"You can," she whispered as he closed his eyes. "I know it's there for you, my love. Just out of reach. Sleep and dream of the answer."

He stretched out on the cot. Pray God that he could.

KERRI PUT DOWN the book and stretched. She looked over at Cody. "Had enough? Ready for TV? Or I can keep reading."

Her nine-year-old shook his head. "You've been crying, Mom."

Not this hour, she thought as she forced herself to

smile. "I'm fine. Better than fine. I'm ready to do an ice-cream run."

"I'm not hungry. It hurts to eat. It hurts to just be in bed. Mom, you have to let me go."

Kerri felt her self-control start to crumble. She'd managed to pull it together after Nathan had left a few hours before, but she didn't have much in the way of reserves. If Cody pushed too hard, he was going to see a breakdown that would scare the life out of him.

How much would that take? How much life was left?

Her eyes began to burn as her throat tightened. No, she told herself. No! She wouldn't lose it like this.

She cleared her throat. "Excuse me, but last time I checked, I'm still the mom so I get to make the rules."

Cody didn't smile. He was pale, his features drawn. The combination of drugs and pain had sucked the strength out of him.

"Mom, I mean it. I'm done here. I need to go. I'll be okay. It's heaven, right? I've been good enough."

She slid onto the bed and carefully gathered him into her arms. He winced, but she didn't let go. She needed to be holding him.

"You've been amazing. You're a great kid and I don't know how I got so lucky."

"Dad sent me," Cody whispered. "And now he's

waiting for me. I want to see him, Mom. I won't hurt in heaven. I'll be able to run and play baseball. We'll wait for you together."

The tears started slowly, then rolled down her cheeks faster and faster.

"Cody, I can't," she breathed. "I love you too much."

"You'll be okay. Nathan will take care of you."

"I'm not sure about that."

"He loves you. He told me. He'll be there, Mom."

Maybe he would have been, before she'd gone crazy and sent him away.

She still didn't know what had happened. It was as if by telling her he loved her, he'd opened a scary place inside. One that didn't let her believe in second chances—because that's what he was.

Even though Cody should be the only thing she thought of, she missed Nathan. She wanted to call him but didn't know what to say.

"Cody, please. Not yet."

"Not today," he agreed. "But soon."

She knew he was in pain every second of every day. She knew it was only going to get worse. Asking him to hang on was selfish and wrong and yet she couldn't let go of her child.

"I love you," she whispered.

"I love you, too."

The nurse came in. "Time for your next shot."

They both watched the liquid injected into the IV. In a matter of minutes, Cody relaxed.

Kerri stood and waited until he was asleep. He would have a couple of good hours now, she thought gratefully. Hours when he didn't have to deal with the agony.

She wiped her face on her sleeve, then walked out of his room. The last thing she wanted to do was eat, but she needed to get something into her system. She honestly couldn't remember her last meal.

One of the nurses walked by. "I just saw Nathan down in the cafeteria, if you're wondering where he is. That man cares about you two so much. You must be happy to have him here to help you."

Kerri nodded without speaking. Nathan here? Was it possible?

She raced to the elevator and when it took too long, she ran down the stairs and burst into the basement. She'd been there so many times she didn't need the signs to get her to the open double doors.

She stumbled inside, then came to a stop as she looked over the tables, searching for a familiar man who couldn't possibly still be here. Then she saw him.

"You're here," she breathed as she hurried over. "You didn't leave. I told you to leave."

He put down his coffee and stood. "I don't usually listen to what you say. It's a guy thing."

She grabbed the chair to keep from falling to the ground. She couldn't feel her legs, or any other part of her body. There was only hope and joy and aching sadness.

"You're here," she whispered again. "I can't believe it."

"I love you both, Kerri. Where else would I go?"

Back to his rich world with its beautiful women. Back to a place where kids were healthy and death was years and years away. Back to where it was easy.

"He's going to die," she said, which wasn't at all what she'd meant to blurt out. "He wants me to let him go."

"You don't have to agree. Hang on. There might still be a miracle."

She stared into his dark eyes, finding strength there. "I don't know if I can. I'm so tired. There's nothing left."

"Then you rest and I'll stand guard. We'll take turns."

He could have left her. He could have not bothered. He could have done a thousand things, but he'd stayed.

His presence gave her the courage to say it at last. "I have to let him go. I have to tell him it's okay."

Nathan pulled her close. "No, you don't. You hold on as long as you can."

She pushed back. "Nathan, we both know that isn't helping him. You were right with Daniel. Children don't always know. They don't want to hurt us by leaving. You've been right about all of it. About Brian being disappointed in me because I made Cody my whole life. He's just a little boy. He never deserved such a big burden."

"Kerri." He kissed the top of her head.

"I have to tell him. If I don't, he'll just suffer more. And for what? Because I'm too weak and selfish to do the right thing? I'm better than that and he deserves more than that."

"God, I love you."

"I love you, too," she told him. "Talk about bad timing."

He nodded, then took her hand. "Whatever you want to do."

She led the way back to her son's room. Outside, in the hallway, she dug deep for strength, for faith. She let the love wash over her, straightening her spine and giving her the words that needed to be said. Then she walked inside.

But Cody wasn't alone. Dr. Wallace stood beside him, injecting several vials into the IV hookup.

"It's the enzymes," he said as he worked frantically. "I knew it was there. They're like a switch we'll turn off. We had the solution yesterday, but there was a mistake in the equation. I realized that this morning. I dreamed about it. When I awoke, I knew what was wrong."

He handed Kerri the empty vials. "It is time to pray. We'll know in twenty-four hours if I'm right. The progression of the disease should stop by then. Then we work on strengthening his body again. A long journey, but a hopeful one. If we can make it through the next day."

THE SUMMER SUN WARMED the air. Nathan waited in the open foyer of the Portland, Oregon, residential facility. If he ignored the bars across the windows, he could almost convince himself he was in a four-star hotel.

It had been two weeks since Frankie had arrived here. Two weeks with only brief reports telling him she was doing better. But he hadn't spoken to her and now, as the far door opened, he braced himself.

For a moment, he nearly didn't recognize her. Gone was the long, dark hair and the haunted eyes. Instead a petite young woman with short hair and flushed cheeks walked toward him. The frumpy, ill-fitting clothes had been replaced by a pretty summer dress. Even more unexpected...she was smiling.

"You look shocked," she said as she approached. "It's the haircut, isn't it? I told them to warn you. There's a beauty salon here, along with a boutique. It's very upscale. I guess if you're going to be crazy, it's best to be rich. I should warn you, I've been charging up a storm. You're probably going to have to cut me off to teach me a lesson."

"Frankie?"

"Want me to start counting to prove it?"

Impulsively, he reached for her, then stopped himself. Her smile twisted slightly as she took a little step to the side.

"I can't hug yet," she told him, tucking her hands behind her. "I want to, but the touching thing is still weird. The drugs are helping, though. The doctors would say it's more about the therapy, but I like the pills. They're easier. Swallowing is a whole lot faster than cognitive behavior therapy."

"I don't know what to say," he admitted. "I didn't know what to expect."

"The good news is I'm not frothing at the mouth."

This was the sister he remembered. The bright, funny girl who had her whole life in front of her.

"You want to go for a walk?" he asked. "Do they let you outside?"

"On a leash." She smiled tentatively. "Yes, I'd like to go for a walk."

They went out into the sunshine.

"It's pretty here," she said. "I thought it would be horrible, but it isn't."

"I'm glad. I was worried."

"Don't be. It's helping. I can feel it. I'm still not where I need to be, but I get flashes of hope."

He wanted her to promise that she would be all right. He wanted to know he hadn't lost her forever.

"Hope's a good thing," he said.

She paused by a long row of roses. "Nathan, I'm really sorry about what I did. I never meant to hurt your friend. What I did was so horrible."

"Don't," he told her. "It's my fault. You were right about everything. I did take the easy way out. I left you to handle the worst experience of your life by yourself. You were so young. I should have been

there for you and I wasn't. I'm ashamed of myself.
I would give anything to go back and change that."

She nodded slowly without looking at him. "Me,
too. I have a lot of anger built up inside. I'm just
starting to look at it. Damn therapy." She raised her
head. "I don't blame you. Not really. You got out and
I don't regret that. One of us should have escaped."

"I wish it had been you."

"I doubt I would have made billions."

"It's not about the money."

She smiled. "I'm glad you said that. I'll keep
shopping."

Her humor only made him feel worse. "I want to
fix things."

"As you don't have a professional degree, I don't
see that happening. Being there helps. Telling me
you want us to have a relationship helps. Time will
help."

"You're not going to cut me out of your life?" he
asked. "It's what I deserve."

"That would be the easy way out, big brother.
You're going to be stuck with me forever."

"I'm glad," he said, and meant it.

They continued walking along the path.

"How are things going with you?" she asked.
"How's Kerri's son?"

"Doing well," Nathan said, still amazed by the
boy's spectacular recovery. "Dr. Wallace found a
cure. Cody's getting stronger by the day. He'll be out

of the hospital tomorrow and should be back in school within a few months. If all goes well, he'll get a chance at a normal life. He'll always need to be careful and take medication, but compared with what he's been through, that's easy."

Frankie smiled. "Really? Wow. That's incredible. You must be…" Her smile faded. "Is it okay? Does it make you sad about Daniel?"

"Sometimes. I wish he could have been saved, too. I miss him."

"So do I. I always loved him a lot. Paige was another matter. What were you thinking?"

Nathan chuckled. "It seemed like a good idea at the time."

"Men can be such idiots."

"Thanks for the vote of confidence."

"You're welcome. Kerri seems nice."

"She is."

"You going to marry her?"

"If she'll have me."

Frankie stopped. "She will. Would you mind waiting until I'm out? So I can come to the wedding?"

"We'd both like that."

"Good."

They started walking again. She touched one of the roses. "I'm sorry about the tower."

"Don't be."

"Are you going to appeal?"

"No. I'll find something else."

She lightly touched his arm. "I love you, Nathan. Thank you for helping me."

"I love you, too." He grimaced. "I keep wanting to apologize for being such a selfish bastard."

"I'm glad you feel that way. Based on what I've told them about you, they're planning extra sessions." She smiled.

THE WELCOME HOME BANNER was the size of an aircraft carrier. Kerri had ordered a big cake with the sweet, sticky frosting that Cody liked so much and later Nathan would pick up fried chicken. There were balloons and streamers and a wrapped box containing a new pair of athletic shoes, the theory being that now Cody could actually walk enough to wear out a pair.

She stood at the top of the porch stairs, waiting for Nathan to arrive so they could go to the hospital to pick up Cody.

It was a perfect day, she thought, ignoring the light rain and clouds. No matter what happened in the rest of her life, she would always have this moment to get her through. There'd been a miracle. What more could she ask for?

Then the limo pulled up in front of her house and Nathan stepped out. She raced toward him and jumped into his arms.

He pulled her against him and they spun together, laughing, kissing, touching. She never wanted to let go.

"I love you," he told her.

"I love you more."

"Not possible."

"Want to bet?"

He kissed her again, slowly, passionately, lingering, then stared into her eyes.

"Marry me," he said. "Marry me, Kerri. I love you and Cody and I want us to be together always. Like a family."

She'd never thought she could be this happy. It was as if she could float up and touch the sky.

"Marry me. I'll spend the rest of my life making you happy."

"You already do." She kissed him.

He nipped at her lower lip. "Is that a yes?"

"It's an absolutely."

EPILOGUE

THE NEW SPORTS COMPLEX in Songwood boasted a state-of-the-art multipurpose arena, a football field and a baseball stadium. Currently, the youth league team baseball playoffs were in their second-to-last game.

Kerri took the soda Nathan passed her and looked longingly at his grande latte. Unfortunately, she had two months until she was due and the doctor had been very clear about her avoiding caffeine while she was pregnant.

"Did I miss anything?" Nathan asked as he passed her the slice of pizza she'd sent him to get. Her cravings were nothing if not consistent.

"Cody's up next. I know he's gonna hit it out of the park."

Nathan put his arm around her as they both watched the twelve-year-old boy step up to the plate.

He'd grown so much, Kerri thought, delighted and relieved. Thanks to Dr. Wallace's miracle, her son was living a relatively normal life. He wore braces on his legs at night and still tired more easily than other kids his age, but when compared to where he'd been just three years ago, no one was complaining. Least of all her.

Her life was more than she could have dreamed of. They no longer had to worry about Gilliar's Disease, and she and Nathan were blissfully happy, married and expecting their first child together. Frankie was going to college and studying social work. She lived in an apartment close to the University of Washington, but frequently spent weekends with them in the big house they'd built on the outskirts of Songwood.

Kerri sucked in her breath as the baseball sailed toward home plate. Cody swung. There was a loud *crack,* then the ball soared up higher and higher. Cody took off for first base.

Nathan squeezed her hand. "He's got a home run." Pride thickened his voice.

Kerri looked at the man who made it clear every day how much he loved both her and Cody, along with the new baby. "I love you," she whispered.

Nathan smiled at her, then kissed her. "I love you, too. A little more today than yesterday."

She laughed. "How did I get so lucky?"

"It was just one of those things."

An accident? she wondered. No. More of a miracle.

REQUEST YOUR
FREE BOOKS!

2 FREE NOVELS
FROM THE ROMANCE/SUSPENSE
COLLECTION PLUS 2 FREE GIFTS!

YES! Please send me 2 FREE novels from the Romance/Suspense Collection
and my 2 FREE gifts. After receiving them, if I don't wish to receive any more books,
I can return the shipping statement marked "cancel." If I don't cancel, I will receive 4
brand-new novels every month and be billed just $5.49 per book in the U.S., or $5.99
per book in Canada, plus 25¢ shipping and handling per book plus applicable taxes, if
any*. That's a savings of at least 20% off the cover price! I understand that accepting
the 2 free books and gifts places me under no obligation to buy anything. I can
always return a shipment and cancel at any time. Even if I never buy another book
from the Reader Service, the two free books and gifts are mine to keep forever.

185 MDN EF5Y   385 MDN EF6C

Name _____ (PLEASE PRINT)

Address _____ Apt. #

City _____ State/Prov. _____ Zip/Postal Code

Signature (if under 18, a parent or guardian must sign)

Mail to **The Reader Service:**
IN U.S.A.: P.O. Box 1867, Buffalo, NY 14240-1867
IN CANADA: P.O. Box 609, Fort Erie, Ontario L2A 5X3

Not valid to current subscribers to the Romance Collection,
the Suspense Collection or the Romance/Suspense Collection.

Want to try two free books from another line?
Call 1-800-873-8635 or visit www.morefreebooks.com.

* Terms and prices subject to change without notice. NY residents add applicable sales tax.
Canadian residents will be charged applicable provincial taxes and GST. This offer is limited to
one order per household. All orders subject to approval. Credit or debit balances in a customer's
account(s) may be offset by any other outstanding balance owed by or to the customer. Please
allow 4 to 6 weeks for delivery.

Your Privacy: Harlequin is committed to protecting your privacy. Our Privacy
Policy is available online at www.eHarlequin.com or upon request from the Reader
Service. From time to time we make our lists of customers available to reputable
firms who may have a product or service of interest to you. If you would
prefer we not share your name and address, please check here. ☐

BOB07

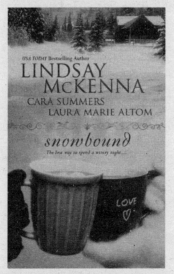

SUSAN
MALLERY

77056	DELICIOUS	___ $6.99 U.S.	___ $8.50 CAN.
77117	IRRESISTIBLE	___ $6.99 U.S.	___ $8.50 CAN.
77210	TEMPTING	___ $6.99 U.S.	___ $8.50 CAN.

(limited quantities available)

TOTAL AMOUNT	$ _____
POSTAGE & HANDLING	$ _____
($1.00 FOR 1 BOOK, 50¢ for each additional)	
APPLICABLE TAXES*	$ _____
TOTAL PAYABLE	$ _____

(check or money order—please do not send cash)

To order, complete this form and send it, along with a check or money order for the total above, payable to HQN Books, to: **In the U.S.:** 3010 Walden Avenue, P.O. Box 9077, Buffalo, NY 14269-9077; **In Canada:** P.O. Box 636, Fort Erie, Ontario, L2A 5X3.

Name: _____

Address: _____ City: _____

State/Prov.: _____ Zip/Postal Code: _____

Account Number (if applicable): _____

075 CSAS

*New York residents remit applicable sales taxes.
*Canadian residents remit applicable GST and provincial taxes.

HQN™

We *are* romance™

www.HQNBooks.com

PHSM0108BL